BOTH SIDES OF THE BORDER

BOTH SIDES OF THE BORDER
TERRY OVERTON

AMBASSADOR INTERNATIONAL
GREENVILLE, SOUTH CAROLINA & BELFAST, NORTHERN IRELAND

www.ambassador-international.com

BOTH SIDES OF THE BORDER

ISBN: 978-1-64960-058-5
eISBN: 978-1-64960-059-2
Library of Congress Control Number: 2021934688

Cover design by Christopher Jackson
Interior typesetting by Dentelle Design

This is a work of fiction. Names, characters, and incidents are all products of the author's imagination or are used for fictional purposes. Any resemblance to actual events or persons, living or dead, is entirely coincidental. Any mentioned brand names, places, and trademarks remain the property of their respective owners, bear no association with the author or the publisher, and are used for fictional purposes only.

Scripture taken from THE HOLY BIBLE, NEW INTERNATIONAL VERSION®, NIV® Copyright © 1973, 1978, 1984, 2011 by Biblica, Inc.® Used by permission. All rights reserved worldwide.

AMBASSADOR INTERNATIONAL
Emerald House
411 University Ridge, Suite B14
Greenville, SC 29601, USA
www.ambassador-international.com

AMBASSADOR BOOKS
The Mount
2 Woodstock Link
Belfast, BT6 8DD, Northern Ireland, UK
www.ambassadormedia.co.uk

The colophon is a trademark of Ambassador, a Christian publishing company.

FOREWORD

BOTH SIDES OF THE BORDER is a beautifully written novel conscientiously rooted in candid authenticity of lived experience—a timely must-read. The stories propel readers along captivating, heart-wrenching, deeply insightful, and thought-provoking intimate views of determination, desperation, and disaster, while providing powerful inspiration for hope.

Terry Overton's brilliant juxtaposition of two women's vastly disparate journeys to the USA-Mexico border draws readers into an exquisite journey of their own into the complex conundrum of our time. Illuminated by the characters' riveting challenges and triumphs, we discover, "After all, we only live a bridge apart." Through the characters' starkly contrasting backgrounds of poverty and privilege, their journeys unfold through relatable tensions, dangers, heartache, and glimmers of beauty, truth, faith, and love. We are compelled to attune to compassion and humanity rather than polarizing divisiveness.

For those who have not witnessed the USA-Mexico borderlands, this insightful novel will transport you beyond the headlines to an intimate, firsthand experience that will illuminate your perspective. For those of us who have lived and learned along the border, it provides validation for embracing the seemingly impossible challenges that face each of us and cultivate compassion for humanity.

KARIN ANN LEWIS, PH.D.
Associate Professor, Teaching & Learning Department
University of Texas Rio Grande Valley

CHAPTER ONE

THE SOUND OF FARAWAY FOOTSTEPS distracted Dolores' thoughts as she sat on a cracked step in the center park of San Pedro Sula, Honduras. In the darkest part of a long, humid night, the moonlight cast strange shadows of the tall buildings. The thickness of the air distorted her senses of sound and sight.

Waiting in the night, the tearful words of her grandmother stormed through her mind again. "Your papá! An accident! He's badly hurt. He can't walk," echoed in her heart. That was two years ago— the last day her father worked.

Dolores felt an ache that she could not shake. The painful memories of failure, when she and her younger brothers couldn't make a living on the farm, were always on her mind. She was no longer a teenager, and she felt a strong responsibility to help her family. But they just couldn't make it work.

It wasn't only the accident that brought the failure. The drought that followed her father's injury hit the family farm especially hard. The state of emergency declared by the government of Honduras brought no direct relief to the family. Famine for the country was imminent. Starvation of her family was more immediate.

Fighting off sleep, her head dropped. Startled, she sat up straight to restore her alertness and looked again through the trees in the park for the possible silhouette of a stranger. Four other girls sat with her, all waiting to make their contact. She didn't know their names. The arrangements of this night weren't discussed in detail. Less information meant more safety.

Dolores heard Emilio, her younger brother, chuckling through the dimness of the remaining moonlight. *Always having a good time,* she thought. Her brothers, Ernesto, sixteen years of age, and Emilio, just barely fourteen, sat with a group of other young men and teens across the park. She and her brothers had secretly planned their trip with a coyote for weeks. Some of the teens in the group were in search of their parents, who had left years ago for the United States. Others simply wanted a job and a better life. A few had been tormented by gangs or corrupt officials. But they had one thing in common: they wanted to leave Honduras.

The first time the family discussed the trip, Emilio—the younger, raucous, and slightly more athletic brother—asked Dolores with excitement in his voice, "How far will we travel?"

"More than fourteen hundred miles to get to Texas," Dolores replied, already feeling anxiety about leaving her family.

"From San Pedro Sula we'll go to Guatemala?" Emilio asked.

Dolores recalled the animation of Emilio's face, giving away his eagerness. He was too young to understand the sorrow of leaving home and the risks of the journey. He likened the journey to a treasure hunting adventure with a chest of gold at the end.

"Yes, we'll begin in eastern Honduras, follow the lower lands of Guatemala to the west, then cross the Mexican border," Dolores said.

"I can't wait! Imagine everything we will see," he said as a smile radiated across his face.

"Yes, we'll see many new things," Dolores agreed, with a tone of sadness. *He has no idea what is ahead,* she thought.

"It won't be all fun and games." Ernesto, the middle child in the family and older brother of Emilio, looked penetratingly at Dolores. His eyes conveyed that he knew about the possible dangers they might encounter. Ernesto was the more serious and reserved of her two brothers. He was analytical, thoughtful, and methodical. She could count on Ernesto to help her make decisions as they traveled.

"And Mexico! I've always wanted to see it," Emilio added. He jumped up from his chair and cheered, "Mexico! Here we come!" He danced in a circle around the small family room, waving his hands in the air. Ernesto shook his head in disbelief.

For the people waiting in the park that night, the travel through Mexico would be the longest leg of the journey. Their families and friends had scraped together the equivalent of a few hundred American dollars for each traveler. With limited funds in their pockets and a few belongings in plastic bags, their families said their goodbyes and prayed their children would find a new life and better future.

Dolores' heart ached at the thought of leaving the safety and security of her family. She loved the family farm and the life in the country with her parents. She felt content within the walls of the humble house that overflowed with memories of growing up with her extended family. The house was set on a fairly small, but sufficient, piece of land. The flowers, banana trees, and coffee plants of the countryside were plentiful. It was a simple and good life.

In their small farming community several miles from San Pedro Sula, if a family couldn't farm the land, there were few options.

Dolores knew the options. Young women her age, and even younger girls, lived in the city and resorted to prostitution to sustain their families. Dolores wanted to keep her virtue, work for a good life, and someday have a family of her own. She would do whatever she needed to do to help her family. After much family discussion, many tears, and even a few cross words, it was decided that Dolores, Emilio, and Ernesto would forego their lives in Honduras and endeavor to make a better life for their family in the United States. It would be safer there.

Earlier that morning, Emilio and Ernesto ganged up on Dolores and made a last-minute effort to convince her not to make the trip. "It'll be too dangerous for you. As a girl, you'll take more risks. Let us go, and we'll send for you later, when we have the money to travel," Ernesto pleaded.

"I'll be fine. I'm older than both of you. I know my way around. I can take care of myself. Remember, I took care of you muchachos when you were just babies. You two better concentrate on looking out for each other and stop worrying about me," Dolores replied.

Even at his young age, Emilio understood the dangers involved for his sister and disagreed with her. "Ernesto is right. You should stay and take care of the rest of the family. They need you here."

"I can't take care of them if I can't make any money. They need money more than anything else. I'll go with you. We'll send money back home."

This conversation continued for nearly an hour. Ernesto and Emilio sensed their older sister could not be persuaded. Reluctantly, they gave in.

"You're so determined. If you want to go, then go! I'm not happy about this. But we will try to look out after each other," Ernesto said.

Dolores stared at her brothers, who had grown into lanky young men. She remembered carrying both of her younger brothers on her hips at the same time, feeding them, bathing them, and clothing them. She'd wiped tears from their eyes when they were hurt and especially when they hurt each other. She felt responsible for them. She was uneasy about taking them on such a trip as this.

The bleak night crawled on, and Dolores thought their contact wouldn't come.

"Do you think he'll show up tonight?" one of the other young girls asked Dolores.

"Let's pray he does."

Dolores pretended to be brave for her brothers and the others in the group, but in her heart, she feared she would have to stay in the city overnight and try again tomorrow. She was tired and beginning to wonder whether she was doing the right thing. Would her mother and grandmother be able to take care of her father? Would she be safe? What if she became ill or injured and couldn't make the trip? Suppose she was stuck in Guatemala or Mexico? Would she be able to get back home? Would her brothers be able to travel the long distance together if something happened to her? Her stomach was in turmoil. Her heart raced and would not be calmed. *It will work out*, she thought. *I can make it*. She said a prayer and made the sign of the cross on her chest. She would trust that God would watch her. At that moment, she scanned the sidewalk across the street.

"Look. Over there," Dolores said to the other girls as she pointed. "I think that's the man we're waiting for." She motioned to her brothers to look at the man walking in the street.

Across the park, a fast-paced man in cowboy boots, jeans, and a plaid shirt walked nearer to the group of young men. Ernesto and Emilio spoke to the man, the coyote, who then walked toward the group of girls sitting on the steps. After a few words, money was exchanged.

"You come with me now. Don't talk. Stay together. We'll walk to a truck," the coyote said in a quiet, yet gruff, voice.

The group silently followed the man through the city.

Dolores looked at the shadow-covered streets and remembered how she had admired the city of San Pedro Sula when she was a young child. People visited the city for the markets, local government offices, and the Cathedral San Pedro Apostol across from the park. She was amazed the first time she visited the cathedral. She had never seen such a majestic structure, and it was a stark contrast from the more modern buildings in the city. Before Dolores understood the danger, she thought she might live in the city as an adult and have a good job. It had always appealed to her.

In her mind, she wandered back to an earlier time when she had talked with her mother many years ago. "I could work there in a store or in a business," she told her mother when she was only eight years of age.

Her mother smiled and said, "We'd miss you too much, pequeña. You need to stay with your mamá and papá."

"You'll see, Mamá. I can work there and *still* come home to you," the eight-year-old Dolores said as she danced on her toes.

"Oh no, no, little one," her mother said as she picked up Dolores. "You'll always stay with your mamá." She hugged Dolores especially tight for the longest time.

Dolores smiled, recalling her mother's words. Now, she knew the reality of city life. The economy of the city hadn't been stable. The gang activity, organized crime, and murder rates sky rocketed. Dolores heard people say the crimes in the city made it one of the most dangerous cities in the world. *God has His own plan*, she thought as the group softly walked past the magnificent cathedral.

For a moment, Dolores was optimistic. She was walking to her new future. She would find a job, start a new life in a new country. She was confident that with God's help, she could send money to her family. She would have a safe life. She would have an untroubled life. She would learn to speak English and find a job. *Dolores Sanchez, living and working in America*, she thought with a smile.

Dolores heard the other girls breathing beside her as they walked tightly together in the dismal night. The young men and teenage boys followed the girls through the meandering streets, not saying a word. Dolores' group from the park joined another larger group of travelers waiting in a long, old, military truck. The truck would take the group to the Honduras-Guatemala border and then beyond. The coyote would escort them across Guatemala to the Suchiate River crossing, where they would enter the state of Chiapas, Mexico. From that point, it would be a mix of walking, train rides, and trucks for the remainder of the trip.

"¡Ándale!" the coyote shouted to them as they packed into the truck. "We need to stay on schedule."

Each one climbed aboard the truck and scooted down to make room for the next person. The nervousness could be felt in the night. The coyote closed the back hatch of the truck with a loud clunk and took his place in the front passenger side of the vehicle.

The common risks for the group of travelers in this part of Honduras were gangs, thieves, rapists, and murderers. Once they left Honduras, the risk of being sent back to Honduras would be an additional and constant fear of the voyage.

* * *

The large group traveled by truck across Guatemala. The young travelers from the park stayed together. Dolores, curious about the other women traveling with her, introduced herself to two of the women nearby. Lola and Olivia shared their experiences with Dolores.

"This is my second time to try for the United States," said the young, thin woman named Lola.

Dolores could hardly hear Lola over the bouncing noises of the truck. But she wanted to know Lola's story.

"What happened the first time?" Dolores asked.

"I was caught by the authorities in Mexico. We all were," Lola replied, nearly shouting.

"Who was with you? How'd it happen?" Dolores asked.

"I was a young girl, traveling with my mother, father, and three sisters. We made it into Mexico, but not far. We were off the road, trying to walk some distance around the checkpoints. A patrol man saw us through the trees and ran after us. My youngest sister fell down, and my mother and father stopped to get her. We were all captured."

"That's horrible."

"The man said he would let us go if we gave him enough money. My father showed him all of the money he had in his pocket. He turned his pockets inside out so the man could see we had no more money. The man took all of the money we had, then took us to the other authorities, and they sent us back."

"Oh, no!"

"It was horrible. My sister still blames herself. We lost all of our money to the coyote who didn't protect us and to the corrupt official who captured us."

"I'm so sorry that happened to you," Dolores said, fearing similar consequences could happen to her and her brothers.

Lola brushed the hair out of her face and continued as the truck bobbled along. "Many years have passed since that time. My family saved the money to send me by myself this time. It's important to us that our family make money in the United States. I want to send the money back to them in the future so they can come, too. We all want to live there."

Dolores made the sign of the cross on her chest and added, "I'll pray for your future and our safe journey."

Olivia, the slightly larger girl of the group, spoke out of the darkest corner of the truck. "My second time, too. My luck wasn't good the first time, either."

"What happened?" Dolores asked.

"Like Lola, I traveled as a child with my parents," Olivia replied. "We made it on foot and on the train for quite some distance into Mexico. I was separated from my parents at a train stop, and within a few minutes, they were taken by the authorities and later sent to Honduras. I stayed with a lady in our group. She promised she would help me go to the United States. We traveled a little while longer, and I told her I wanted to go back to Honduras and find my parents."

"And did you find them?" Dolores asked.

"I found my father," she said, hanging her head downward. "My mother was killed before they made it back to Honduras."

"That's so sad, Olivia. I'm sorry for you and your family."

"It was painful and a hard time for us. My father said they were robbed by some men who took all of their belongings and then killed my mother. They tried to kill my father, too. He was hurt but didn't die. My father wants me to go to the United States for the sake of my mother. He said he wanted me to know that she died for us to have a better life, and we should try again for her."

"I'll pray for you, too," Dolores said as she turned away from the group. She didn't want the other girls to see her crying. She questioned her own decision to leave Honduras. Perhaps she should've stayed with her family. She missed her mother, father, and grandmother. She worried that they needed her. *No*, she thought, *I couldn't send my two little brothers alone.*

Dolores looked across the truck at her two brothers. Despite the thumping, rocking, and bumping of the truck, they were sleeping. She prayed for their safety. As hard as she tried, she couldn't stay awake a moment longer.

During the night, the truck made its way across the Honduras-Guatemala border. The trek through Guatemala would require a couple of days across the hidden backroads. Once they reached the river, the coyote would help them cross it to Mexico.

The truck stopped abruptly and pulled to the side of the dirt road near a clump of trees. Dawn was approaching, and the sky turned from black to light gray. The coyote opened the door and got out of the front of the truck. He walked to the end of the truck bed, where the travelers had been sleeping, and opened the hatch in the back.

"Wake up. Everyone out. We'll travel through the night and take a break in the daylight hours. It's easier to travel the roads during the night. Less risk," the coyote said.

One by one, the weary passengers unloaded from the truck as the coyote had instructed.

"Okay. Now, you can go find some places to rest or eat. Some of you brought food. Others can look for fruit in the trees over there," he gestured. "When it starts to get dark again, we'll load up and go back on the road."

Dolores and her brothers adapted to resting during the day under the trees or behind bushes and traveling at night. Dolores stayed close to her brothers but within her own group of women.

"We need to stay together as a group," Olivia said. "Some women have been attacked while traveling."

"It's true. I saw this happen when I traveled as a young girl. It's frightening." Lola nodded her agreement.

All of the male travelers were being respectful of the women and girls in the group. Many of the male travelers had mothers or sisters traveling with them. There were only two intact families that traveled as parents with their young children. Dolores worried for them and said many prayers.

In the afternoons, the group looked for fruit that grew in the area. Sometimes, they were lucky. People living nearby who saw the group searching for food gave the young children meals or fruit. Others who brought food with them shared with the children. In turn, the children offered it to their parents or to some of the women who were helping the families. Dolores looked at her brothers. They looked thinner than they had been just a few days ago.

"Ernesto, have you and Emilio eaten any food today?" Dolores asked.

"No, we had some fruit yesterday. We're fine. And we have a bottle of water we share," Ernesto replied.

"Look what one of the children gave to me," she said as she handed the boys a single large tortilla. Ernesto tore the tortilla into three even pieces.

"What do you think Mamá is fixing for dinner tonight?" Emilio asked.

"Probably a large tortilla," Ernesto answered.

"No, a giant one!" Emilio said with outstretched hands.

The three siblings shared the tortilla and talked and laughed together. For a moment, they were a family again. They already missed home and the quiet countryside. Longing for the small house surrounded by lush plants with their loving family inside, silence took over, and their faces became sullen.

To cheer up her brothers, Dolores whispered, "We're blessed. So far, we haven't had to use any of our hidden money."

Both brothers nodded as they chewed bites of their share of the tortilla.

The week before Dolores, Ernesto, and Emilio left for the trip, Dolores had sewn small pockets with button-down flaps inside each of their shirts. Inside each pocket, they had placed some money. They agreed the money wasn't to be used for food if at all possible, but only for travel. Dolores anticipated multiple people along the way would ask for money to take them to their next stop. So far, the three had been able to hold on to their money. She wasn't sure they had enough, but she trusted that God would watch over them as they went on their journey.

After they finished their tortilla, Dolores commented, "The other women who have been here before told me we are getting close to the river."

"Maybe we can cross it tomorrow," Ernesto said.

"That'll be great," Emilio remarked. "We will soon be in Mexico, and next, we will be in the United States! Not long now," he said and laughed.

"That's right," Ernesto said.

Dolores smiled, but she was terrified about what was ahead. She feared it might be treacherous crossing at the river or that there'd be violence in Mexico. The women had told her so many frightening stories in the past few days.

The coyote signaled it was time to board the truck and move closer to the river.

"This will be your last time in this truck." The coyote seemed distressed. "Then, I take you to the edge of the river. Maybe we can cross tonight. I'll tell you what to do. Once you are on the other side, in Mexico, you can find another coyote to help you, if you want, to take you to Tapachula."

The coyote, with a serious tone in his voice, warned the group, "The train makes many stops. You might need to leave the train and then board again at multiple cities and towns. If you can't get on the train in Tapachula, you should make your way to Arriaga and get on the train there."

Dolores hoped to get on the train in Tapachula. She didn't want to travel further on foot. The more they traveled on foot, the longer the journey. Once they found the railyard, they would need to catch a train and later jump off at each stop and catch the train again as they traveled through Mexico. Crossing over to Mexico would be the first difficult task.

The passengers traveled through the night in fearful silence. Each one staring out the back of the truck thinking about the difficult journey across the river.

CHAPTER TWO

THE BUTTERFLIES IN EVA'S STOMACH worked overtime as she stepped on the glossy white front porch of her mother's small Cape Cod home and opened the squeaky screen door. Eva's excitement about her move to another state was tempered by the knowledge that her mother fiercely objected to the idea. As much as Eva loved her, it seemed to Eva that her mother doubted Eva's self-reliance.

"I thought you would've been here earlier," her mother hollered from the kitchen.

"Sorry. I had to finish packing up the apartment."

Eva entered the kitchen, filled with the familiar smells of home-cooked food. She knew the long, silent pause lingering in the air was her mother's way of telling her once again that the move to south Texas was not approved.

"That smells wonderful," Eva commented, hoping to lighten the mood for the evening.

"Just the same chicken-fried steak and mashed potatoes," her mom replied.

Eva quickly grabbed for a small bite of the extra crunchy crust already on the platter. She loved those little fried tidbits, even if they were unhealthy.

Her mother slapped Eva's hand gently and, in one motion, returned to the frying pan. "No sneaking ahead of time," she warned as she shook her finger.

Her mother turned the sizzling meat over in the pan and went back to loading slabs of butter in the creamy mashed potatoes.

"Anybody else coming over to join us?" Eva asked.

"You know your sisters are all busy with their kids," she said, shaking her head as she started the gravy. "I never heard of so many activities. Baseball, soccer, basketball, piano, science club. You would think your sisters didn't want their own kids around. Seems this generation has forgotten the important things."

"Now, Mom," Eva calmly scolded, "you know they want their kids to have lots of opportunities."

"Even so," her mother commented. "Your sisters have busy lives. Too busy, if you ask me."

"I'll call them before I leave and tell them goodbye," Eva said. "I was hoping to see them tonight."

Eva was not the prettiest girl of the four girls in the family. But she might be the second prettiest. Second only to her older sister, who was, after all, the winner of their high school beauty pageant. Not having the natural beauty her sister possessed contributed to Eva's self-determination. She had to make decisions and fend for herself when her sister merely gave a smile and a wink and things happened automatically. Eva trudged on behind the scenes with clearly defined goals. Goals like finishing college, marrying at a certain age, and starting a great career. Her goals hadn't included a nasty divorce from an abusive husband, working as a housekeeper, and using food stamps as she worked her way through school. Her plans didn't include asking for a loan to pay the divorce attorney. Her original plans were to reach particular achievements and live happily ever after.

When Eva's plans fell apart, her mother attempted to comfort her by saying, "If you want to make God laugh, just make a plan." But Eva got through it. She was strong. She had an unwavering conviction to have a better life, a life better than her mother and sisters, who married disappointing men and then quickly produced a multitude of children.

"Let me put these on the table," Eva said, once again hoping to prod her mother into a happier frame of mind.

"Thank you. Now, Eva, please explain to me one more time—this time so I understand—why in the world you are moving to Brownsville, Texas?"

"Mom, you know it's for a job. I'm going to be a professor. And I am very grateful that they extended the offer to me since I just graduated."

"Now, look here, just because you have a Ph.D. doesn't mean you know everything. In fact, there's a lot you don't seem to understand."

"Such as?" Eva knew what was coming. Her mother could voice any number of objections.

"Well, for one thing, Brownsville, Texas, is dangerously close to Mexico. And why in the world do you want to move down there with those liberal Democrats?"

Eva's mother bragged that she was one of the few people in Southside, Virginia, who voted for any Republican candidate on the ticket. As for Eva, she often told her mother that she considered each candidate for their platform. In reality, she rarely voted and didn't care much about politics. Eva clearly understood that her mother did not approve of her move or of "those liberal university people."

"Oh, Mother," Eva replied, "I'm sure there are conservatives and liberals in south Texas."

"And don't you know what is going on down there? I mean, those illegals come across every day. I saw on the news—"

"Mom, you have got to stop watching cable news all the time. You need to get out more and, you know, talk to people."

"Oh, for goodness' sakes. I see plenty of people! I see people at church and in the women's prayer group. And even *they* are worried about you. And *me* talking to people? You're one to talk," her mother said, giving her "the look."

"Okay, Mom. Let's eat," she said, trying to change the subject before her mother could begin the "When are you going to start dating?" questions.

"Seriously, honey, when are you going to date someone again?"

Too late, Eva thought.

"I know that scoundrel of a husband you had was just awful. But there are others out there just waiting to meet a nice girl like you. Plenty of men out there, you know."

Eva's divorce was still raw. She didn't want to talk about that with her mother again. She was over that dark phase of her life. She was moving on to a better future.

"Mom, I'm hardly a girl. I'm twenty-nine you know," she said, diverting the conversation.

"Of course, I know you're twenty-nine. I was there when you were born." They both laughed.

"This is delicious," Eva said, taking another bite of mashed potatoes and chicken-fried steak totally smothered in gravy.

"I'll bet you won't get food like this down where you're going," her mother remarked, taking a second helping of potatoes.

"No, probably not, Mom." Eva agreed with her mother to keep from going down the road of comparing Mexican food with Mom's Southern cooking.

"So, as I was saying, when will you start dating? All of that hard work and studying is over. Now you will have time for a social life," her mother said, patting Eva's hand.

"We'll see, Mom. You know I will have to work really hard now to get tenure."

"Oh, good grief. Don't use work as an excuse. There's nothing like a good, strong marriage to help you through everything."

Her mother talked about perfect marriages as if she'd had one. Eva's own father had abandoned the family when Eva was quite young. Perhaps being raised by a single mother provided the foundation for her own autonomy. She'd been expected to take on responsibilities from an early age that did not burden most children. She was proud that she didn't need anyone. She could achieve whatever she set her mind to.

"Are you excited about the new job?" her mother asked.

Eva was shocked. The job offer was extended two months ago, and this was the first time her mother had asked her about her new position.

"I am very excited."

"Tell me what you already know about the job," her mother requested as she scooped up another spoonful of gravy.

"The faculty members are pretty amazing. They're doing research in the local schools. And one woman—her name is Maria—a senior

faculty member, was very impressed with my teaching and disserta-
tion research. I'm thinking I'll ask her to be my mentor."

"What? Land sakes. You get a Ph.D. and still have to have someone
mentor you? I never . . . " She just shook her head instead of finishing
her sentence.

"It'll make getting tenure easier. That's what people tell me, anyway."

"Okay, now to the important question. How long will you be
there? I mean, you'll move back here, won't you?" Her mother's question had a hint of desperation in her voice, and her eyes pled with her.

"Maybe. But I have to be there for six years before I can apply
for tenure."

"Six years? Six years? You'll be thirty-five by then! You'd better
find someone by then."

"Mother, good grief. That would be nice, but that *isn't* the reason
I'm going." Eva could not deny that at some point she would like to
meet a perfect someone.

"You know, something else . . . well, I'll just say it." Her mother
hesitated for a bit.

"What?"

"You know, I'm a worry wart." Her mother's eyebrows raised up
and came together when she was worried. Eva could see clearly that
something was upsetting her.

"Okay, Mom, what?"

"It's the location. I mean, besides being right there at Mexico, you
are in hurricane territory."

"Mom, you know the good thing about hurricanes? You have
plenty of warning."

"Eva, I'll be watching the news, and if I see so much as a hint of a tropical storm—"

"You'll call me," Eva finished the sentence for her mother.

"Yes."

The evening ended without any major conflicts. Her mother, heartbroken and not understanding Eva's motives at all, gave her a lingering hug as Eva stepped out on the porch.

"Now, you call me," her mother said, taking a tissue from her apron pocket and wiping her eyes. "And don't forget to call your sisters to tell them goodbye."

"Okay. I'll call you often, Mom. Don't worry. I'll be fine," she answered with only a twinge of doubt.

* * *

One last check, Eva thought. She scanned the efficiency apartment. Everything she owned, which was scant, was packed. *A clean break; that's what this is,* Eva thought to herself.

She crammed the last of her clothing into her overflowing suitcase. Her overnight bag, a few boxes of books, and a box of kitchen items were neatly packed in her second-hand car. Eva rolled her suitcase out and loaded it into the trunk. She was off to a new life exactly 1,602 miles away. Her planned route included stops at two economy hotels at strategic points. It was possible to make the trip in two very long days, but she opted to make the drive in three. Her new apartment, conveniently near the university and a short thirty-minute drive from the coast, was waiting for her. She would arrive two weeks before the first day of class.

The uncluttered sky presented no issues for driving. Music was her only accompaniment in the small, overpacked car. The open car windows invited the Southern humid air inside as she drove, blowing through her hair, providing an even stronger sense of freedom. For a moment, she felt as though she was in a car commercial zooming down the highway to the music. Passing through the mountains gave her pause.

"Goodbye," she whispered as she buzzed by the Virginia-North Carolina state line. *Goodbye to the bad memories.*

The Tejano music she discovered when she interviewed at the university played loudly as she moved along the highway. Listening to this music every day was a good way to learn casual Spanish, even if the songs mostly dealt with love and loss. "Mi amor, no quiero que me dejes . . . " Nevertheless, the rhythms and the melodies were adequate company for the ride.

Eva followed her GPS to the hotel, marking the end of the first day's drive.

"Good evening. How can I help you?" The welcoming hotel clerk smiled.

"I have a reservation for Jordan."

"Let's see. Ah, here it is. Eva?" he asked.

"Yes."

"Very good. Here you go. Your room number is 208, but it's also marked on the inside of the key holder."

"Thank you. Oh, where can I get some dinner?"

"You can walk about a half-block south, and you will have a couple of options there," he replied. "You can choose between a steak house or a diner."

"Great, thanks," she replied, feeling a sense of self-reliance having driven one-third of the way.

Eva opted for the diner. Not as good as her mother's cooking, but walking to and from the diner gave her the opportunity to stretch her legs before bed. When she finally got back to her room and into her bed, she was asleep in no time.

Eva awoke too early. *Forty-five minutes until my phone was set to go off,* she thought. She popped out of bed, eager to get on the highway. By the end of the day, she would be just inside the Texas state line. She smiled. *Texas, my new home state.* She delighted thinking about being completely on her own. Gathering her makeup kit, overnight bag, and other necessities, she checked out.

Deep blue morning skies with bright streaks of gold shooting out from the sun and no traffic to speak of presented a perfect day for driving. Eva turned up the music and headed southwest. As her car rambled down the highway, so did her thoughts. Music did not serve as a distraction today. Regrettably, Eva intensely focused on self-analysis. For a moment, anxiety intruded into her happiness. Unexpectedly she found herself questioning her move.

Seriously? One thousand six hundred and two miles away from the life I have known? Was this a good thing? Will I find the happiness that has eluded me all my life? Will I make enough money to afford a social life? And the finer things in life? Or will this be another phase of unfulfilled dreams, false promises, and shallow relationships? She interrogated herself.

This is nonsense, she thought. She pushed her thoughts aside. Her achievements so far were accomplished by her own ability and effort. She would do the same in Texas. She slowed her breathing rate and focused her thoughts on the road ahead and her future. The location would be perfect. Semi-tropical weather, Gulf Coast beach nearby, and Mexico even closer. She would be the minority there. Being absorbed into a new life would be exciting. She would master Spanish and be on her way to traveling around Mexico whenever she wanted. She dreamed of an untroubled life full of joy, excitement, challenges, and someday, maybe love.

There, that's better. She turned the volume up and attempted to sing the few Spanish words that she knew. Gazing out the window, she noticed the mountains of yesterday had given way to rolling hills, trees, and, subsequently, flat land. She was making good progress. A short stop for lunch would be great.

Eva turned into a small café in Georgia for an early lunch. The slow-moving waitress's dialect was as thick and sultry as the Georgia air.

"Our specials today are fried catfish, barbecue sandwich, and a slice of buttermilk pie," the waitress said.

Eva listened to the list of daily specials and was especially interested in the way the waitress elongated the word pie, "Puh-eye" into two syllables. *How could she do that?* Eva wondered.

"Uh, I'll have the cobb salad and a cup of coffee." She would forgo the pie. Maintaining her appearance was one of the battles she had won.

"Outta coffee. I can make some if you wait, or how about sweet tea?" the waitress asked.

"Unsweet please," she replied.

The waitress gave her a look that clearly said, "This is Georgia. Who drinks unsweet tea?"

Eva finished her lunch and filled the car with gas. Cruising down Highway 10, the increasing number of oil rigs and refineries in southern Louisiana signaled she would soon be in Texas. She skipped dinner, hoping to cross the state line before her appetite caught up with her.

Without warning, there it was. A large sign on the side of the highway: "Welcome to Texas."

Home, she thought. Now, she could call it a day and check into the hotel.

The next morning, Eva woke earlier than the day before. With a full tank of gas and a biscuit to go, she was off. An hour and a half outside of the city of Houston, a proliferation of mesquite trees, cactus, and oil rigs lined the road. Eva sped by Corpus Christi Bay and followed the GPS to Highway 77 to the Rio Grande Valley. *Not long now,* she thought.

The fields south of Kingsville were dotted with Border Patrol cars, vans, and trucks among the mesquite trees and brush. State trooper vehicles were abundant as well. *Wonder if there is something going on today?* She didn't know this was just a typical day in this part of south Texas.

The King Ranch sprawled along both sides of the highway. This region had few gas stations. The sparse gas stations doubled as cafés. Eva stopped to fill up her car and went inside for something to eat. The menu, all in Spanish, listed ten different breakfast tacos and twenty additional kinds of tacos. "Hmm . . . well . . . " She studied the pictures of tacos.

"I guess I'll have a taco," she said to the clerk. And with uncertainty in her voice, she studied the menu and said, "I guess just a beef one?"

The clerk shot her a look, indicating her choice was not specific enough.

She randomly chose one of the options. "Uh, a beef fajita taco?" she asked in a timid voice.

The clerk asked, "De maíz o de harina?"

Eva was not sure what the clerk said.

The clerk repeated in English, "Corn or flour tortilla?"

"Uh, I guess corn? Is that good?"

The clerk quickly slapped the beef onto the tortilla and whispered, "Gringa," as she smiled and wrapped the taco up in paper.

Several miles from the cafe, she saw a building with lines of cars stacked up and Border Patrol agents inspecting cars. Trained canines were walking with the Border Patrol agents around the stopped vehicles on the lanes driving north. *Must be some kind of a checkpoint.* There was no checkpoint on her side of the highway going south. She drove past the check point and saw dozens of cameras and other types of surveillance equipment.

Within forty-five minutes, the number of palm trees increased. The palm trees multiplied and lined the highway on both sides. *Getting closer,* she thought. She checked the GPS. "Only sixty-one more miles," she whispered with a smile as she ventured on.

The GPS guided her to the apartment parking lot. She stepped out of her car and felt like she had opened an oven door. "Good grief, it's hot," she murmured. She walked past the swimming pool landscaped with palms and oleanders to the manager's office and obtained the keys to her new home.

Stepping inside her new apartment, she glanced around the room. She smiled and said, "Nice. Very nice!"

The furnished apartment was more charming than she remembered from the online photos. Saltillo tile, stucco walls, a nice sized kitchen with a large window. It was more like a two-story townhouse. She quickly arranged her few belongings, then drove two blocks down the street to the grocery store. *Just get enough for a few days to get started,* she thought. She had been frugal over the last year and stashed away all the money she could in a savings account. She needed to stretch her funds over the first month or two if possible.

Eva surveyed the supersized grocery store. It was different than any she had experienced. The produce section was enormous and had more types of peppers and beans than she knew existed. And the fruit . . . it was beautiful. Papayas, mangos, all kinds of citrus, Asian pears, and a host of fruits she could not identify. She loaded up more than she had planned to buy; but it looked so delicious, she couldn't help herself. As she rounded the produce section, she found fresh tortillas, fresh tamales, and a multitude of salsas. *Can't wait to try these,* she thought.

Checking out, she heard no English whatsoever. She was struck by how little Spanish she understood. *Oh, my goodness! They talk fast,* she thought. *I'm gonna have to pick Spanish up quickly.* She'd find a way to learn the language as soon as possible.

She took her grocery bags and walked to the exit door. Her eyes were drawn to a display of travel brochures in a rack. She skimmed across the titles. One brochure had colorful pictures of a tour of Mexico's historic sites. Without a second thought, she picked it up and tossed it into her grocery bag.

Back at the apartment, she unpacked the groceries, made a fruit plate, and sat down with the brochure. Eva read the travel details from front to back. The name of a travel agency office was stamped on the back. "Open Monday-Saturday 9:00-6:00," she read aloud. *I'll be at the agency door at 9:00 a.m. tomorrow.*

CHAPTER THREE

DOLORES WOKE FROM HER AFTERNOON sleep energized. Today, they would reach the river. The coyote gave the group specific instructions that were to be followed exactly. At dusk, they would leave the parked truck and follow the coyote toward the river. Once they approached the riverside, the coyote would determine the safety of crossing. If the river was busy, they could sneak across undetected. They were to watch for the signal for the group to come forward in smaller groups of five or six. Although there was no danger from the Guatemalan side of the river, Mexican officials watched the river crossings for undocumented travelers. Mexico didn't allow people to enter the country illegally. If caught, they risked being sent back across the river—or worse.

The group gathered together and listened to the coyote.

"I'll go ahead of you. Watch for the signal. Then move up closer to the river until I tell you to stop."

The group followed the coyote's instructions. He went further and signaled them to move up to another spot closer to the river and behind a few trees. This routine was repeated several times.

The coyote didn't want anyone—Mexican authorities or criminals—to see the group approaching. The coyote knew exactly where the group was to wait to move across. When the group was close to the river, he said, "I know a *balsero* who will ferry you over on a raft. If you want to wade out and then swim across, you can. But wait for the *balsero* to get the raft about halfway across, and then you swim out."

The region was a popular crossing spot for Hondurans, Guatemalans, Salvadorians, and anyone else who happened to be traveling to the United States from Central America. It was easier to cross here than other spots. Crossing the river was on the route of travel for entrepreneurs who wanted to sell their goods in Mexico. For undocumented people, the trick was to cross when the river was busy so that the small groups of travelers would go undetected. The merchants used rafts and small, shallow boats to cross. Many people swam across with little difficulty unless the river was up. Today, the river was up.

"Are you ready?" Dolores asked her brothers.

"I am," replied Ernesto.

Emilio nodded his head zealously.

Dolores took a moment to pray with her brothers for a safe journey and thanked God for helping them to reach the border of Mexico. They hugged each other and smiled.

"Soon, we'll be together in the United States," Emilio said.

"Yes. Soon," Dolores agreed, yet she knew the journey would be long and dangerous. She knew they would be safe once they reached their destination.

The coyote climbed up a spindly tree to have a better view of the other side of the river. He shimmied down quickly and said, "We must wait for a while. Sit over there." He pointed. "In the shadows. Some Mexican authorities are checking papers."

Dolores and her brothers rested in the darkness. She knew they were all hungry and wished they could've eaten before they crossed the river. But she believed that God would provide food for them on the other side.

Ernesto and Emilio anxiously stood up every few minutes to look for the coyote. No sign of him.

Ernesto asked, "What if he left us here? What if he took our money and left us to cross alone?"

"Yeah," Emilio chimed in. "What would we do? Would we still try to cross on our own?"

The brothers turned to their older sister with worried looks and waited for a response. "Yes, we'll still cross. But I'm not giving up on the coyote. He could've left us many times. He has had our money for days and stayed with us."

"She has a good point," Ernesto said.

"Okay," Emilio said, allowing himself to smile again. "I believe he'll come back, too."

Sweltering, hot, humid air encouraged the mosquitoes to swarm the group. All of the travelers were tired and hungry. Their exhaustion couldn't be missed, but neither could their optimism. As a group, each day they traveled closer to the river, their spirits lifted a little more.

"You know," Olivia said to the group, "I feel good about this trip. I believe this time I *will* make it to the United States."

"Me, too," Lola said.

Without warning, the coyote reappeared.

"We go now," he whispered. "But no talking!" he warned. "If you want to cross with a raft, come with me. If you want to go on foot and swim across on your own, go over there by the largest tree and watch. When the raft is in the middle of the water, you start out. And stay quiet. The Mexican authorities left, but they may return any time."

Unsure of her swimming abilities in deep, rapidly moving water, Dolores opted to cross the river in a raft. Her two brothers were both strong swimmers and believed they could swim across. She didn't want to be separated from them but felt this was the quickest way for the three of them to get across and stay out of sight.

The coyote addressed the group by the river. "Too many want to cross by raft, so we'll take turns. You, on this side, will go first," he said, pointing to his right. "I'll come back for the rest of you."

Dolores was in the second group. She watched as the first group climbed onto the raft. The *balsero* slowly steered the raft across, keeping it beside a larger raft carrying goods to Mexico from Guatemala. The moonlight beamed down like a spotlight on the water. Dolores could see the group gently slide across the river in the raft. Ernesto and Emilio swam unnoticed behind the raft. *What would be waiting for them on the other side?* Dolores wondered.

Ernesto and Emilio swam with a group of several boys and young men. The water was warm and fairly shallow, except in the very middle of the river. As they neared the other side, they felt large tree roots, stones, and plants along the bank. Emilio grabbed a slippery root and pulled himself up ever so quietly. With his younger brother securely on the bank, Ernesto grabbed another root and was on the shore in no time. They crawled up on to the firm ground and stayed low.

Both of the intact families opted to go the short distance across the river in the raft and would have a turn with Dolores. It was more time-consuming, loading up the toddlers and children with the parents. Dolores boarded the raft, and a mother asked, "Please, can you help watch my three children? I'm afraid the toddlers might try to crawl out."

"Yes, I'll watch them with you," Dolores agreed.

The raft left the bank, and Dolores strained to see her brothers on the other side of the river. The bank was completely dark. Were they safely across? Would she be able to find them right away?

The raft teetered a bit as it set out to cross the river beside a larger trade raft. About midway, the larger raft with commercial goods bumped Dolores' raft. Before she knew what happened, the mother screamed, "My baby! My baby!"

"Be quiet! Stay still!" the coyote said.

Others in the raft said," Shhh! Be quiet! We'll be caught!"

The mother hysterically waved her hands above the water off the side of the raft, causing the raft to bounce up and down in the water. Water seeped into the raft.

"Stop! Stop!" the others in the raft screamed to the mother.

"We'll sink!" another screamed.

Dolores reached down into the black, warm water and grabbed the baby's shirt, pulling the baby back onto the raft. The baby was not breathing. The frantic mother was crying; the coyote was trying to quiet everyone. The *balsero* was nervous and scolded the coyote. The other children on the raft cried and screamed with fear.

"Shh, shh!" the parents said to their children. "Quiet."

Dolores feared the Mexican officers would hear them and stop them on the other side. After a minute or so, the baby coughed, and water spewed out of his mouth. He cried. The mother took the baby in her arms and quieted him.

Dolores was uneasy as she looked across the river. *Did the authorities hear the commotion? Did my brothers? Had they come out to see what was wrong?* she wondered. She prayed they were safe and would remain out of sight from the authorities.

Minutes later, the raft ebbed to the bank. The coyote helped everyone off one by one and told them to disappear into the wooded area. "Hurry, go!" he said. Then he wished them luck in their travels.

"Wait, sir," Dolores said in a panic. "Where do we go now?" She didn't know where to go. She only knew that Guatemala and Honduras were behind her.

The coyote pointed and said, "There. Follow the road, but don't travel on the road; you'll be caught."

She nodded and ran toward the other part of the riverbank looking for her brothers.

"Dolores," she heard someone whisper. "Over here."

Dolores walked quietly in the direction of the voice that she recognized as Emilio's. In the shadows next to a tree, she thought she made out a figure in the darkness.

"Emilio?" she asked.

"Yes," he said as he reached for her. She hugged Emilio, then Ernesto. They were wet from swimming, but she didn't care. They were safely across.

"What happened out there?" Ernesto asked.

"A baby fell into the water. I grabbed him by his shirt and pulled him back to the raft."

"Oh, my goodness. That's why we heard a lady screaming and everyone talking." Emilio frowned.

"Yes," she replied.

"I hope the authorities didn't hear the woman or the baby," Ernesto said.

"Where do we go now?" Emilio asked.

Dolores pointed and said, "We'll follow that road. The checkpoints are on the road, and the authorities often patrol. We must walk a distance from the road."

A tap on the shoulder startled Dolores. Alarmed, she turned, thinking it was a police officer or government military personnel. It was the mother of the baby who fell into the water.

"You frightened me," Dolores said.

"I'm sorry. I didn't mean to scare you. I'll say a blessing for you for saving my baby," said the mother.

Together, Dolores and her brothers bowed their heads as the woman said a prayer. Then she turned and offered Dolores some food.

"I've been saving this, but my husband said we'll get more . . . and you look hungry."

"Oh, no, I couldn't take your food," Dolores objected.

"Please. For me. You saved our baby. We'll get more food."

"Thank you. My brothers and I haven't eaten today," she said as she handed the rolled-up tortilla and beans to her brothers.

The mother thanked Dolores again and walked back to her family group.

Each took a bite and savored every morsel. Dolores couldn't remember when she had last tasted such delicious beans, even if they were cold and the tortilla was a little damp from the river.

Olivia and Lola joined Dolores and her brothers. They hugged each other.

Olivia asked, "What happened on the raft? We crossed on the first raft, but I could hear screaming on the second one."

Dolores explained the event and then asked, "Olivia and Lola, do you want to walk with me and my brothers?"

"A small group would be good. I remember how to get to the trees on the other side of the road." Olivia nodded.

"Lead the way." Dolores motioned her forward.

She and her brothers walked a few paces behind Olivia and Lola. The bright moon of the early evening was now behind clouds, and the view of the land was obscured. They moved without saying a word. The trees and brush were thick, and Dolores' blouse caught on a limb. She fell behind the group and was afraid to be alone in the trees. Her brothers, paying attention to Olivia and Lola, hadn't noticed their sister had fallen behind. She caught up to her brothers and whispered, "Every once in a while, we should check to make sure the three of us are still together. It's dark here, and we can easily become separated."

Her brothers agreed. She didn't want to scold them, but she did want them to be more watchful of their surroundings and each other.

The group walked parallel to the road and through the trees. Olivia held her hand up to halt the group. Loud voices penetrated the night. Bright lights indicated a checkpoint was just ahead. Dolores' heartbeat increased.

Olivia whispered, "We must be careful." She motioned to the checkpoint and the lack of trees for several yards. "Let's go, one by one, to that group of trees over there. Stay down low, behind those bushes. Don't speak or make any noise."

The members of the group nodded, and Olivia pointed to each one in turn to make the jaunt. One by one, the group made it past the checkpoint to the cover of trees. They walked several more yards into the deep cover of the trees and away from the road.

Three miles further, Lola stopped the group. She motioned. "Up there. We must travel closer to the road for just a few yards. The brush up ahead does not look passable, so we must get out from the cover, just up to that next clearing of the brush to those trees ahead; and then we can travel out of sight. Be careful. We will go one by one again. Agreed?"

The group nodded their heads in silence, and Lola pointed out each one in turn. Lola would be the final one to make the walk nearer to the road.

Olivia made it through and ducked behind the trees. Next, Ernesto and Emilio each ran in turn. Last, Dolores made it across. After they moved into a hidden position, Lola began her walk toward them.

From nowhere, tires loudly skidded to a screeching halt. A van stopped on the side of the road. The doors were thrown open. Three men with tattoos covering their faces jumped out and ran across the short distance of the field. They snatched Lola. One of the men grabbed her and covered her mouth. She screamed frantically when they pulled her into the van. Another man scanned the trees, looking for others to take. The group, huddled within the trees, remaining perfectly still, was not visible to the men on the other side of the road.

One of the men yelled to the driver, "Go ahead; get her to the safehouse."

The doors slammed shut. The van sped down the road into the dark jungle.

Dolores, Olivia, Ernesto, and Emilio slowly stood up, shocked. They had no warning of the van. It just appeared.

Dolores' shaking was uncontrollable. Olivia cried and tried to be quiet as she covered her face with her hands. Dolores put her arm around Olivia to calm her.

"I know what will happen next," Olivia said through her tears. "They will use her in a brothel or sell her to someone else who will."

Dolores and her brothers were speechless.

Ernesto asked, "Should we try to find her and bring her back?"

Dolores panicked. "I don't think so." She knew her brother meant well, but he didn't understand the risk involved. If the boys found Lola and attempted to retrieve her, they would be killed.

Olivia said, "We can't. They'll take her into Tapachula or Salina Cruz or Oaxaca, and that's where they will sell her—or use her in their own brothel. They're part of a gang. Probably Salvadorian."

Ernesto and Emilio didn't grasp the horror that Lola would be suffering.

Olivia pulled herself together and advised, "We should move away from this spot and hide and get some rest. It will be light soon. Tomorrow, we'll figure out where we'll go to get on the train or find a truck of other travelers."

The group agreed.

Dolores, Olivia, Ernesto, and Emilio found a hiding spot within the trees and up on a hillside. They began to understand the seriousness and peril of their journey. Sitting on the hillside provided a better view of the trees, undergrowth, and fields. During the remaining few minutes of night, they witnessed other travelers quietly making their way in the obscurity. They could distinguish shadows, figures, and silhouettes moving in the midst of the woods. An occasional crackle of leaves as the travelers worked their way through the night and faint sounds of insects and moving reptiles were the only sounds they heard.

How many people must be on this journey, Dolores wondered.

"Dolores," Emilio whispered.

"Yes?"

"Are you okay?"

"Yes. Just a little tired." She didn't want to worry her brother by speaking of her uneasiness.

"Me, too. Think it'll be safer tomorrow?"

"We can pray for God to watch us," she replied.

As each member of the group sat in silence, they felt intense apprehension. They had been across the Mexican border for a few short hours. A baby almost drowned, and one of the members of their group had been kidnapped. Dolores prayed for their safety in the coming days.

CHAPTER FOUR

"GOOD MORNING," EVA SAID TO the travel agent.

"Good morning. How can I help you?" the agent asked.

Eva admired the natural beauty possessed by Hispanic women. Jet black hair, long eye lashes, dark eyebrows, and such beautiful skin. The travel agent was neatly dressed in a black dress with a bright pink jacket and large silver earrings. Eva focused again on her purpose for the visit.

"Oh, yes. Hi. I picked up this brochure in the grocery store yesterday and wanted to know more about this tour."

"I can help you with that." The agent looked at the brochure, then quickly said, "This is a tour that starts in Monterrey, Mexico. So, you'd fly or drive into Mexico. But the trip leaves in three days. Let me see if there is availability."

Eva was optimistic. It was crucial for her to make this trip before the semester began. She needed to improve her Spanish . . . fast. Understanding Spanish would give her an advantage in assimilating to her new city and her university position. She was a quick learner and was confident her skills would improve in a week of intense language immersion.

The agent made a call to the tour director. Eva listened closely, hoping it was not too late to join the tour.

"I see. Okay, yes. Hold on." The agent covered the phone and asked Eva, "Are you ready to make a deposit today? They'll hold your spot. Or you can pay in full today rather than when you arrive in Monterrey."

"Oh, sure. Today is great. Credit card will work?" Eva asked.

"Yes." The agent took the card and gave the tour director the necessary information.

The agent handed the card back as she said, "Okay, you're set. I can access the details about the hotels and stops online for you and give you the complete itinerary."

"Oh, perfect. And is there another option to get to Monterrey?" Eva didn't want to risk getting lost in Mexico and miss the tour. "I don't want to drive, since I've never been to Mexico."

"Never?" She questioned with a surprised look. "Sure, you can catch the bus from the bus station downtown. I'll give you that information, and you can purchase your ticket right now if you like."

"Excellent," Eva replied.

This seems too easy, Eva thought. A vacation! And a learning experience! A double treat.

"Oh, look at this. Here's a lower-priced ticket for the bus trip to Monterrey. It can save you a little money," she said.

"Saving money is always good," Eva said.

"Now, I think I can get you the pass from the city bus station to the travel agency. You'll only need to find the bus line and board the bus without having to buy the pass in Monterrey."

She printed off the itinerary and the passes and went over the details with Eva.

"The trip is billed as an historic tour which leaves on Saturday and lasts for one week. It includes several states in Mexico and goes south all the way to Veracruz, making stops along the way in Dolores Hidalgo, Guanajuato, Morelia, San Miguel Del Allende, some of the attractions in Michoacán, and Puebla on the way back to Monterrey. It goes around Mexico City, so that is one city not included on this tour."

Eva looked at the pictures. The cities in Mexico looked enchanting.

"It is a semi-inclusive package with some meals and all hotels pre-arranged. The hotels are rated as five stars in Mexico, which is the equivalent of three to four stars here. There are some optional excursions available. You can sign up for those with your tour guide."

Eva reviewed the plans in her mind. She would ride a bus from Brownsville to Monterrey. She didn't think that would be difficult. In fact, it would be fun to let someone else drive. Then meet up with the tour group. *It sounds simple,* she thought.

The agent added, "Your bus from Brownsville first travels to Reynosa, another large border city west of here, and then to Monterrey. Don't get off of the bus in Reynosa. It's not very safe in that part of the city, and you're on the same bus all the way to Monterrey. Monterrey is a busy city of over one million people and sits in the mountains of Mexico. You'll go into the large Monterrey central bus station and find the correct city bus that is shown on your pass to make a connection to the other travel agency located across town."

"Okay," Eva said.

The agent continued, "There, you will meet your travel guide and other fellow travelers. The other tourists are from Mexico. You'll meet them there and depart for the actual tour. It will take you most of the day to get from Brownsville to the other travel agency location. Any questions?"

"Do you know if any of the other tourists speak English?" Eva asked.

"Most will only speak Spanish. I know your guide personally, and he speaks English as a second language."

Eva had only begun to study Spanish. *What better way to get immersed in the language?* she thought.

"Now, you do understand there are some safety risks associated with this trip?"

Eva was thinking there might be some challenges, but she was eager to go.

"I thought there might be. You mean like the hiking?"

"Well, that does pose some risk. But be prepared for a high level of security officers, Mexican federal police, military, and such."

"Oh. Is it that dangerous? I've heard about people traveling in caravans through Mexico from Central America to enter the U.S."

"Not dangerous when the security officers are present with the tour group. You'll probably not travel to the same areas as the caravans. Just pay attention. We also know there may be cartels operating in the larger cities, so you should stay with your group at all times."

Eva's face gave away the squeamishness she felt as she listened to the agent.

"And don't worry. You'll be traveling under the tour company's visa, so you can't be anywhere without the group or the tour guide. Don't be concerned. This tour takes place every couple of months, and we haven't had any incidents reported."

"That's reassuring."

"Remember to take your credit card, your passport, spending money, and driver's license. There is a checklist here on the back of the tour itinerary that tells you what you need. Don't take too much money. You can exchange your dollars at the Cambio stand near the bus station. Keep your documents and money on your person at all times. It might be helpful to get one of those small passport purses you can wear inside a jacket or blouse. Keep your documents on you, but out of sight. Be sure you read all of the precautionary information on the back of the itinerary."

"Okay, thank you."

"And . . . there's a number on the back of the brochure if you need to reach the other tour agent before you leave . . . you know, in case you change your mind about going. Just be sure to dial the country code listed there before the actual phone number."

You obviously don't know me. Of course, I'm not going to cancel. I can do this, Eva thought. She gathered up her brochures, tickets, and itinerary and thanked the agent. She felt a perfect mix of excitement and anxiety about her travel plans.

That evening, Eva's mother called to see how the move-in was going. After Eva told her about the drive down to Brownsville, the apartment, and the grocery store, she found the courage to tell her mother about the upcoming trip.

"You're doing what?! Have you lost your mind? A single woman traveling to Mexico, in Mexico, for a week with people you don't know? With people you can't even talk to?"

"Well, Mother, that's the point of the trip. I have to learn to speak Spanish."

"You are crazier than your crazy uncle Fred. Now, he was crazy, certifiable. But you are downright insane! Don't you know it's dangerous there? You don't have any legal rights or protections there. Oh, my goodness, I may have a stroke."

"Well, Mother, I need to learn Spanish as quickly as possible—"

"Buy one of those computer language programs. I've seen them on TV. *Rosetta Stone* I think it's called—"

"Mom, it won't be the same as being in the country and being forced to speak the language. Besides, you know I'm independent and can do this. I can make it on my own. I always have."

Nothing Eva said put her mother at ease. Eva had never heard her mother talk so hysterically. But she had to admit, she, too, was a tiny bit apprehensive about traveling alone in Mexico, but she was not going to let that stop her.

"Mom, I'll call you in a couple of days from Mexico."

"Mexico. I never . . . "

"It'll be fine," Eva said, trying to reassure her mother.

"I'll be watching the news for problems that are happening in Mexico," her mother said, emphasizing the words "in Mexico."

"Okay, Mom. I'll talk to you soon."

* * *

Two days was not very much time to get ready for the trip. Eva selected her clothing carefully so she would take just the right amount and her suitcase wouldn't be too heavy. "I can always buy clothes there if I need to," Eva whispered to herself. She checked her bag several times, then went to the bank. She got a little cash to change at the Cambio stand downtown by the bus station.

The morning of the trip, Eva called a taxi to take her to the bus station in Brownsville. The bus station was a combination of people in a hurry and people asleep on the benches. Many of the people arriving in Brownsville crossed the border every day to work. Trucks and vans parked outside, waiting in the fumes and heat, ready to pick up the workers. Eva watched as the people scampered from the bus terminal to the vehicles that would take them to their employer for the day.

Eva's excitement covered her face. *Might be better to not be so notice-able, so obviously a tourist,* she thought. *I'll try to blend in.* She laughed to herself, realizing she was the only Anglo in the entire bus station. *Blend in. Right.*

She checked the clock and the boarding time for the bus. As usual, she was early. She sat in one of the few vacant orange plastic chairs in the lobby of the bus station and watched the people for nearly an hour. The air conditioning wasn't quite enough to cool the lobby area stuffed with so many people. Parents hushed their busy children, who were not fans of the waiting process. Others greeted incoming family members, speaking rapid Spanish with great bravado and tightly squeezing the arrivals with prolonged hugs. It wasn't uncommon to see multiple members of extended families, three or four generations worth, picking up a single relative.

The announcement of, "Ten-fifty bus for Monterrey, all passengers to the terminal," blasted over the speaker in Spanish and then in English.

Eva handed the attendant her suitcase to be loaded with the others under the bus and presented her pre-purchased ticket to the bus driver. She squeezed down the narrow row of seats holding her travel bag so that it did not accidentally hit anyone sitting in aisle seats along the way. The bus seemed nice enough. Cushy chairs in plush, royal blue fabric and air conditioning running full blast. She noticed the restroom in the back and felt at ease. She didn't know how long the ride to Monterrey would take. Her passport purse with all of the documents was tucked inside her jacket. Everything was in place.

With all of the passengers on board, the bus wobbled through the city streets a short distance past the rows of duty-free shops to the Brownsville International Bridge. As it moved across the bridge, she saw groups of barefoot children extending their hands out to the people walking across the bridge. Occasionally, a pedestrian would toss a coin over the bridge to the children below with outstretched hands. One lucky child would catch or find the coin along the river-bank. The other children then followed the person who tossed the coin as they cried out for more money.

Eva's heart broke for these children in tattered clothing running under the bridge with their hands reaching out for coins. She wondered if another kind person would toss a coin. She would later learn that some of these children lived on the street.

She was energized as the bus crossed the International Bridge, and she knew she was already in Mexico. Traveling out of the United States was something new to her. Eva believed all of her life she was meant to be a world traveler. She remembered getting her first passport years ago. It had not been used until today. This would be her first of many trips to other countries.

Within minutes, the bus entered a parking spot on the other side of the bridge. The bus driver, speaking only Spanish, instructed the passengers to leave the bus, and he gestured to Eva to come along with the group. Everyone stood outside the bus and presented their papers. Eva reached into her purse and pulled out her travel visa the agent had given her. She gave her passport and the papers to the official.

Another officer motioned toward the bottom of the bus and instructed the driver to open the hatch and unload the bags. One by one, the luggage was removed from the bus as the officer inspected each parcel and suitcase. After several minutes, the luggage and parcels were loaded back under the bus, and the passengers were directed to board the bus. Eva followed the group. She wondered if unloading the complete bus and searching each piece of luggage was standard routine or if the officials were looking for something specific. No one on the bus seemed concerned. The bus driver shook hands with the officials and returned to the driver's seat.

Eva settled back into her chair and looked out the window. A few passengers were speaking very rapid Spanish. Others gazed out the window or read newspapers. The bus negotiated the nearly deserted narrow streets of Matamoros. Sand bags were stacked around the corners of the road. There was a military presence of Mexican federal authorities. A sand-colored tank was at the end of one road. A passenger across the aisle noticed Eva's worried look as she surveyed the street. He leaned toward Eva and said in a very thick accent of broken English, "No worry. Es safe. Safety for you. Safety. Cartel."

"Oh. Thank you," Eva replied.

She felt on edge. Once again, she questioned herself. *What had she done? Would this trip be her end? Was her mother, heaven forbid, right?* No, she coached herself, *I can do this. I can do anything I decide to do.*

She realized she was now on the outskirts of Matamoros. Don't think I'll visit this city again. She hoped Monterrey and the other towns would be more tourist-friendly.

About an hour and a half later, the bus parked in the Reynosa station. Several passengers left the bus and were replaced by new passengers. The woman sitting next to Eva slept. Concrete buildings; pitted, rough, dirty streets; and a few people moving about were all that Eva could see outside the bus terminal. The larger, unattractive industrial buildings, scarcity of people, and nonexistent landscaping depicted a city victimized by crime and high rates of poverty. She did not see anything that would attract her to return to this city.

A mere thirty minutes later, the bus was back on the road headed south to Monterrey. The landscape outside Reynosa, in the state of Tamaulipas, was flat, dry, and overrun with cactus, mesquite trees, and yucca plants. The scenery was about as unfriendly as anyone could imagine. The terrain didn't improve as the bus entered the state of Nuevo León. Eva thought about the thousands of individuals who must have crossed this land on foot throughout history, looking for a better life either in Mexico or the U.S. How hard those trips must have been.

The bus continued southwest for some time and then slowed down to a halt. Out the window on the other side of the bus, Eva saw what appeared to be an outpost. The bus door opened, and a man in military attire, sporting a machine gun, stepped on board the bus. He walked down the aisle, eyeing the passengers. Eva's heart raced. Being the only Anglo on the bus, she was not sure what to expect. The man with the machine gun walked to her row of seats and looked her directly in the eye. He walked back to the bus driver and said a few words in an authoritative-sounding voice. The driver responded, "Sí, sí," and showed him a list of what Eva figured was passenger names. The man checked over the list and the papers. He looked up again and looked straight at Eva again. He spoke Spanish to the bus driver as he stared at Eva. Her face turned red. A sensation of unexpected panic came over her, and she thought she might faint. He returned the list to the driver and stepped off the bus. The door closed behind the man, and the bus began to roll forward.

Eva took slow, deep breaths to calm herself down. She had no idea who the man was or what he was doing. The passenger who had reassured her before was now asleep. She couldn't ask anyone on the bus because she didn't know how to ask. She felt helpless and vulnerable.

Eva looked out the window and continued to calm herself. The wilderness stretched on for miles. She saw a tiny village in the distance and wondered about the people who lived there and how they lived in such stark terrain away from populated areas. Based on her observations of Reynosa and Matamoras, perhaps living in a desolate village was safer than living in a city.

A few hours later, the bus slowed to a stop at a gas station. A new passenger entered the bus. The driver took the ticket and motioned to the entering passenger to have a seat. Slowly, the bus angled back out to the highway.

The trip to Monterrey took longer than she expected. With all the stops and starts, it had been more than five hours since the bus left Brownsville. The travel agent mentioned that if Eva drove her own car, it would probably take three to four hours of actual drive time from Brownsville to Monterrey. But traveling by bus required additional time to cross the bridge, undergo inspections, and make additional stops along the way. Unbeknownst to Eva, the trip would take more than seven hours.

She settled back in her seat and looked through the front window ahead. Eva could now see mountains climbing up from the flatlands. The late afternoon sun surrendered to spectacular colors of early dusk. Oranges, pinks, even a slight purple tint were displayed around the edges of the mountain range. *Incredible*, Eva thought.

The bus neared the large city as the lights twinkled from the mountain sides. Once in the city proper, the bus entered a freeway and soon exited toward the city buildings. The bus struggled through the smaller roads to the very large bus terminal.

Eva checked her papers and noted the bus line number she would take to go across town to the travel agency. She felt a slight wave of dread as she exited the bus and retrieved her luggage. *Maybe the driver can help me,* she thought. She showed the bus line number to the driver, and he motioned for her to go inside the building.

Inside the massive station, there were posted signs, all in Spanish. She couldn't ask for help. Feeling scared and distressed, she worried about making her connection on time. What if she missed it and was stuck in the bus station? Her mother's words were ringing in her head, "You are crazier than your crazy uncle Fred. Now, he was crazy, certifiable. But you are downright insane! Don't you know it's dangerous there?"

She stood there, not knowing what to do when a small, older lady with red hair approached her and, in broken English, asked, "I help you?"

"Oh, thank you so much." Eva showed the lady her bus connection.

The lady attempted to answer Eva, but mostly Spanish came out, so she simply motioned for Eva to follow her.

The bus station terminal was a combination of concrete, motor oil spots, and exhaust fumes. Yellow-tinged lights provided little assistance to passengers reading their passes and looking for their buses. People talked loudly and bumped into each other. A man was asleep against the wall. The little lady with red hair stepped carefully around the sleeping man and scurried past, then stopped in front of another bus.

The lady motioned to the door of the bus as she said "¡Rápido!"

Eva knew what that meant. She rolled her suitcase quickly to the bus.

"Thank you again, uh, gracias," Eva said.

"De nada," she replied and sped away to another bus.

Eva was grateful that the woman had noticed her worried look. She wondered if the lady with the red hair fully understood how helpless Eva felt standing in the bus station alone and unable to talk to anyone. She typically could figure things out on her own, and eventually, she probably would have found the right bus. She was certain of that. But she was grateful for the help.

The driver for the designated city bus took Eva's ticket and waved her on board. She surrendered her suitcase to the attendant, who stowed it under the bus. Most of the other passengers had no luggage but only shopping bags, brief cases, and other items that were evidence of daily living in the city. Eva supposed most of the passengers were just going home after work or going to another part of the city.

Exhausted, she found a seat near the front. She was ready to get to the other travel agency to board the final tour bus with fellow travelers.

The bus sped down a large freeway to the other side of the city and then exited and turned into a parking lot of what appeared to be a shopping center. A group of people in the parking lot were talking to each other. Each one of them had at least one piece of luggage.

At last, I'm here, she thought.

CHAPTER FIVE

DOLORES WOKE BEFORE THE OTHERS. She sat for quite some time thinking about home. *I wish I could let Mamá and Papá know where we are and that we're okay,* she thought, knowing they were worried. She watched the sun getting lower in the sky. Such a vibrant display of God's work. *I wish I could be watching it from my home in Honduras with all of the family together.* Her heart was sad.

Dolores couldn't think of the past. She needed to stay strong for her brothers and think only about the future. *What would it be like in the United States? Do people really get to eat every day? Do they have warm clothes? Do they live in nice houses? Does everyone have shoes? Does everyone get to go to school? Does everyone get to work? Is everyone protected from gangs and violence?* Dolores had heard so many fascinating things, it was difficult to believe all of these things could really be true. Her thoughts were interrupted by Emilio.

"When will we start to walk?" Emilio whispered.

"Soon. We should wake the others. It's getting dark," Dolores said.

Olivia stretched her arms and legs. "Oh, my legs are sore," she said.

Ernesto awoke. He shook some dirt off his pants. He took off his shoe and examined his blisters.

"That looks bad," Dolores said.

"This one is pretty sore," Ernesto said, pointing to the large, open blister on the bottom of his right foot. "And red."

"Yes. It looks like it might get infected. When we get to some water, you should wash that off," Dolores said.

Emilio asked, "Do you have any idea where we might find some food?"

"I see some plants over there," Olivia responded. "There may be some jicama."

The group made their way to the edge of an unkempt farm field. Ernesto and Emilio dug up large clumps of dirt with their bare hands under a jicama plant and pulled up the edible root.

"Ah, come here, you little delicious fruit," Emilio said with a smile.

"Wish we had a knife," Ernesto said.

"I have a small one," Olivia said. "We can do it, I think."

"Good," said Dolores.

Emilio gave the piece of fruit to Olivia. She took a tiny, thin, bladed knife from her pocket and took off a piece of the skin. She peeled the remainder of the piece of fruit.

"I don't know if this knife will be able to cut it into nice pieces; but it might be able to cut some slivers, and we can eat those."

The three stared at the fruit as Olivia worked. She handed each of them pieces of the fruit as she shaved off slivers.

"Oh, my goodness," Dolores said, placing the moist piece of fruit in her mouth. "I did not know I was so hungry!"

Occupied eating fruit, the others said nothing.

When the last sliver was eaten, Olivia said, "We should start walking in that direction." She gestured northeast.

Step after step, the tired legs and blistered feet continued. No one talked. Each one scanned their surroundings incessantly as they plodded along in the dark. Sparkling stars contrasted the black sky. They walked far enough from the other larger groups, so they couldn't see them. Nevertheless, they heard the others talking.

"We must keep our distance. It sounds like that group is growing," Olivia said.

Without saying anything further, they moved away from the road several more yards and moved at a slow, tired pace.

* * *

The four travelers were walking as the darkness gave in to the morning light. They heard whispers and low voices coming through the trees and fields. In the distance, they saw people converging on the side of the road.

"There are many more people here this morning heading north," Ernesto told Dolores. "It's a crowd over there."

"It looks that way," Dolores agreed.

"Is that bad?" Emilio asked.

"I'm not sure. But it may help us to find our way," Dolores said. "There'll be plenty of people to follow."

"I suppose so," said Ernesto.

"Good morning," Olivia said to the others. "Are you ready to walk toward La Bestia? We can get on the train in Tapachula. It'll take us to Arriaga. From there, we'll decide which route to take to the United States."

Ernesto spoke first. "I know I'm ready to get on the train. We've been walking so much that I have sores on my feet."

"We still have a walk ahead of us. You notice many more people have gathered?" Olivia asked.

"Yes," replied Dolores. "We should all be very careful. Some of these people may not be travelers but criminals."

"I wondered about that, too," said Ernesto.

Dolores whispered to Olivia, "There are so many gang members in El Salvador, Guatemala, and Honduras. It might be difficult to distinguish the gang members from the people fleeing their own countries because of violence and poverty."

Olivia agreed. "Yes. Better just to keep our distance from the group. You know, keep space between us and the group over there."

They walked within sight of some of the other people from Honduras but kept watchful eye on people they did not know. There were as many people from El Salvador and Guatemala as from Honduras. There were a few others from undetermined countries.

Dolores. Olivia, Emilio, and Ernesto remained some distance from the road and scavenged for any possible fruit or other food to eat. They were all hungry. They came upon a house that was tucked behind some shrubs. They did not approach the house, but a woman opened the door and called out to them.

"Here. Come over here. I have something for you," a small, older woman called out.

Olivia and Dolores went to the woman, and Ernesto and Emilio watched. The woman with a face full of tanned wrinkles looked to be of Mayan descent. She gave them a handful of tortillas and some fruit in a small bag.

"I will say a prayer of thanks for you and bless you," Dolores said. She made the sign of a cross.

Tears streamed down Olivia's face. Her heart was full of gratitude. She hugged the woman and said, "Blessings to you."

Dolores and Olivia called out quietly to Ernesto and Emilio. They didn't want anyone else to hear for fear they would take the food from them.

"Ernesto. Emilio. We have something. Come and see," Dolores said in a hushed voice.

Dolores opened the bag so her brothers could see inside. Ernesto's eyes opened wide. Emilio stood frozen, anticipating the first bite.

Dolores counted the tortillas. "One, two, three . . . there are four, one whole tortilla for each of us," she said to Olivia. "And look at the fruit. Mamey, rambutans, pomegranates, and plantains."

Ernesto asked, "Should we save a piece of the fruit for later?"

Emilio added, "We can eat half of a tortilla now and save the other half and eat that with some fruit later when we get hungry again."

Olivia said, "I think that's a good idea."

They divided the food, and each one put a piece or two of fruit and their remaining tortillas in their pockets. They felt reassured knowing they would have something to eat later.

"Let's find a place to rest while it's daytime and then walk after it's dark," Olivia advised.

The four weary travelers looked for a place within the brush that wasn't noticeable from the road. It was a typical hot and humid August day with off-and-on light rain. They decided to rest just a few hours, wake, and then discuss their plans.

In the late afternoon before even a slight promise of dusk, Ernesto was awakened by the sounds of footsteps not far from where he was sleeping. Without making a sound, he slinked over to Dolores and nudged her.

"Yes?" she whispered.

Ernesto motioned in the direction toward the road. "Over there."

Dolores woke Olivia and Emilio.

"Shhhh," she whispered.

There were more people walking within sight. Dolores, Emilio, Ernesto, and Olivia moved away from the others into an area with a few more small trees.

"We should get started with our walk," Dolores suggested.

They all agreed.

The trek from the Suchiate River to the town of Tapachula was just a little over twenty miles. They would travel through benign terrain of clumps of trees and farming fields attempting to remain undetected.

Dolores watched the people walking nearby with rough expressions on their tattooed faces. They looked similar to the gang members from El Salvador she had seen in San Pedro Sula. She monitored their movement, looking for any indication that they might be edging closer to her own group.

Olivia was keenly aware of the gang appearance of the men traveling nearby. She was saddened by what had happened to Lola. She felt protective toward the group.

"Your brothers remind me of my family. I feel like they're my brothers, too," Olivia said to Dolores.

"Yes, they like you, too. They're good boys. But I'm also missing the rest of my family," Dolores whispered.

"It's hard not to miss family when we're on a trip like this," Olivia said. "You feel good about making progress on the journey but know you are moving further from your family."

They continued to move stealthily through the trees that lined the crop fields. Although they weren't far from the Pacific Ocean, the drought had taken a toll on these fields just as it had the farm in Honduras. The dusty and dry fields did not provide much cover. The group was relieved when darkness finally came.

It was difficult to detect other figures moving toward Tapachula in the twilight. Dangerous strangers could suddenly come up on the group. Olivia touched Dolores on the shoulder. Emilio and Ernesto stopped walking to listen.

"Should we try to find a more protected path?" Olivia asked Dolores.

"We could go over in that direction." Dolores pointed. "There are more trees. But there could be more people walking over there for the same reason."

Ernesto and Emilio listened, not saying a word, not knowing what would be the best choice.

"Good point," Olivia said. "Might be best to stay over here."

They agreed to continue near the farm fields since some of the fields were lined with small bushes and high grass. They would travel further away from other people who, like themselves, crossed at the river and were heading for the train. Blackness now engulfed the sky.

They were on pace to make it more than halfway before the sun came up. They were about nine miles from Tapachula by daylight. Their footsteps were disguised by the ear-piercing singing of the Mexican cicadas as they continued their trek toward town. Houses became more frequent nearer to the town.

They traveled at a pretty good clip. Fatigue set in. Dolores methodically placed one foot in front of the other. Her feet were sore; her legs ached; and like Olivia and her brothers, she needed a break.

"Dolores," Ernesto said, "should we eat the rest of our food now— you know, what we saved from yesterday?"

"Ernesto, I had forgotten about that," she said, pulling out pieces of a tortilla and a piece of fruit from her pocket.

"Oh, yes," Olivia added. "I hadn't thought about eating at all."

They sat down and pulled out the remaining food. Without speaking, they each ate their food, concentrating more on their walk than the nourishment.

After a short break, Dolores said, "I know we're all tired. There's no good place right here to hide and sleep. Let's go a little further and look for a place to rest before we go in to Tapachula."

They agreed and continued to move along, darting between the fields and houses.

"Wait! Wait!" a shouting, desperate male voice cut through the early morning air. "Stop! Don't hurt her! Stop!" A man shouted in desperation.

The group stopped and turned toward the panicked screaming. Men from El Salvador had ambushed a man and a woman. The man was thrown on the ground, dust flying up from the scuffle, as the woman struggled, screamed, and then cried.

The woman shouted loudly, "Stop! Stop! No!" And she sobbed. "No! No! Stop hurting me!"

They could not see what was happening to the people who were on the ground. They only heard the yelling and screaming.

"We can rescue them," Emilio said.

"No!" said Olivia. "They have weapons. Look."

"Oh," Emilio said, "knives. Very long ones. Should Ernesto and I get weapons? We might need weapons for protection the rest of the way."

"Shhh . . . let's get out of sight," Dolores said as she pointed. "Over there, fast."

They skirted further from the group for safety. They scurried to a small stand of bushes and trees even further away from the road.

"Okay," said Dolores, almost out of breath from the rapid pace. "We can stay here for a while. Let's rest."

Dolores regretted she was not able to help the couple fighting against the Salvadorian men. She knew her first concern was to keep her brothers safe. She wished she could've done something. She prayed for protection for the couple and for all the travelers going north.

Ernesto and Emilio went under some bushes and laid down on the hard, dry ground. Dolores and Olivia sat under a tree a short distance away. The group was silent. The danger surrounded them wherever they went. It would be tomorrow before they reached the train yard. They planned to walk covertly to the train yard in the daylight, which would add more risk to their journey, but they would reach the railyard sooner.

CHAPTER SIX

EVA STEPPED OFF THE CITY bus and collected her bag. She turned toward the group of fellow tourists, and a man appeared in front of her.

"Hello," he said. "My name is Adrián. I'm your tour guide this week," he said as he extended his hand.

Eva took his hand and replied, "English! So glad to meet you Adrián." A sense of relief washed over her, evident by the smile spreading across her face.

Adrián was charming and attractive but also quite a bit younger than Eva. She was embarrassed that a romantic thought had entered her mind—even for a fleeting second. *I'm not on this trip for that, no matter what Mom said.*

"I'll be able to answer any questions you have and tell you about the many sites we'll visit."

"Thank you. I'm looking forward to it."

Adrián added, "We're still waiting for two others to arrive, and then we'll board the bus."

"Okay, great. Do you know if anyone else on the tour speaks English?"

"I'm not sure. The other tourists are from Mexico. Actually, most are from Monterrey. They're taking this trip as a vacation. Many of the people on the tour are retired, although not everyone. Come over and let me introduce you to the others."

Eva followed Adrián. He introduced her to each passenger. "Eva is from the United States. She is a professor in Brownsville, Texas."

Upon hearing the words *Estados Unidos* and *profesora*, the other travelers responded "Ah, oh," or "bueno." Each one expressed how glad they were to meet her. She could only nod. She turned her back to the others and asked Adrián, "How do I say I am glad to have met them?"

"Easy. When they say they are glad to meet you, you say *igualmente*."

"Oh, okay. Easy enough. Thanks."

Adrián went about getting everyone situated, and the other two passengers arrived.

When Adrián introduced one of the late arriving men as Esteban Garcia to Eva, he replied, "Or Steven in English."

"Oh, good. Thanks, Steven. You speak English?"

"Yes," he said with a smile that would begin to melt an iceberg on the North Pole. "I went to college in the United States. I'm a manager of a *maquiladora* near Brownsville."

"I see. Excuse me for not knowing, but I just arrived in Brownsville a couple of days ago. What's a *maquiladora*?"

"Just think of it as a factory. A large facility where Mexican workers make things, often for sale in the U.S. Most of the time, the factory is owned by an American company."

"Oh." She was about to ask him the type of factory when Adrián introduced the other passenger to Eva.

"And Eva, this is Tomás," Adrián said.

This time, when Tomás expressed that he was glad to make her acquaintance, she responded, "Igualmente."

"Very nice," Adrián said with a smile.

Adrián handed each passenger a badge to wear on their clothing or around their neck. Then he said, "Okay, once you have your badge, your itinerary, your ID, and the travel visa all tucked away, you may board the bus. We will take off in about five minutes."

The luggage was loaded, and the last bit of light disappeared. The sky became completely dark as the bus left the city to begin the weeklong adventure.

Adrián stood up in the front of the bus and said, "Good evening and welcome to an historic tour of Mexico!" He said everything in Spanish first and then in English. "As you may know, we'll be traveling all night tonight to get the trip underway. In the morning, we'll be in the city of Dolores Hidalgo for breakfast. But for now, get comfortable. Chat with your neighbors and get ready for a wonderful week."

Eva knew she would not remember all the names of the passengers. But she had no trouble remembering Steven. He spoke English and was very easy on the eyes. She couldn't help but wonder about him. She wanted to learn more about him while on the tour. She was curious to know more about his work and his family. His English was very good, and he certainly had his share of charisma.

She sat in her window seat next to a woman who spoke no English, which gave Eva the opportunity to rest. She was excited and drained. She took her travel pillow and blanket from her carry-on bag and moved around a bit, trying to settle in for the night. The bus rolled over the highway causing a steady thumping sound, which lulled her to sleep.

* * *

The tour bus progressed on the route through the night. In the emerging morning light, Eva looked out the windows at the quaint narrow roads and colorful buildings as the bus entered the town of Dolores Hidalgo.

Adrián greeted the tour group. "Good morning and welcome to Dolores Hidalgo. This is where the fight for Mexican independence began. Across the road, you can see the Church of Our Lady of Sorrows. Legend says this is where the fight for the freedom of Mexico began. It is open for you to go inside and see the beautifully ornate interior as well as the impressive towers outside of the front wall. We'll all gather here in about two hours."

"Oh. One more thing," Adrián said. "We've arranged for you to tour the Museo de la Indepencia Nacional just over there," he said, pointing. "Enjoy; see you in two hours."

Adrián said, "Another one more thing." He laughed and added, "On your left down the road a few steps, you'll find a small restaurant. Your badge will get you in for your breakfast. See you in a couple of hours."

Adrián turned to Eva and said, "Be sure you have a cup of their coffee. It is true Mexican coffee. The beans are grown in the mountains of Mexico, and the coffee is flavored with a touch of cinnamon. You'll love it."

"Thank you for the tip. I'll order some," Eva said.

Eva was famished and thought she would enjoy the Church of Our Lady of Sorrows more after a meal. The décor of the restaurant was quite appealing. The Saltillo tile floor, stone and stucco walls, sturdy wooden tables covered with linen cloths, and quaint wooden chairs made the interior charming. Some of the other people from the tour entered the restaurant just ahead of her.

"You join us?" said the wife of a middle-aged married couple, inviting Eva to sit at their table.

"Yo soy la señora García y el es mi marido el señor García. We practice English?" the wife asked Eva.

Eva smiled and said, "I am Eva Jordan. I want to practice Spanish."

The husband and wife interpreted the menu for Eva. She repeated the words as precisely as possible. The couple asked Eva how to say the names of various objects around the restaurant in English. She, in turn, repeated the words in Spanish after the couple pointed to each object. They all laughed as each one struggled to pronounce the words.

Eva thanked the couple for their help and finished her cinnamon coffee.

The Church of Our Lady of Sorrows was magnificent. The inside was exquisite shades of pink and beige. The altar, trimmed with golden color, was remarkable. The sanctuary was eerily still. The people inside sat in silence. A strange sensation of reverence came over her as she sat in the pew. Eva surveyed the room and noticed Steven was sitting near the front. He remained there for some time.

Eva examined the sanctuary and noticed flowers and candles placed around at strategic points around the worship area. The sun streamed in through the windows, accenting the ceilings that appeared extraordinarily tall. *What a splendid structure*, she thought. It was clear why the people here loved this church. It had a holy feeling within the walls that washed over her, and she could not shake it.

Steven arose from the pew and walked back through the church, nodding at Eva as he passed. She wanted to speak to him, but the words she thought about saying were clumsy and superficial. Nice church? Are you enjoying the tour so far? *Superficial,* she thought, *dumb.* She would look for opportunities to talk with him about something meaningful. In the back of her mind, she heard her mother telling her she needed to date. Her mother's comments played back in her mind over and over, *"Seriously, honey, when are you going to date someone again? I know that scoundrel of a husband you had was just awful. But there are others out there just waiting to meet a nice girl like you."*

Feeling less confident than when she entered the church, she left and joined the group outside. They gathered on the stone street and listened to Adrián tell the group about the attractions in Spanish and then to Eva in English.

"You'll have more than an hour to walk through this part of town. Be sure to notice the large *zocalo,* or town square, just up the street. You're in the tourist area of the city, so you will be able to shop and see some of the sites of the city. The vendors will be opening about now. These vendors may not barter as much as the ones you might know closer to the border, but you can ask. In the zocalo, you'll also see a gazebo. It is a great place to take pictures. Stay within sight of each other and meet back at the bus in, oh, let's say about an hour and thirty minutes. Any questions?"

She shook her head no, not wishing to be singled out from the group.

The group walked around the *zocalo* and visited with the vendors. Children were playing around the square and the gazebo. Eva admired the local crafts and jewelry in the shops. She studied the vibrant colors of the Mexican blouses and skirts displayed by the vendors. She felt quite safe here. She didn't see any of the Mexican security officers in the area. She walked back to the meeting place for the tour of the Museum of Independence.

"Hello," Adrián said. "I think we're all here. Show your pass at the door. There will be a local guide there to explain the exhibits if you want to hear the details. But once inside, feel free to tour the museum on your own. We'll all meet back here in about an hour and head over to a late lunch."

Museums weren't her thing, but Eva was interested in the history of Mexico. She showed the clerk at the door her badge and went inside.

The local guide greeted the group and beyond that, Eva could not understand a word. So far today, her mother's words replayed in her head, encouraging her to hurry up and date someone, and now she felt the inadequacy of not knowing any language but English. She sighed and leisurely walked through the large hallways examining the exhibits. The décor of the museum was impressive—polished wood and stone floors, archways, a courtyard, and even a stained-glass window of Hidalgo, the priest-turned-fighter for independence. It was a great part of the Mexican history.

Steven walked with the large group but turned toward Eva when he saw her.

"Too bad they don't have a guide here who provides the tour in English," he said.

Eva, feeling embarrassed that he approached her, laughed and said, "Yes. I could understand a little of what was said, but I think I get the general story from the exhibits."

"It was quite something. A priest who called his people together to fight for independence."

"Yes, you don't see that every day," Eva said.

They both laughed, and then Steven said, "Our hour is almost up. Think I'll go grab a bite of lunch."

"Okay," she said.

Okay? She thought. *Why didn't I say mind if I go with you?* Dumb! She was kicking herself for missing the opportunity to walk with Steven and get to know him a little better. For all she knew, he was married. Then she reminded herself her goal on the trip was to learn Spanish, not meet someone to date, no matter what her mother said.

Adrián greeted each member of the group and pointed out various cafés near the bus. "Once you have eaten, come back to the bus. We will leave for San Miguel de Allende in an hour. That will put us at our hotel by six."

Eva didn't see Steven. She assumed he was somewhere eating. She found a small café and had a delightful taco and rice. She learned to dine alone in public years ago. It took some practice, but eventually she figured out the key was to think of something else instead of reminding herself that she was alone. She almost convinced herself that she preferred being alone. Scooting her chair back under the table, she walked away feeling more confident. She was one of the last members back to the tour bus.

As the bus meandered through Mexico, Eva listened to Adrián and learned some of the historical facts about Mexico. Adrián discussed the early aqueduct system, revolutions, battles, independence, the social caste system, the origination of the Day of the Dead, the Spanish settlements, and other historical facts. She enjoyed the climate and the company. The food had been wonderful; the shopping was fun. She was learning some basic Spanish that she could use in everyday conversation. The day had been a wonderful experience.

Tonight would be spent in San Miguel de Allende. Approaching the city, Eva spotted the red, orange, pink, and yellow buildings. The churches poked out across the city, and the clusters of houses could be seen on the hillsides. Colorful vines and plants were spilling over the balconies. The streets crawled up the steep hills, and the town grew up on the hillsides. She was mesmerized by the colorful city.

Eva was struck by the number of Americans, Canadians, and others who made this city their part-time or full-time home.

Eva commented to Adrián, "There are certainly a lot of people here that look like they are Americans or Europeans."

"Yes, there are," Adrián agreed, then addressed the group. "This city is one of the places in Mexico where Americans and people from other countries come to retire. The weather is marvelous year-round. Many retirees come here because they like the community culture. This city provides arts, markets, and other ventures."

Then he added, "Your hotel is right across the street. It's a nice, Spanish-colonial style building with small gardens and a terrific courtyard. Show your badge and passport as you check in. Your luggage will be placed in the lobby. So, get your suitcase; and after you take it to your room, go out the door off the lobby and into the courtyard. The hotel staff will be serving you there. They have prepared a wonderful meal."

He added, "Tomorrow, you will have the morning to tour the city, and then we will meet at noon to board the bus. Eat a late breakfast or snack before you board the bus. Stay in small groups and keep your badges with you."

The tourists from the bus crossed the narrow cobblestone street and entered the hotel. It was a small but pleasing lobby with a tiny gift shop on one side. Eva checked in, took her suitcase, and located her room. She took hold of the sturdy, wrought iron handle and opened the tall, heavy, Colonial-style wooden door to her room. It was nicely appointed and very clean. She dressed for dinner, then walked down to the courtyard that was overflowing with potted plants and fuchsia bougainvillea on the walls.

"Hello," Steven said as Eva entered the courtyard.

"Hi," she replied.

"Care to join me?" he asked.

"Sure, thank you," she said as her heart sped up a little. *It would be nice to have company.*

"So, what do you think of Mexico so far?" Steven asked.

"It's beautiful, and the towns we've seen are charming." She felt nervous. She hadn't had a friendly conversation with a man in a long time.

"I agree. These old cities are intriguing. The history, the architecture—all very alluring for tourists. We're seeing such a beautiful part of the tourist side of the cities."

"Oh?" she asked.

"Yes. We're seeing the pretty side of things, not the ugly side."

"I think I saw some of the not-so-pretty side of cities before I got to Monterrey."

"You came from Reynosa?" he asked.

"From Matamoros and then through Reynosa," Eva replied, feeling a bit more at ease.

"The border towns can be especially bad. There's some infighting within the cartels and between the cartels," Steven said.

"But you work there, in Matamoros?"

"Yes. Matamoros has changed over the years. There's so much violence now. That's why I wanted to take this trip. I wanted to see the Mexico I remember, and I thought being a tourist would let me see the wonderful part of Mexico. This is like the Mexico I knew as a boy growing up. The crime's not visible, but I know it's around."

"So far, I have to agree that this tour has been different from what I saw in Matamoros and Reynosa," Eva said.

"I know Matamoros quite well. I grew up in a town not far from there. The things I have seen in Matamoros . . . I can't speak about them. As far as San Miguel de Allende, it's charming, but the whole city isn't like this. Not far from here, you'd see poverty, violence, and who-knows-what. There are crimes here. But the tour buses won't show that part of the city. And that's a good thing because everyone here is on vacation. People don't take vacations to be in reality. Vacations are for escape."

"I suppose that's true," Eva agreed.

"As an American, you should be watchful of people targeting tourists," he added. "And in Mexico, if you have any trouble, you wouldn't have the same rights as in the United States. Police may not be as responsive."

"Well, that's troubling," she said, feeling a touch of anxiety.

"I'm wondering, what do your university students say about Mexico?" asked Steven.

"I haven't met them. I don't begin teaching until after I return from this trip. I'm looking forward to meeting the students and finding out more about the area. I have to admit I had no idea that Mexico was so beautiful and yet had so much criminal activity."

"But think about it. You have violence in the United States, too. In the bigger cities, in the poor parts of town, you'll find the same types of things going on."

"I guess so."

Eva and Steven enjoyed their dinner and talked about the next day's itinerary.

"I'd like to see a little more of the city before we depart at noon. Maybe eat breakfast in the courtyard here before we leave. Would you like to come along?"

"Yes," Eva replied, almost too quickly. She'd feel better exploring the sights with someone rather than by herself.

"Great. Would nine o'clock work?"

"Yes. Meet you in the lobby?"

"Okay."

Back in her room, Eva replayed the conversation she had with Steven. He was so charming, and he had the kind of face that seemed to become more attractive the more he talked. Eva was troubled by their conversation about Mexico, though. Steven's perception of what was happening across Mexico was disconcerting. Surely, he was overestimating the amount of violence and the deterioration of the country. She knew it was risky in the border towns, but she hadn't been aware of the status of the other parts of Mexico.

Thinking about the dangers of Mexico reminded her of her conversations with her mother. *I'll give her a call*, she thought. Then I'll touch base with my sisters. I know they are probably worried about what I'm doing.

Eva followed the instructions about using her cell phone to call the United States. She heard some clicking noises and then the sound of her mother's phone ringing.

"Hello?" her mother answered with uncertainty in her voice.

"Hi, Mom."

"Oh, good, you're okay. Glad to hear from you. I have been worried sick about you," her mother said. "Your sisters have been calling me to find out if you are okay."

"Of course, I'm okay. Why wouldn't I be?"

"Well, you're in Mexico, alone, and you don't speak the language," she replied.

"I'm having a great time. And I'm not alone. There are forty-five people on the tour with me. There are two people on the tour who speak English. And the tour has already been to two towns," Eva said. She dared not mention any of the anxiety-provoking incidents she experienced on the way to Monterrey.

"I'm so thrilled to know you're okay. Do you trust all of those people on the tour? Are they good people? I keep hearing on the news—"

"Mom, you have got to stop watching cable news night and day," Eva warned.

"Do you even know what's going on down there? I saw there is another caravan, and it'll be heading through Mexico this week. Thousands of them. Do you hear? Thousands coming our way."

"Well, Mom, I haven't seen any sign of any caravan or any other problems. All I've seen is interesting countryside, charming towns, good food, and great shopping."

"Promise me you'll stay very alert and aware at all times?" pleaded her mother.

"Of course, Mom. I'll call you again in a few days. I'll call the girls and say hi."

"Good. Your sisters would like that."

They said their goodbyes, and Eva sighed with relief. She was surprised she didn't hear even more lecturing about Mexico.

She gave her sisters each a quick call, laid out her clothes for tomorrow, and climbed into bed.

CHAPTER SEVEN

"ERNESTO, EMILIO," DOLORES SAID IN a hushed voice as she touched their shoulders. "Wake up. Ernesto, Emilio, time to go. We'll walk in daylight to the train yard."

Ernesto and Emilio sluggishly came out from under the bush, stretched, straightened their clothes, and smoothed their hair.

"I can tell your younger brothers about getting on the train," Olivia said with a bit of nervousness in her voice.

"I want to hear about it as well," Dolores said.

"Ernesto and Emilio, Olivia wants to talk to us about the train."

The boys turned their eyes to Olivia and listened.

"Today will be different from our journey so far," Olivia told them. "We'll be going into the train yard near the town. You'll need to be ready when we get there. We'll all jump onto the train while it's moving and try to stay together. But the most important thing is to hang on to the train. You'll need to grab hold of the train as it's moving, then climb up one of the ladders to the top. You'll see things you've never seen. Someone might fall off the train. It's dangerous when that happens. People get hurt on the train. Hold on as tight as you can. Once you're on the train, you can reunite with each other or wait until the first stop to find each other."

With fear in their eyes, Ernesto and Emilio listened to every word Olivia said. Dolores' heart pounded faster with each word Olivia spoke.

"When we get to the railyard, we may have to wait for the right time to board the train. If something does not look right, then protect yourselves. Hide if you need to," Olivia added. "We may not be able to get on the train today. But if that happens, we'll get on the next train that comes in another day or so."

Focused on their destination, they walked toward Tapachula. The houses, now interspersed on some of the roads, indicated the nearness of the town. They tried to look as if they were locals rather than strangers. When the sun came up, Dolores could see that the whole area was congested with people from Honduras, Guatemala, and El Salvador. In fact, Dolores could not distinguish who lived in the town due to the high number of people who, like her, were just passing through.

Olivia signaled for Dolores, Ernesto, and Emilio to gather closer. "Be aware of the Mexican authorities. If they stop you, they'll ask for papers. If you do not have papers, they'll send you back to Honduras. We'll see more authorities in the town. Some may be local authorities, and others might be federal authorities."

Dolores thought about all of the risks. The gangs, the criminals, the Mexican authorities, and jumping on a moving train. *Have I brought my younger brothers into a hopeless situation?* She continued the walk.

They traveled until they reached the edge of the town. Olivia knew the location of the train yard. Olivia looked around and said, "No Mexican officers."

"God watches us," Dolores whispered to her brothers. "We're blessed."

Ernesto and Emilio nodded.

They followed others to the train yard. No one talked. They walked down several streets and then back to the edge of the town. The railyard was within view.

"It doesn't look like I thought it would," Dolores said to her brothers.

They stared down the empty rails with grass growing between the tracks throughout the train yard. Other people were milling about. Some were standing; a few were sitting next to run-down buildings; and others were sleeping in grass by the walls of the buildings. People were sleeping under the disconnected railcars on one side of the yard.

Olivia saw a woman sitting on the ground and asked, "Do you know when the train will come?"

"They told me it will arrive around three o'clock this afternoon. Are you going to get on?" the woman asked Olivia.

"Yes," Olivia said.

"I've been on this train before."

"Oh?" Olivia asked.

"Yes. I want this time to be better. Last time, I was robbed before the stop in Arriaga and had to come back and wait to earn more money," said the woman.

"Did it take you a long time to earn the money?"

"No. I went into the town and worked for a few nights." And then she began to cry. Through her tears, she said, "I never had to do that before. I am ashamed. But I was hungry and wanted to try to get on the train again."

Olivia hugged the woman and told her, "It's okay. It's okay. You're going to get another chance now. It's okay."

Olivia left the woman and joined Dolores, Emilio, and Ernesto. The day wore on. The group sat in the overgrown grass outside the train yard as the heat of the sun increased.

Emilio looked at Dolores and asked, "What do you suppose is happening at home now? Do you think that stupid, old rooster is screaming?"

She and Ernesto laughed.

"Mamá's getting some food for Papá and Grandma. Mamá probably made some pan de coco if she had the ingredients. If the chicken had eggs, they will eat breakfast when Papá is up. Do you think they've been able to get some coffee beans by now?"

"Gosh, I don't know. They have nothing to trade for the beans," Ernesto said. "Boy, I would love some of Mamá's coconut bread!"

The group sat in silence in the tall weeds. The heat from the sun was beating down on them. They moved to some trees closer to the railyard.

More people were gathered near the railyard. Families with young children, men, young adults. All were dreaming of a future in the United States.

A Mexican federal officer walked out from around the corner. He asked each person, whether standing or sitting, to show their papers. People ran away and hid. Others talked with the officer.

"Look," Olivia whispered to Dolores.

"I see him."

Ernesto and Emilio watched and waited to see what their sister would do.

Dolores observed a man handing money to the officer. The officer then waved him toward the train rails. She watched the officer approach another man, and he took a greater amount of money from the man.

"He is a corrupt officer. He'll take whatever you give him," Dolores said. "I saw one man give him a lot of money, and another person gave him very little."

"So, what do you want to do?" Ernesto asked.

"Let's all give him the same amount. Let's each give him . . . " Dolores counted out a few bills. " . . . this much."

Ernesto and Emilio took the bills out of the inside secret pockets. Olivia had a few bills in her pants pocket and got them out for the officer.

They walked toward the officer to give him money, but Olivia said, "Wait. Not yet. Come here."

They gathered around Olivia. "We must not get on this train. We'll wait for another train. See," she said and pointed to the other end of the train. Behind the last car, a group of Salvadorian gang members were gathered.

"They intend to get on this train. We mustn't get on with them. They'll take your money and throw you off the train. I've seen it happen before," Olivia said.

Disappointed, they agreed.

The train came and left. They watched as others ran to gather speed and jump on the train. The gang members were all on board. Many other unsuspecting, innocent travelers were on the train as well. They watched the train until it was out of view. The railyard was empty.

* * *

Another day passed as they waited for the train. Having rested for a whole day, they were ready to make the jump onto the train. They were hungry, but excited. Olivia told Dolores and her brothers to stay near the train yard. She walked beside the track for some distance to some trees. She found two plantains and brought them back to share with the group.

There was no sign of the Mexican officer. It was quiet, except for the arrival of additional people wishing to catch the train.

After eating the plantains, Olivia approached an older woman waiting in the train yard.

"Have you seen any officials here today?" she asked the old woman.

"No. Those men . . . " She pointed. " . . . said there was trouble at the market, and the officer had to go over there."

"That's good for us, yes?" Olivia asked.

"Yes. No trouble for us," the old woman agreed.

Olivia walked back to the group and told them the good news.

"We should be safe to go today if no officers show up. No officers are here to take our money or ask for papers."

A loud, metal clanging caught the group's attention.

Dolores said, "There it is."

"Yes. *La Bestia* approaches," Olivia said.

Dolores' heart pounded quickly. She thought it might beat right out of her shirt. Her hands were sweaty. She hugged her brothers and Olivia. She made the sign of the cross and said a prayer for protection on the journey.

The train slowed to a halt. Olivia began to walk out to the end of the railyard. The others followed.

"We'll wait here until the train starts again. Once you see it moving, get ready to run and jump on. You'll grab the ladder and pull yourself up. Then climb to the very top and move down the car a little, so others can get on after you."

At last, the train began to move. They watched as it approached.

Olivia went first. She had experience and knew what to do. They watched her take hold and quickly pull up on the ladder. Ernesto followed Olivia. He was able to run at exactly the right speed and grabbed the ladder tightly.

"You go," Emilio said to Dolores. "I want to come after you."

Dolores didn't argue because she knew her younger brother was the fastest runner in the family. She ran, grabbed the ladder, and with shaking arms, forcefully pulled herself up and climbed to the top. She was trembling but safe.

Emilio ran right behind Dolores. The train picked up speed quickly and looked like it would leave Emilio behind.

"Emilio!" Dolores screamed. "Emilio!"

He was running but wasn't able to catch the same ladder to get up on the same car.

"Emilio! Get the next car!" Ernesto screamed and pointed to the car behind his car.

Emilio ran as fast as he could. At the last minute, he reached for the ladder; but he had trouble pulling his legs up because of the increasing speed. Another man climbed down the ladder part way to help Emilio.

"Emilio! Pull your legs up! You can do it!" Dolores screamed.

Finally, Emilio held onto the ladder and climbed up. He was on a car behind Dolores, but she could see him sitting with other young men. She could watch him from her car.

Another man came out from some tall bushes and ran to get on the car with Emilio. He ran as fast as he could but couldn't catch it. He tried for the next car. The man grabbed the ladder with one hand, but the train was increasing its speed. He couldn't hold on. He screamed and then fell under the train, making a loud thud. He screamed so loud, it could be heard above the sounds of the train. Dolores looked back and saw a mangled body on the track. Her stomach was sick. She quickly prayed for the man and for all the travelers on the train.

As the train journeyed further from Tapachula, Dolores had to duck or lie down when the train went under trees. She covered her face with her hands. The branches scraped across her arms and the rest of her body, leaving scratches on her hands and arms. Once they got to a clear area, Dolores could see the fields, trees, and mountains in the distance. Her view had opened up to a panoramic landscape of Mexico. She felt the hot breeze as the train rapidly moved on the track. They were at last on their way north.

The loud and constant shaking of the train was unlike anything Dolores had experienced. It shook her whole body, and the noise was constant. She looked across at Ernesto, who was smiling, enjoying the ride. He wasn't worried about anything, and Olivia seemed relieved and tired. She glanced back at Emilio among a group of other young men. Dolores worried about him. She didn't know if the people he was with could be trusted, and she wasn't sure if Emilio would be able to protect himself.

A man sitting next to Dolores tapped her on the shoulder.

"Look. This is for you. We have extra." He handed her some rope. "Tie yourself to the train. Keep you from falling off," he yelled with a smile.

She took the rope and gave it to Ernesto. He tied it around his leg and then gave some back to Dolores. She tied it to her leg and to the rail on the side of the car.

"Now, if you sleep, you'll stay on the train," the man said.

"Thank you," she said.

Dolores could see a great distance from her position. This area was lush and green. *This part of Mexico was lucky to have more rain than we had in Honduras.* The mountains of Mexico protruded ahead and went forward for miles. There were fields of tall grass, trees, and other plants growing toward the mountains.

Dolores took deep breaths and attempted to enjoy her journey. Her worries about the future prevailed. She knew they'd be required to jump off the train before it entered the railyard in Arriaga. She didn't know what they would do for food.

The man who had given Dolores the rope asked, "This your first time on the train?"

Dolores nodded. She could hardly hear him over the train.

"It'll be fine," he yelled. "We'll be in Arriaga soon. Much faster than walking."

Dolores smiled as she thought of her sore legs. "Yes, much faster," she said as loudly as possible. Then she asked, "What do you know of Arriaga?"

"Some tell me there are places to rest and to get something to eat. The town has a shelter near the railyard. It is for people on the way north."

Dolores nodded.

"Be careful. Mexican authorities are there to stop us. Get off the train before it gets to the railyard."

"Yes. We will."

As the car pitched along on the tracks, she faintly heard some people talking. Ernesto was lying down. She could only see the top of Emilio's head. Olivia was sleeping near the front of the car. She prayed they would all make it safely to the next stop and that there would be no trouble in Arriaga.

CHAPTER EIGHT

EVA WAS GREETED THE NEXT morning by vivid rays of sunshine as the city of blooming jacaranda trees, bougainvillea, and climbing vines awakened the streets. She was dressed before the scheduled rendezvous time with Steven. Eva took a quick walk down the Spanish colonial street and stayed near the hotel, eager to return in time for breakfast. The morning air was invigorating. The ideal temperature served as an introduction to another enjoyable day in Mexico. She was delighted she made the impulsive decision to take the tour. She was overjoyed that Steven seemed to have an interest in her.

The local vendors on the street arrived to open their shops and display the goods on their carts. The cobbled streets welcomed the local residents as they scuttled to their daily responsibilities. She leisurely strolled, taking in the ambience of the area. Fascinated by the pink, prominent steeples some distance away, she hoped Steven would want to visit that church. She glanced at her watch. Better get going.

She walked briskly back to the hotel. Eva reflected on her conversation with her mother the night before. *Thousands of people in a caravan moving to the United States,* she thought. *Ridiculous.*

She entered the hotel lobby and saw Steven waiting by the gift shop.

"Good morning." He was grinning from ear to ear.

"Buenos dias." She smiled.

"Ah, practicing your Spanish today?" he asked.

"Not so much. But I am anxious to see more of the city."

"Me, too. Shall we get a little breakfast?" he asked.

They went to the courtyard. A breakfast buffet was set up for the tour group.

"This is nice," Eva said. "Look at the interesting variety of fruit."

A large, decorative collection of fruit was displayed on the table beside a self-serve fruit tray.

"That's one thing we have plenty of here in Mexico—fruit. We can grow just about anything here. See this? It's called carambola. In English, a star fruit. You see, here it is on the tray, cut up and ready to eat. Try it."

"Oh, wow, it is kind of, like, sweet and a little tart."

"And this one—"

"That is kind of creepy-looking," Eva said.

He laughed. "It is called a dragon fruit. But over here, see how it looks cut up? This one is red inside and sweet. Take some and give it a try."

Eva added a slice of star fruit and a piece of dragon fruit to her plate.

"And this is a plantain."

"I guess it's a banana-type fruit?"

"Similar. They can be bland or sweet depending on the ripeness. Want to try?"

"I think I'm good for now. I'll try these today, maybe a plantain tomorrow," she said and laughed.

"And this is a type of sausage here, chorizo. And papas, oh, potatoes. And, of course, you can get some eggs down there on the other table. They'll cook them however you like them."

"And these are pastries?" she asked.

"Yes. *Pan dulce*, or sweet breads."

"*Pan dulce*," she repeated.

"Yes. Not as sweet as many in your country. But they are good. My problem is that I like them more than the fruit." He laughed as he took several for his plate.

They added their breakfast items to their plates and sat at a small table in the courtyard. They talked about the tour, their hotel accommodations, and what they might see in San Miguel de Allende.

"I saw a church, some distance away. I actually could just make out the steeples. But it looks very interesting."

"That is Parroquia de San Miguel Arcángal. We can see it after breakfast if you like."

"Yes, I'd like to see it closer," she said.

They left the hotel and walked through the historical tourist district of San Miguel De Allende.

Steven said, "Many of the buildings here, like in other cities in Mexico, have been rebuilt several times. Some have plaques with stories about their origin. But the church of San Miguel de Allende offers its own interesting beginning. What you see now is a reconstruction of a deteriorated church. The man who created these Gothic-like structures was a *mestizo*."

"I remember Adrián used that word when he spoke about the various races and mixed cultures on the first day of our tour. Do you know about this particular man's ethnicity? Or race?" Eva asked, not knowing why she was curious.

"I read about him. His name was Gutiérrez, and he was both Spanish and indigenous. That is the meaning of *mestizo*," Steven said.

"Looking at this work up close, it is miraculous," Eva said as her eyes scanned from top to bottom and left to right.

"Yes, it is," he said and then paused as he looked up to the towering steeples. "Can you believe that he taught himself how to do this work?" he asked as he turned his gaze toward her.

"I can't imagine. It is magnificent."

"Legend has it that he saw some postcards of churches in Europe, and he used those pictures to design the steeples," Steven said, still gazing in her eyes.

"Truly amazing," she said, trying to dismiss his stare.

"Yes, it is," he said, still gazing at Eva.

They turned and entered the church, noticing the elevated ceilings with detailed stone work. Opulent archways and enormous chandeliers added to the splendor of the church.

"There are no words to describe this place," Eva said, amazed at what she saw.

Steven agreed.

They walked outside the church and continued their walking tour of the city. The streets were lined with colonial buildings, shops, and vendors. A manicured park was nearby. Eva noticed the brightly painted murals on the walls of buildings.

Steven pointed. "You see, this mural tells the history of Mexico. Here, we see the indigenous people; here, the Spanish coming; here are the farmers, the church, and so on. It's a common practice in Mexico to paint the walls with murals that tell stories."

Eva admired Steven's love for Mexico he displayed without hesitation. She spent a few minutes studying the details and vivid colors depicting years of changes in Mexico. "I wonder what it was like back then?"

"Mexico has had so many changes over time. And tragically, it's had many changes in my own lifetime," he said with sadness in his voice.

They continued their walk by the colonial buildings and Jardin Principal, the park near the church, and the center plaza. The park, with its uniquely trimmed circular trees and gazebo, provided the perfect place to sit and talk.

"Tell me more about the changes. You said the country has changed since you were younger?" she asked, noting his sparkling smile and dark eyes as he turned to answer her.

"Yes. When I was a boy, my childhood experiences were simple but fun. My family was close, and we all lived near each other. We easily walked a couple of houses one way or the other to visit everyone in the family," he recalled. Then he added, "The city, Matamoros, was the most exciting place for us to go. Near the *zocalo*, we often stopped for a coffee at a little coffee shop, and we visited with each other for hours. The city was a busy, thriving place with markets, restaurants, a theater, businesses, and government buildings. Everyone got along. People were kind to each other." Steven's face lit up when he talked about his childhood.

"That sounds just like this place, where we are now. Look around; it's a thriving city with wonderful people," Eva said.

Steven smiled, then said, "Yes, it is in a protected area. Someone is paying the cartel for protection, or like in many places, the local government is controlled by the cartel. The police look safe enough, but many are corrupt and allow the cartel to do as they wish for money."

"It is hard to believe—it seems so calm and friendly here—"

"I wish it wasn't true. What if I told you that we are sitting in a region that is influenced by, or in conflict with, as many as ten different organized crime or cartel groups?"

"Really? It doesn't look like it is in conflict," Eva said.

"I know. Unfortunately, it is. Los Zetas, Los Caballeros, La Familia Michoacána, Beltran-Leyva Organization, and Cartel Jalisco Nueva Generacíon are the most well-known. It changes often. There are small, organized crime groups and large groups in constant conflict. Always fighting, shooting each other, or brutally killing by some other method. All so unnecessary."

"Well, it seems peaceful here," Eva said as she glanced around the area.

"In general, this territory, like much of Mexico, is in turmoil. These cartels are so power hungry, money hungry, that they have forgotten about our beloved Mexico and the people," he said with sadness.

"But why? To make money from drugs?"

"That is part of what they do. Guns and weapons running, human trafficking, prostitution, and, of course, drugs," he said with a strange tone. It was as if he was either apologizing to her about his country or felt guilty that the cartel situation had escalated.

"How sad for Mexico," Eva said. "To ruin this beautiful place."

"Not just here. You know the cartels have influence in the United States?"

"You mean to sell drugs there?" she asked.

"For many types of business. In fact, right now, the Zetas and Gulf Cartel are located right along the border of Texas, inside the state of Texas, and beyond."

Eva was dumbfounded. Her mood was paralyzed by this news. *It can't be true, can it?* she wondered to herself.

"I'm sorry. I shouldn't have said so much. I don't want to ruin your trip. We should go back. The bus will leave in an hour."

"Oh, yes," Eva said, looking at her watch. "We should go."

Eva and Steven walked back to the hotel with little conversation. A quick "See you on the bus" was all Eva could muster. She was sad and in disbelief about Steven's information. He was familiar enough with Mexico to know the facts about the current affairs. But it just didn't seem possible.

Eva returned to her room and gathered her belongings. She walked to the lobby and tried to put the seedy elements of Mexico out of her mind.

* * *

The tour group was accounted for and ready to start on the next leg of the journey. Steven sat in a seat across the aisle from Eva, talking to a man sitting beside him in the window seat. Nevertheless, Eva was pleased that he sat near her. The elderly couple sat in front of her. The lady turned and smiled at Eva.

"You like trip?" she asked Eva in broken English.

"Very much," Eva replied.

"Es una hermosa ciudad." The woman winked at her and turned back around to her husband.

Eva smiled and nodded. She assumed the woman thought the city was pretty.

Adrián stood at the front of the bus and asked, "Did you enjoy San Miguel de Allende?"

The heads of the tourists on the bus nodded and gave positive reviews.

"Good! Because we have another exciting stop coming up. Not far from here, about an hour and a half, we'll arrive in Guanajuato. We'll spend the night there and then head off fairly early tomorrow for Michoacán. I'll tell you more about what we'll do in that state when we board the bus tomorrow. Let's just say we have some outdoor activities planned in Michoacán.

"Okay. Now, more about Guanajuato. It is an old and interesting city. It has a tunnel system of roads under the town. These were actually put in to help keep the water from flooding the town and the early mines that were there. Now, the tunnels are part of the roadway system. The route we'll take to the hotel includes driving through one of the tunnels."

As the bus made its way to the outskirts of San Miguel de Allende, Adrián continued talking to the group.

"You'll see the streets are narrow, and many people in the city walk rather than have cars in Guanajuato. We will do a fair amount of walking while we are there and . . . "

Adrián stopped talking. He was bothered by something out the window. The group followed his gaze in unison to determine what was happening. Local police redirected the bus to turn down a different street.

Eva gasped as she turned in her seat. She saw yellow tape around a section of the road. Two bodies were lying face up in the road. They appeared dead.

"Sorry about that, folks," Adrián said. "As you know, in some parts of the larger cities, we might have crimes committed. This is a good time to remind you all to stay within our designated area on the tour. Always keep your credentials with you and stay in a group."

Steven leaned across the aisle toward Eva and asked, "Are you okay?"

"Yes, fine, thank you. It's just that I have never seen that before."

"A crime scene?"

"Yes. And dead bodies in the street like that."

"Yes. If you go into enough big cities, on the wrong side of town, you will see this—in Mexico and in some of the cities in your country, too."

Eva nodded.

"Are you sure you are okay?"

"Yes," she said, feeling a little queasy.

The elderly lady in front of her turned and gave Eva a sympathetic look and said, "Está bien."

Eva nodded back. She had to admit it had shaken her. She believed she must make a more concerted effort to stay near the tour group. She would travel only in the specified areas. She may have been a little careless in San Miguel de Allende.

She sat back in her seat. None of the other travelers seemed to be disturbed by what they had seen. *How can a country have two separate identities? Two personalities?* she wondered. No matter how upset she was, she could not say anything about this to her mother. It would be too upsetting to her.

The bus rocked along now, well outside the city. The countryside with its rolling hills, houses, and trees was picturesque. Peaceful. As the bus left the San Miguel de Allende area, the terrain changed to one of rocky ridges jutting out from the wooded hills.

Eva thought about her breathing. She concentrated on slowing her rate and calming her thinking. In her mind, she revisited the morning she had with the scenic views of San Miguel de Allende, breakfast with Steven, and touring the historic tourist area. That was the town she wanted to remember, not the last few minutes.

The bus neared the city of Guanajuato. Another stunning view of multicolored buildings and houses built up on high hillsides. In some ways, it was similar to San Miguel de Allende.

Adrián stood back up and addressed the group.

"Here we are in Guanajuato! Are you all ready for another great visit?"

Once again, the heads bobbed in unison, indicating their excitement.

"Good, good. We'll be staying in a hotel right in the middle of the historic and tourist district. You'll want to see the museums; there are three or four right within walking distance—the Juarez Theater, the Jardin de la Union—and don't forget to see the Alley of the Kiss. I'll be happy to take a group for a walking tour this afternoon after lunch if you like. Down from the Alley of the Kiss, there is a terrific *mercado*. Mercado Hidalgo. If you want to do some shopping and eat a really fresh meal, you must go there. You might want to ask for a taxi if you want to go straight there and spend some time. It would be a good place to eat lunch . . . " He glanced at his watch. "Or an early dinner," he said as he laughed. "And now, we are about to enter into a tunnel."

Steven leaned over to Eva and smiled. "Any of those places get your attention?"

"There are a lot of options for sure. I think I would like to go to the market. How about you?" She was thrilled he had asked.

"That sounds interesting. We could go to the park and then see other historical buildings on the way back."

"Okay. Sounds great," Eva said, excited that he included her in his plans.

"The market would be a good place to eat some fresh, authentic Mexican food. They use the market produce for the dishes they prepare," he said enthusiastically.

"Perfect," Eva said. "Meet you in the lobby once we are checked in?"

"Okay. I'll get a taxi, and we can go eat first. It seems like breakfast was a week ago," Steven said as he laughed.

Eva laughed. "Yes, it does." She was looking forward to spending more time with Steven.

Eva recalled that much had changed since breakfast. Not only had she heard disturbing information about Mexico, but she also had witnessed a crime scene firsthand. She wouldn't think about it. There was too much of the tour yet to enjoy, and Steven added to the pleasure of the trip.

The hotel was a mix of modern touches and bits of old Mexico. It was larger than the first hotel. The light fixtures were modern, and some of the walls were made of old stacked stone. There were modern-looking fountains inside and outside, and the hotel had one quaint restaurant. In another area, there was an upscale lounge with brightly colored chairs and modern lights.

"Interesting," Eva whispered as she looked at the interior of the hallway and sitting areas.

Eva's room was modern, small, and had all the necessities. She stowed her luggage, brushed her hair, and touched up her lip gloss.

Eva made it to the lobby as Steven was asking the concierge to call a taxi to take them to the market.

"The concierge said the taxi will be here in five minutes," Steven told her and smiled.

"Okay. I hope it's a short ride. I'm hungry."

At that moment, the concierge called to Steven.

"Your taxi, sir."

In no time, they entered the market. The arch over the doorway and the raised, arched ceiling gave the market building a unique character. Inside, there were numerous vendors selling a variety of goods. Eva could smell some of the food being prepared by the vendors. The market was bustling with people buying produce. Others were sitting on stools at counters eating their lunches. There were sections of the market with tall shelves stacked with canned goods and specialty foods. Another part of the market displayed clothing, dolls, and an assortment of merchandise.

"Oh, my!" said Eva. "I don't know where to start."

"Let's go over there." Steven gestured. "Where they are cooking food."

Steven explained all of the entrées on the menus hanging over the vendor booths.

"Hmm . . . I think I'll try the chile relleno. That looks delicious."

Steven placed the orders, and they sat on the stools watching the cook make a batter and roll the stuffed peppers to cover each one. In a large pan, she fried the peppers, placed each one on a plate, covered them with sauce, and added the beans and rice.

"*Buen provecho,*" she said as she handed each one their plate.

"My goodness!" Eva said after the first bite.

"You like it?"

"Oh, yes. It is quite an unexpected taste. Very good!"

Steven smiled and watched Eva as he continued eating.

Eva glanced around the market at the wonderful products of Mexico. She wanted to examine some of the booths for more detail. Being in the market had lightened her mood. Today had been a mix of emotions. She felt safer with Steven and more secure taking a taxi. She hoped there would be no additional unanticipated grave events for the remainder of the tour.

CHAPTER NINE

THE TRAIN SLOWED DOWN JUST short of the railyard in Arriaga. Dolores tapped Ernesto on the shoulder.

"When we see the first people get off the train, we need to jump off."

"I'll get off when you do," Ernesto replied.

"Can you get Emilio's attention?"

"I'll whistle. He knows my whistle."

Ernesto whistled, and Emilio turned to him. Ernesto gestured to him to get off the train and to watch Dolores.

Emilio nodded in agreement.

The train's wheels screeched as the train's speed slowed. Olivia jumped off, then Dolores, Ernesto, and Emilio. All were off safely with no problems. Emilio ran to catch the group.

"I'm so glad you're safe," Dolores said.

"Yeah. Me, too," Emilio replied.

"You gave me a scare. God had to listen fast because I was praying fast."

They laughed.

"Next time we jump on, I'll start sooner, before the train is going so fast. Did you see that other man who fell?"

"It was tragic," Olivia said. "I've seen that happen before. You must be very careful."

The man who had given Dolores the rope hopped off and walked behind Dolores. He tapped Dolores on the shoulder and said, "If you want to go to the shelter, they'll have something to eat, and you can rest."

"Yes, we would like to go," Dolores said.

"I show you," he said.

The group walked behind the man on a pathway overgrown with grass. The path led to a gravel road and then to a white stucco building trimmed in red paint. The words Casa del Migrante Hogard de la Misericordial were painted on the front above the door. Inside the fairly large building were cots, bunk beds, hot food, and a first aid station. Numerous restrooms and several showers were in a separate area that was divided into rooms for men and women.

"Ernesto, look," Dolores said as she pointed to the first aid station. "You can have them look at your sore feet. They can help you."

Ernesto smiled. "I will ask for help. I have more pain today. But first, food?"

"Yes," Emilio agreed.

The food table had three hot trays with rice, beans, and tortillas. Neatly organized on a long table were a stack of plates, a tray of utensils, and water dispensers and cups.

"This is outstanding," Dolores said.

Olivia followed Dolores in line, and they each took a plate of food. Ernesto and Emilio followed and stacked their plates full and drank several cups of water before they sat down to eat.

"How long has it been since we've had hot food?" Olivia asked.

"We were blessed to have fruit and tortillas along the way. But this is wonderful," Dolores said.

Ernesto, Emilio, Dolores, and Olivia were silent. They were all eating and smiling.

Emilio rubbed his stomach and said, "Now, I want to go to sleep."

"There are cots over there. We can all rest," Dolores said. "I think I'll go and wash up a little."

"Great idea," Olivia said and accompanied her.

Emilio went to the area with cots and laid down. Ernesto went to the first aid station. A kind woman was attending to another traveler who was sick. Ernesto waited for his turn.

"How can I help you?" the lady asked Ernesto.

"Oh, it's my feet. I've been having trouble because of the walking."

"Take off your shoes and let's have a look."

Ernesto grimaced as he peeled off his shoes. The blisters caused the shoes to stick to the bottom of his feet.

"Okay. Let's wash these first and let me see what we are looking at here."

The lady brought a large pan of water and antiseptic and washed his feet. The soap stung the blisters. Then, the lady took a cloth and scrubbed the sores. Ernesto groaned.

"I'm sorry. I know it's painful."

She treated the sores and bandaged his feet. Then she added, "Now, you need to stay off these feet for a day or two."

"But we are going to go get back on the train," Ernesto protested.

"If you can wait at least one day, you will be able to use your feet. I can give you a tube of this." She held up some antibiotic ointment. "Keep it with you and put it on each day until you can wash your feet again. But you need to stay here until tomorrow. Rest. And have another meal."

Ernesto walked over to the cots and told Dolores and Emilio what he was supposed to do. Then he added, "But I feel okay to leave later today if you want. I don't want to keep us from going. It'll take longer to get to the United States."

"Don't worry. We can all use the rest and food," Dolores said.

Ernesto found a cot and laid down. They rested for a while.

When Emilio awoke from a short nap, he saw Dolores sitting on her cot observing the other guests in the shelter.

"Dolores," Emilio said, "What's the first thing you want to do in the United States?"

"I haven't planned it out yet, but we'll need to find a place to stay. Maybe with a nice family or in a shelter. And then, I'll find work," Dolores replied.

"Sounds like you do have a plan," Emilio said.

Ernesto woke and asked, "What are you talking about?"

"We were just thinking about being in the United States," Emilio said.

"We have a long way to go. One of the men over in the first aid station said it could take two weeks to get there from here. We'll stop at the towns, and then we will have to catch the train again," Ernesto said.

Emilio looked down.

"Don't worry," Dolores said. "We will get there as soon as we're able."

"Look, over on that wall," Olivia said as she pointed to a large map of Mexico.

Dolores, Olivia, and Emilio went to the wall and studied the map. Ernesto remained on the cot, trying to stay off his feet.

"I think I should go this way," Olivia said as she pointed to a western route. "I want to go to California. My aunt lives there, and I will try to find her."

"We're going to go this way," said Dolores, pointing to the eastern side of Mexico. "It's a shorter distance, and we do not want to travel more days than necessary to get there. We'll go through Veracruz and then up this tip of Texas."

Olivia added, "I think I'll eat one more meal and then catch the next train."

"Of course. You have a further distance, and you want to get started. We'll wait with Ernesto another day," Dolores said. "Maybe we'll see you in another town when we get off the train again."

"Yes, that could happen for sure before the train routes split," Olivia agreed.

"You've helped us so much. We're thankful for your help. I'll pray for your safe journey," Dolores said.

"And I'll pray for yours," Olivia said.

Later that day, after they had all eaten dinner, Olivia hugged each one and said goodbye to Dolores, Emilio, and Ernesto.

And just like that, the group that originally was five, who left Honduras together, was down to three—Dolores, Emilio, and Ernesto. Dolores was saddened and knew she would miss Olivia. She had given them advice all along the way. Now, they'd be on their own.

* * *

Many other travelers entered the shelter during the night. Each person had their own story. Dolores heard accounts of gangs, corrupt officials, unstable governments, abusive family relationships, and countless others. But she also heard stories and dreams of hope. Hearing the hope of so many energized her. She would use her energy to help her younger brothers get to the United States. She felt positive about her goal. At last, she relaxed on a cot and fell asleep.

"Ernesto, how are your feet today?" Dolores asked.

"Better. It helped to get them clean," Ernesto said.

"Emilio, are you awake?" Dolores asked.

"Yes. I hear every word you are saying," he grumpily replied. "But this bed feels so good. No rocks, no tree roots, no dust."

"I know it feels good, but we should eat and get ready to catch the next train. It will be here soon."

"Okay." He sat up.

They walked to the food table and saw rice, beans, tortillas, and a large tray of fruits.

"I am going to eat like a king this morning," Emilio said with a smile as he rubbed his belly and took a plate. "Can you give me a little extra?" he asked the volunteer.

She nodded and scooped more rice and beans for his plate.

Ernesto was second to get a plate. He asked the volunteer to give him more on his plate, and the volunteer handed it to him. The volunteer piled Ernesto's plate even higher than Emilio's. Dolores followed Ernesto. She savored each bite of her breakfast. She knew this might be the last food they would have for some time. She was not sure what she would find in Ixtepec.

"Hello," a neatly dressed man said. "I'm the director of the shelter. Are you finding everything okay?"

"Yes, sir. Thank you so much for this shelter and the food, and showers, and everything. It's a gift from God to us," Dolores said.

"It is part of a church operation here. It's our calling to help those in need. I wanted to speak with you. You're all traveling to the United States?"

"Yes," Dolores replied. "These are my younger brothers."

"And you came from where?"

"We're from Honduras."

"You've made your way very well so far. No trouble for you?"

"Not for the three of us. We've seen other people have trouble, though."

"Yes, I am sure by now you have. I wanted to warn you about something. There are many, many women who come here and have already been attacked by men along the way. There are some very dangerous and evil men who hunt for the women travelers. So, brothers, can you watch out for your sister at all times? Do not leave her side."

"Yes, sir," Emilio and Ernesto said simultaneously.

"And which direction are you heading from here?" asked the director.

"We are going to go east to Veracruz and then up the coastline to Texas."

"Ah, okay. I know that you will next stop in Ixtepec. Then you will go through Veracruz."

"Yes," Dolores said.

"Okay. Ixtepec is a very small town. There are checkpoints near the town. It's so small, that you will be noticed right away as travelers. You must be very careful there. It's one of the places that evil men watch the tracks for women coming into town and leaving. It's because there is not as much cover as you might find in a larger city. I don't think there are any shelters for you for quite some distance. I'm not as familiar with the eastern route. Know that I will be praying for your safe journey."

"Thank you. We'll be especially careful," Dolores said.

"And we'll watch out at all times," Ernesto said.

"Very good. Let's have a prayer together."

They bowed their heads, and Dolores began to sense fear from the warning she was just given. As the director prayed for protection and safety, Dolores felt a warm sense of safety envelop her. She was thankful for the feeling. She felt more determined than ever to make their way to the United States.

Not long after they prayed, they heard the train coming in the distance.

"Time for us to go?" Emilio asked.

"Yes," Dolores replied. She didn't want to leave the safe place, but she knew it was time.

"Each of you check your pockets. Your money is still okay?" she whispered.

They nodded.

"Okay. Let's go."

They thanked the staff at the shelter, then walked down the tracks to the outside of the railyard. They all carefully scanned the area. No presence of local police or anyone that looked like trouble. They sat under a tree and waited.

The sun soon heated up their hiding spot under the tree and in the tall grass.

"Why is the train so slow to start up?" Emilio asked.

"Patience. Be ready when it begins to move," Dolores said.

At last, the train began to inch its way forward toward their location.

"Let's try to get on the same car," Ernesto said.

The three emerged from the tall grass and moved toward the train. The first car was already loaded with travelers. They targeted the second freight car. Ernesto, Emilio, and Dolores successfully held on to the ladder and pulled themselves onto the train. As they climbed to the top, others followed them and soon, their car was full. The remaining cars behind them had fewer people aboard.

Dolores scanned the cars, examining all of the people that were visible from her car. They looked like ordinary travelers. She didn't notice anything indicating gangs or other criminal types. Several of the cars behind her had families traveling together.

Good, she thought. *This crowd appears to be safe.*

The train rocked along, revealing landscape of dry fields nearby, overgrown vegetation in the distance, and mountains as a backdrop. Dolores had never seen so much open country. She saw green, grassy patches alternating with dry fields, red and brown dirt, dead-looking trees, flatlands, and rolling hills. It was a vast view of land with no evidence of people.

The rural area reminded her of her farm home in Honduras. She wondered how her family was. She wished she had a way to let them know that their children were doing fine on the journey. For a moment, her heart ached. She said a prayer for God to watch her family and for her to be able to protect her brothers.

A teenaged boy riding on a freight car behind got her attention. He was waving to his mother on Dolores' car.

"Stay there," the mother yelled.

"I can come to you. I will jump across."

"No. It's not safe. Stay there," she pleaded.

"What?" the teenaged boy asked, not able to hear his mother's soft voice.

His mother motioned for him to stay, but he was already moving forward. He ran to get a running start and leapt high into the air. The train cars shimmied, causing them to be unaligned with each other. His mother gasped. The boy miraculously made an accurate jump to the other train car.

In no time, the boy was reunited with his mother.

"Don't ever do that again," she begged as tears ran down her face.

"I'm fine, Mamá," the boy said.

"If we get separated again, don't jump. Wait until the next train stop. Do you hear me?" his mother pleaded through her tears.

Dolores' heart was beating so loudly, she could hardly hear the train. She hoped her brothers would never try that. She looked at Emilio and Ernesto, who both had panicked looks still on their faces.

Emilio said, "You don't have to worry about me. I wouldn't do that in a thousand years. When I had trouble yesterday getting on the train, that was enough for me."

"Good," Dolores said.

The riders were quiet now, enjoying the view and knowing they would soon be at their next stop. This was one of the shortest rides of their journey.

The miles clicked by, and Dolores saw the small town of Ixtepec ahead.

"Look," Ernesto told Emilio.

"Oh, good. We'll get off again?" Emilio asked Dolores.

"Yes. And remember the town is small with checkpoints. We'll have to hide from authorities and from anyone who looks suspicious."

"We'll look very closely," Ernesto said.

The train slowed as it approached the town. All three were able to jump off the train. They walked into a barren field and continued to walk in the direction of the town, staying away from others. Several of the travelers passed them, walking at a faster rate. Ernesto's feet were bothering him. He required a slower pace, and Emilio and Dolores walked slowly with him.

"Look," Emilio said as he pointed up ahead.

From out of the fields, two Mexican officers appeared and captured several of the travelers ahead of them. They were on their knees on the ground. The authorities tied their hands and wrists behind their backs and instructed them to accompany them to Ixtepec.

"We'll walk further away from the tracks," Dolores said as she motioned. "And keep looking. More officers might be hiding."

They continued their journey to a place they could spot the train as it began to leave Ixtepec. They would hide the rest of the day in a spot where the train would be visible to them. They didn't talk for fear of being heard by someone they could not see. Dolores said prayers all along the way for protection. She wanted this part of the journey to be over soon.

CHAPTER TEN

EVA AND STEVEN SPENT HOURS in the market. Steven explained the exotic fruits and vegetables of Mexico to her. Eva was having one of the most enjoyable days she had experienced in a long while. She waved at others who arrived in the market from the tour bus who waved back and smiled. The elderly couple were visiting the vendors and examining the items.

Then Steven turned her attention back to display. "Do you want to see a delicacy? Look at these. Do you know what these are?" He had a mischievous look on his face.

She hesitated, then answered, "Uh . . . not sure, but they look creepy."

"Yes. Creepy they are. They're considered a delicacy by some in Mexico. These are spicy grasshoppers. Would you like to try some?"

"Oh, gosh. I think I'm gonna have to pass," she said.

"I don't blame you. I try not to eat bugs unless there is nothing else to eat," he said with a laugh.

Eva continued her shopping, investigating each trinket and piece of clothing in the market.

"Are you looking for something in particular?" Steven asked her.

"Not really. I thought I might look for souvenirs here to take to my mother and sisters."

"You can look at this market, but you might find more interesting souvenirs in some of the other towns. The state of Michoacán has many unique, authentic Mexican gifts. And some of these items over here," he gestured to a table, "are from the cities and towns we will be visiting, so—"

"Oh, so they may be priced better in Michoacán?"

"Exactly."

They left the market and visited the park and other colonial-style buildings along the way back to the hotel.

As they passed by a museum, Steven asked, "Want to go inside?"

"You know, the weather is perfect. I'd prefer to keep walking," she said, hoping he would go along.

"Okay," Steven agreed.

As the evening made its initial appearance, Eva heard the sounds of a local mariachi band playing. She and Steven walked closer to the band. People were spilling out on to the streets for the evening. Eva felt the music gave the evening an air of romantic mystery as it cascaded out into the gathering crowd and the evening sky. *What is Steven feeling?* she wondered. *A new friend? Potential dating relationship?* She wanted to know.

Eva and Steven looked in a few of the shops near the hotel before calling it a day.

When they entered the lobby, Adrián was talking to other tourists. He gestured and said, "Eva, Steven, come over."

"How was your afternoon?" Adrián asked.

"It was fun," Eva said. "We took your advice and went to the market to eat."

"Ah, good. Just needed to let you know, the bus will leave at eight o'clock in the morning. The hotel will have a breakfast set up for us at 6:30. We have a full day planned for tomorrow."

"Thank you," Eva said.

"Guess that means we need to get some sleep," Steven said. "Are you as tired as I am?"

"I could use some rest," Eva agreed.

Steven gave her a smile and a wink and said, "See you in the morning then."

"Okay." *Yes!*, she thought.

When Eva returned to her room, she was still smiling from the day. She decided she should call her mother to check in. No need to have her mother worry. But she would not mention anything about Steven either. She didn't want to hear the list of questions about him that her mother would ask. Besides, she didn't even know the answers to most of the questions her mother would ask her.

"Mom?" she asked when the phone picked up.

"Eva? So glad it's you."

"Just wanted to check in and let you know everything is okay."

"Good. I was watching the caravan on the news on TV when you called—"

"Oh, Mom—"

"Now listen. They have moved into Mexico. They were in Guatemala, and now they are in Mexico. There are—"

"Thousands, Mom, I know."

"You have seen them, then?"

"No, Mom. You told me there were thousands when we talked the other day."

"Oh, oh yes. Well, listen, they are saying there are gang members from El Salvador and Honduras and other criminals from who-knows-where—"

"Hey, Mom. I'm having a wonderful time, and I haven't seen a single caravan."

"Well, that's good. Where are you?"

"I am in Guanajuato."

"Whato? Haha."

"Anyway, tomorrow we're going to another state in Mexico called Michoacán."

"Is that near Guatemala? South? Near the caravan?"

"No, Mom."

"I'm just worried about you."

"It's okay, Mom. We are in a big group, traveling together, so it's okay."

"If you say so," her mother said. "You know your sisters and I are concerned about you."

"I know, Mom."

"Your sisters enjoyed talking with you the other day. I'll let them know you are doing okay.

"Thanks, Mom. I'll call you in another day or two, and tell the girls I'll call them again soon."

"Now, don't forget. You watch your back. Check your surroundings."

"Yes, Mom. Goodnight now."

After her shower, Eva fell onto her bed, smiling and thinking about tomorrow.

* * *

Eva took a plate off the stack for the breakfast buffet and selected star fruit, eggs with chorizo, and two small Mexican sweet rolls. She was chewing her first bite when she heard, "What . . . no plantain?"

She looked up to see Steven smiling and standing beside her with his plate. *So glad to see you*, she thought to herself.

She laughed. "Have a seat." She was glad to have his company for breakfast. It was a good way to start the day.

The other members of the tour group staggered in and smiled as they passed by Eva's and Steven's table. Eva greeted each one and smiled at her ability to say hello and good morning in Spanish.

They finished their meal and had a little more coffee before going to the bus. This time, Steven sat beside Eva, which made her quite happy, but she tried not to make her smile too obvious.

Adrián greeted the group. "Good morning! I visited with each of you yesterday evening, and it sounded like everyone had a wonderful time in Guanajuato. Today, we'll be traveling from Guanajuato to Morelia in Michoacán. Morelia has some terrific shopping and restaurants that you may try in your spare time. I say spare time in jest because we'll be very busy when we get there." He laughed.

Adrián continued, "Once we are all checked into the hotel in Morelia, we'll load back on the bus for a ride over to Nuevo San Juan Parangaricutiro. It takes a little over two hours to get there. Now, this will be an outdoor adventure, and there'll be some horseback riding required. Following that, you'll hike up to see a village where a volcano erupted many years ago. You'll see where the eight-year flow of lava swallowed the village almost in its entirety. The volcano began to erupt in 1943, so, you see, it is a young, new volcano."

One of the elderly passengers asked, "What if we don't think we can make that horse ride and hike?"

"If you'd prefer to stay in town and shop or see some of the other sights, just let me know," Adrian replied. "I'll need to get a head count of who is going to see the volcano site. For now, sit back and enjoy the ride."

Steven, leaning in next to Eva, said, "This will be an adventure you don't want to miss."

"Sounds interesting, and a change from looking at colonial buildings and parks."

"Yes, I've never been to see the place where the lava ran over the village, but I've heard stories about it all my life."

"Oh?"

"I know that the lava from the volcano covered the whole village just like Adrián said and that it was the village of San Juan Parangaricutiro. But after it was destroyed, when they built the village back, it was named . . . "

"Oh—Nuevo because it was the new village."

"Yes. And the most fascinating part of the history is, that out of all the village, everything was completely destroyed, except the altar and steeple of the village church."

"Wow. So, is that what we'll see?"

"I imagine we'll see it. I'm not sure how close we will get to the church, though."

Eva and Steven chatted the rest of the way to Morelia. The more they talked, the more Eva was convinced that he was an interesting person whom she wanted to know better.

When the bus parked in front of the hotel, Adrián presented the details to the tour group.

"We'll leave here in about thirty minutes. You will have time to check in with the hotel clerk and be back here on the bus. We'll stop in the village near the volcano. If you need a snack or a drink before the horse ride and the hike, you'll have a few minutes in the village. Wear shoes that are good for hiking when you come back to the bus."

The hotel was nice, but not as quaint as the first hotel and not as modern as the second. In fact, it was a little disappointing. But her room was clean and had the essentials. She hoped she wouldn't spend too much time in her room, anyway.

Within minutes, she was settled in. Eva kicked off her sandals and put on a sturdier pair of shoes. She checked her hair and makeup. She went down the hallway to the lobby, then out to the bus.

"Well, that was a quick stop," Steven said as he took his seat next to Eva.

"Yes. It was. But I'm ready for an adventure," Eva said.

Steven and Eva sat together on the bus. About half of the group on the tour opted to go shopping rather than on the volcanic site excursion.

Promptly, the bus was back on the road. The bus seemed to make the two-hour-and-fifteen-minute drive to the village in short order. Perhaps it was just the company and the conversations with Steven that made the time pass quickly.

The large bus had to creep into the small streets of the village of Nuevo San Juan Parangaricutiro. The driver parked the bus, and Adrián instructed the group to walk a block further down the street to a tourist center.

Adrián added, "You'll ride in a small van to the location where the horses are stationed. Local guides will take you up on horseback to the place that you must continue on by foot. Once you dismount and walk down the path, the guides will wait with your horses until you return. Here are your passes to present to the van driver."

"Sounds simple enough," Steven said.

Eva and Steven walked down to the vans waiting to take tourists. A short and winding road took the members of the tour to the horse station. They walked to the run-down stables covered with a tin roof and found the local guides waiting. With a little help from the guides, Eva and Steven mounted their horses and listened to the brief instructions about how to turn and stop a horse. Steven appeared to know how to handle the horse easily. Although Eva had ridden horses, it had been several years. *Just hope I don't make a fool of myself,* she thought.

The local guides, boys of no more than fourteen years of age, led the line of horseback-riding tourists up a steep path lined with black lava rocks. As they rode along the path, the church steeple became more distinct.

Eva and Steven arrived at the designated stop with the other members of the tour group, and the guides instructed them to dismount. Eva was surprised at the shakiness in her legs after getting off the horse. She and Steven began their walk up the narrow and rocky pathway.

Eva attempted to give the appearance of walking with self-assurance with her shaky legs, but soon the rocks caused her to slip.

"Careful," Steven said as he held on to Eva's arm.

"Thank you," Eva said. "This is quite something. These rocks are massive."

"And sharp," Steven added. "You sure don't want to land on one of these."

"You're right about that," Eva said.

Steven helped Eva along the rocky path by holding her arm or hand as needed. The landscape was barren. Only occasional stray trees were able to grow between the large lava rocks that caused a swath of destruction years ago. Further out from the direct path of the lava, there were vegetation and mountain ranges in the distance. But the area of the pathway was so desolate that it made Eva think that it might be like walking on the surface of some other planet without life.

"This is really weird. This terrain," Eva said.

"It's kind of like being on the moon or something," Steven said.

Eva smiled. "I was just thinking this is like being on another planet!"

They laughed and cautiously continued the walk.

At last, they made it to the church.

"Will you look at that," Steven said.

"The church is completely destroyed, except the steeple and the altar area," Eva said. Then pointing to the altar, she said, "And look there."

People were climbing on the rocks inside the church and placing flowers and candles on the altar. They stood and prayed.

"It looks like the locals still come here; and for them, this is a place of worship. You want to climb over the rocks and go down there?" Steven asked.

"Sure. If you do."

Eva and Steven carefully made their way over the boulder-sized lava rocks to the altar of the church.

"I think in its day, this was a very beautiful altar," Eva said.

"It's quite interesting. See these stones and pillars? And look at the steeple tower. It looks like there were two towers but only one survived."

"It does," she agreed.

They climbed around for quite some time examining the old church.

"You know the locals here say that God saved this church, protected it," Steven said.

"I suppose that's one plausible theory," Eva said.

At that time, two other local people climbed up to the altar with flowers. Steven and Eva quietly watched them and then continued to explore the church. They climbed around the inside walls and then all around the outside of the church.

After exploring the outside of the church, Steven asked, "Ready to go back to get our horses?"

Eva agreed, and they followed the rocky path back to the horses, where the guides waited to lead them back to the van. A short ride later and they were back on their bus headed back to Morelia.

"What a day," Eva said.

"Yes. You know, I think I'm hungry. Want to get some dinner in Morelia? I heard there are some good places with local cuisine near the hotel."

"Sounds good. I don't want to walk too far," Eva said, not wanting to tell Steven about her shaky legs.

"I agree with that," he said. "That was quite a walk today."

It was dark when the bus arrived at the hotel. Eva and Steven departed straight away for a nearby restaurant.

The décor of the restaurant was authentic Michoacán. The polished wooden tables, colorful plates and tablecloths, and paintings by local artists hanging on the stone walls created a true Michoacán atmosphere.

They were seated immediately. Steven explained the menu items to Eva and helped her to order. She repeated the words in Spanish.

Eva said, "You know, there's something I have noticed about Spanish."

"Tell me."

"Many of the words in Spanish sound like words in English, and they have a similar meaning."

"That is true. Those are called cognates."

"That makes it much easier to understand what I hear. But I still have a hard time speaking Spanish, you know, like in sentences. It's that whole verb conjugation thing, and the male and female forms of words."

"It does make Spanish more complicated for English speakers. Your language does not have the exact same issues."

Just then, the waiter returned with their steaming food, and they began to eat right away. The plates were piled high with authentic Mexican deliciousness.

As they ate, Eva said, "Steven, the other day, you told me quite a bit about the crime in Mexico. Yet, since that first day when we passed the crime scene, things have been wonderful with no hint of crime. Are we traveling in safer places now? Are there just small pockets of crime in Mexico?"

"I thought talking about crime had upset you, so I wasn't going to talk about the violence anymore."

"I'm curious because we have covered many miles, and everything seems so peaceful."

"Now, since you asked, I'll tell something you would like to hear. In fact, the town of Morelia is one town that tries very hard to keep their people safe. Their police force reaches out to the community, like some do in the United States. They make a real effort to have a friendly relationship with the people in the town."

"That is great to hear. But what about the cartel or corrupt officials?" Eva asked.

"The police force in Morelia is fighting corruption. This area may be one of the safest in Mexico."

Eva smiled. She wanted to believe that good always wins over evil. But after the earlier discussion with Steven about the cartel and gangs, she wasn't sure good would be able to defeat evil in Mexico.

Eva and Steven finished their meal and went back to the hotel. In the very small lobby, Adrián was waiting as the tour members returned for the night.

"Good evening," Adrián said. "Did you enjoy the volcano?"

"Oh, my, yes," Eva said.

"And you found a good restaurant for dinner?"

"We did," Steven said, "right down the street."

"Wonderful. Tomorrow, when you come to the bus in the morning, go ahead and check out and bring your luggage. We'll be going to an all-day adventure before we head to Veracruz tomorrow night," Adrián said.

"Where are we going?" asked Eva.

"We're taking an hour-drive over to a lake near here. In the middle of the lake, there's an island. We'll ride a boat to the island and spend the day. When we meet back at the bus, we'll travel all night to Veracruz."

"The lake trip sounds exciting," Eva said.

"We'll leave at eight o'clock in the morning. Breakfast will be across the street at the café at seven a.m."

Steven turned to Eva and asked, "Want to meet over there?" as he looked into her eyes and smiled that smile.

"Of course," she said, again pleased that he had asked her.

Eva decided to call her mother, since she would not be able to call the following night. Traveling by bus all night long made it difficult to get good reception for calling home.

"Hello?" said her mother.

"Mom. Just calling to say hello."

"Oh, good. Well, the caravan is moving in Mexico—"

"Mom, I'm having such a good time."

"So, you haven't seen the caravan?"

"Oh, Mom, you'll be glad to know the police department in this city is very good. In fact, they try to follow a similar model of our police in the United States."

"That is good to hear. But what about in the other cities where you travel? Are the police departments good in those places?"

Eva hesitated for a moment and then said, "No problems so far, Mom. Everything is fine. I rode a horse today up to a volcano."

"You did what? You're in Mexico riding horses? Going to volcanos? Oh, my. Now I'm more worried than ever."

"Mom, I made it down just fine and have already had dinner and am ready for bed."

"So, what crazy thing are you going to do tomorrow?"

Eva hesitated again. She didn't know if it would be worse to tell her mother the truth or to leave out the details of the boat ride. She decided to tell her the details later.

"We're going to visit a village, and then we will go to another city. But, Mom, we'll be on the bus all night tomorrow night, so I will not be able to call you."

"Oh, okay. Well, you call me when you can. And watch out for that caravan. They must be getting closer to you."

"Tell you what. I'll watch out for a caravan if you'll stop watching cable news."

"Oh . . . you!"

"Okay, Mom. Tell everyone hi for me. Talk to you in a couple of days."

CHAPTER ELEVEN

IN THE MIDDLE OF THE afternoon, Emilio jumped up from the tall grass and looked toward the town. He heard the train starting up.

"Dolores, Ernesto," he whispered. "There it is."

They walked nearer the track, ready to grab the ladder and climb up. They scanned the area looking for authorities, but none were near. The train approached, and they were in position. First, Ernesto ran to the ladder and jumped up—then Emilio, followed by Dolores. They climbed up to the same freight car. The train was not as crowded as the previous train to Ixtepec. Dolores wasn't certain why. Perhaps others wanted to stay in Ixtepec to rest.

The journey from Ixtepec to Veracruz would take quite a while. Veracruz was a much larger city than Ixtepec, and Dolores hoped it would be easier to remain undetected there. She prayed they would be able to find something to eat.

She scanned her freight car. The people who were riding on her car were families and young men about the age of Emilio and Ernesto. She examined the cars behind her and didn't see anyone who looked dangerous.

The train moved rapidly through the lush mountainous area of southern Mexico as it shifted from east to north toward Veracruz. Mile after mile, the train continued. Dolores heard the screams of spider monkeys in trees near the track. Their long arms and tails caught her attention.

The rain forest foliage made Dolores long for her home in the countryside of Honduras. Some of the plants here were plants that grew near her home. The banana trees and coffee plants were known to her. She also knew the plumeria flowers. But other plants of the rain forest area were unknown to her, underscoring the feeling that she was in a strange and unfamiliar world.

Clouds moved in, and a light mist began to fall, increasing the humidity even more. It was as if the train was cutting through a low-hanging cloud in the rain forest. Hours passed. Dolores, Emilio, and Ernesto dozed for short periods of time. Emilio was awake and watched while his sister and brother slept. He noticed something unusual on the far end of the freight train. He didn't want to wake his sister until he could determine what was happening. There was movement on one of the cars further behind him. Then he was able to make it out.

Two men at the end of the train were working their way toward the front cars. Emilio was afraid they might try to come to the car that he and Dolores and Ernesto were riding. He watched as they hopped up to another car. It was then he noticed the tattoos on their faces and the clothing they wore. The young man sitting next to Emilio turned to see what he was watching. He nodded and nudged Emilio. "Los Zetas."

"Dolores, wake up. Look. It is Los Zetas down there on that car."

Dolores sat straight up. She watched the two men. This is why more people did not get on this train, she thought. They saw Los Zetas waiting in the railyard.

The Zetas were asking the passengers for money. Dolores watched the two Zetas ask another passenger for money. The passenger pulled his pockets inside out to show the gang members that his pockets were empty. In horror, Dolores, Emilio, and Ernesto watched as the Zetas threw the flailing, screaming man off the train.

"What will we do?" Ernesto asked.

"We have money," Dolores said. "Let's watch and see if we can tell how much they are giving them."

Dolores, Emilio, and Ernesto stared at the two Zetas to see what would happen next. The train was moving too fast to consider jumping off.

The Zetas went to each person on the car behind Dolores' car. One of the Zetas looked slightly smaller and younger than the other. The younger Zeta held a man, and the older one demanded the money. The frightened man hastily emptied his pockets and gave the Zetas all of his money. The Zeta yelled something, then shoved the man face down on the car and went to the next man on the car.

"They're going to jump onto this car next and try to get money from everyone on this car," Ernesto said.

"Are we going to give them all of our money?" Emilio asked.

"No. Quickly, let's get some out of our inside pockets and put it in the outside pocket. Then when we give them the money, pull out your pants pockets, and they'll think that's all we have," Dolores suggested.

"Okay," Emilio said.

Each one took out a small amount of money from their secret pockets and put the rest back. They put the smaller amount into their pants pockets.

The two Zetas went to the next man. He pleaded with them, and he told them he didn't have any money. They wrestled with the man as he screamed and hit them back. Then he yelled even louder and said, "God knows what you do!" The Zetas threw him off the train. The man screamed when he bounced and then hit the ground.

The train shook as it moved along, picking up speed. The Zetas then went to the last person on the car right behind Dolores' car. The Zetas yanked him by his shirt and yelled, "Give us the money! Give it to us now!" and slapped his face repeatedly. Eventually, the tortured man gave them his money. The Zetas stood up, pushed the man out of the way, and walked toward Dolores' car.

"Looks like we're next," Dolores said.

Emilio grabbed his sister's arm in fear and said, "They're coming. They're coming!"

As the shaking train moved faster on a straight segment of track, the Zetas got in position to jump to Dolores' car. The younger Zeta leapt off the car toward Dolores' car. At that instant, the train hit a jagged piece of track, and the car jerked to the right side. With a loud thump, the younger Zeta fell between the cars. He screamed as the train ran over him. He screamed again when the next car ran over him and severed his legs.

"No!" yelled the older Zeta. "My brother! No!" The older Zeta jumped off the train going full speed.

Dolores was shocked. Ernesto and Emilio and the others on their freight car shouted and clapped with relief.

"God watches over us," Dolores said to her brothers. She said a prayer of thanks for God's protection once again.

* * *

With the tension over, Ernesto, Emilio, and Dolores settled back to relax on the top of their freight car, enjoying the ride through the rain forest mountains.

"How long has it been since we left Ixtepec?" Ernesto asked Dolores.

"I'm not sure, but it will be dark soon."

"It will be dark when we arrive in Veracruz?"

"I think it looks that way," Dolores responded.

The train slowed to pass through a small town that was not a scheduled stop. As the trained slowed, women and men unexpectedly ran out from the side of the track to the train cars and began throwing plastic bags up to the top of the cars.

"What are those?" Emilio asked. "What is that they are throwing?"

"I don't know," Ernesto said.

One of the bags flew right toward Dolores, and she grabbed it. She opened the bag.

"Look at this," she said. "It's a bag of food and water."

"What?" her brothers asked at the same time.

"Yes, it has tortillas, beans, rice, fruit, and a couple of bottles of water," she said.

"We'll share it. Scoot over here."

"We haven't eaten since Arriaga," Emilio said.

She handed each brother a tortilla, a packet of rice, and a packet of beans to share. They passed the beans and rice back and forth and drank some water. In her heart, she thanked God for answering her prayers.

"We should save the fruit," Emilio suggested.

Dolores and Ernesto agreed.

Dolores took only a small portion of the rice and beans and let her brothers eat the remainder.

An older man in a gray shirt sitting on their car caught one of the bags and was enjoying his food. He said, "Gracias, Patronas."

"Sir," Dolores said, "what do you mean, Patronas?"

"The women who help the riders on the train. They are known all through Mexico, even in my town. They've been helping riders for many years."

"This is wonderful," Dolores said. "They have big hearts."

Ernesto and Emilio finished their meal as the sky darkened. They put their heads down and slept for a while. Dolores remained awake as the train jostled the cars down the track.

Sitting in the dark, Dolores looked at the even darker jungle the train was passing through. She noticed the older man in the gray shirt was watching her. She felt uneasy.

"It's good we are not out there at night," he said as he gestured toward the overgrown jungle plants.

Not wanting to be impolite, Dolores said, "Riding the train is better than walking."

"Yes. In there," he said, "many ghosts. Many people disappear here and are never found."

"Really?" Dolores didn't know if he was making conversation or if he was, in some way, making a threat.

"Yes. Many disappear. They find them later, in the ground. Nothing but skulls."

Emilio sat up. His curiosity was piqued. He listened closely, then asked, "Who are these people who disappear?"

The old man replied, "Some are people with cartels. Many are people who ride these trains."

"Did someone tell you this? About the skulls?" she asked.

"No. I saw it on TV. In one place, 166 skulls were found. Another, 250 skulls. There is much crime in Veracruz."

"That's awful," Dolores said, finding it difficult to believe him.

The man looked out into the night and said nothing more.

"Wow, that's a lot of skulls," Emilio said to his sister.

"Yes," she agreed.

"And many are people who ride the trains?" Emilio asked.

"That's what he said," Dolores replied.

Dolores looked out in the night sky, now so clouded that the stars could not shine through. She wondered about the people who had gone missing in the darkness. *So much evil in the world,* she thought to herself as the rumbling of the train persisted.

"Dolores," Emilio said, "Why do so many people disappear?"

"I don't know. But you know how important it is to stay together and away from anyone who looks evil or dangerous?"

"Yes."

"Good. Always keep watching and looking."

"I will."

The earlier clouds slowly cleared, revealing a sky full of stars. Dolores gazed at the brilliant stars and thought about God. *He has given us a wonderful sky tonight.*

A crying baby disrupted the calmness. Dolores looked behind her. A mother attempting to quiet her infant. The infant could not be comforted, and the mother seemed distressed. Dolores couldn't imagine making this journey with an infant so small. How difficult that would be for both the mother and the baby.

The humid breeze began to blow through the banana palms and the papáya trees. She smelled the salty air. *Must be getting closer to the water.*

Ernesto stirred from his sleep. He sat up and looked at his sister and brother and asked, "Did I sleep a long time?"

"Not really," Dolores said.

"I didn't think so. I'm still tired," he rubbed his eyes and looked toward the engine of the train.

"Look there," Ernesto said. "The lights ahead."

"Looks like the city," Dolores said.

"Will we get off the train soon?" Emilio asked.

"Uh-huh."

Dolores, Ernesto, and Emilio prepared to climb down the ladder as the train slowed down.

The city of Veracruz, located on the coast of the Gulf of Mexico, was a bustling center of night life, restaurants, and other sightseeing attractions. Dolores, Ernesto, and Emilio left the train far out from the tourist region of the city. They began to approach the buildings in the older part of town. The other riders of the train peeled off the train cars. They walked through the buildings in the shadows. No one talked.

"Let's walk parallel to the tracks. We'll end up on the other side of the railyard, on the other side of the city."

Dolores and her brothers walked tightly together, as they pressed on their route between the concrete, brick, and stucco buildings. There was no sea breeze. The dank, damp darkness in the alleyways trapped the pungent smells of the city. With no breeze, the mosquitoes traveled in large swarms around their arms, legs, and faces. Any exposed area of the skin was a target for the pests. Dolores and her brothers swatted continuously at the pesky insects.

When Dolores and her brothers left the concealment provided by each alleyway to cross a street, they scrutinized the intersection.

They checked each corner, fearing local criminals or gang members might view them as easy targets.

They slowly made progress through the city, block after block.

Emilio stopped and said, "Listen. Music."

"Lots of people, too," Ernesto said.

"Shhh!" Dolores said. "We must stay hidden."

The alleyways and streets were cracked, and water puddled up in every crevasse. The mosquitoes were relentless. Dolores and her brothers continued walking, and she saw men sleeping against a building in the next block. She took Emilio's arm and pulled him back. Ernesto stopped.

"What?" Ernesto whispered.

"We need to go over one block," she said and pointed. "There are men sleeping there. We must be careful."

Dolores, Ernesto, and Emilio walked over another block and saw more people were sleeping in the alleyway. They went over still another block. It was clear.

"Let's go," Dolores said.

At last, the railyard was in view. There was a field on the other side of the railyard. Many people sat against the buildings. A few were asleep under the train cars.

"We can go over there," she said as she gestured, "past this section, by the field, and wait."

Dolores led the way and went to a clump of bushes. There, Dolores saw the mother dressed in the pink and red flower blouse, who was quieting the crying baby earlier on the train. The mother looked at Dolores. She was crying, but the infant was quiet.

"My baby. She is sick," the mother said as tears flowed down her face. She wiped her face with her blouse.

Dolores looked carefully at the baby. The baby wasn't moving at all. As the mother pulled the baby to her, the baby was completely limp. Her tiny arms flailed as the mother rocked her. Dolores feared the baby was dead.

CHAPTER TWELVE

EVA'S FIRST THOUGHT WHEN HER alarm startled her awake was to get packed up quickly. The bus would be leaving early. She was anxious to spend more time with Steven and to see the island in the lake. She knew it would be another amazing place in Mexico. She gathered her things and went to the lobby.

Steven arrived from the other hallway. He pulled his suitcase behind him. Others on the tour pulled their suitcases and carried travel bags.

"Good morning," he said and smiled. "You're early, too. Shall we see if we can load our luggage before breakfast?"

"Sure." Eva followed Steven to the bus.

The bus driver was standing beside the bus having a cup of coffee.

"Excuse me, sir," he said to the bus driver. "Can we go ahead and . . . "

"Oh, yes, yes," the driver said and quickly opened the hatch underneath the bus.

"Thank you, sir," Eva said.

They placed their luggage under the bus and then walked to the designated café for breakfast.

"Do you know about this lake?" Eva asked as Steven opened the café door for her.

"I've read about it, but this will be my first visit," he said.

They walked past a large breakfast buffet table and took their seats in the café. A waiter immediately appeared at the table. He said, "You may help yourself to the buffet or order from our breakfast menu. But I can get your drinks now."

"I think two coffees, correct?" Steven asked.

"Yes, coffee would be great."

Steven thanked the waiter, then turned to Eva and said, "Since we are in a hurry, we might want to get something from the buffet."

"I agree. It looks delicious."

They selected their breakfast items and returned to their table.

"What have you read about the lake and the island?" Eva asked.

"Let's see, uh, the ride over by boat is a short ride. A village covers the entire island, and there is a statue right in the middle of the island."

"Okay. Anything else interesting?"

"It's the place where there is one of the most famous Day of the Dead celebrations in November."

"Day of the Dead?"

"It is very well-known all over Mexico."

"And the statue? Is it something for the Day of the Dead as well?"

Steven laughed. "No, it's of José Maria Morelos. He was a famous fighter for the independence of Mexico."

"I see," she said.

"And now, let's hear you speaking some Spanish today. After all, that was your goal for the trip, right?"

"Sí, sí." She laughed.

After their breakfast, they hurried to the bus. Eva and Steven were among the last to board but were able to find seats together. The bus driver closed the doors, and the bus rolled forward.

"That was close," Steven said laughing.

"Yes, it was." She smiled.

Adrián took his position in the front to make his morning announcements. "Good morning. Are you ready for another terrific day?"

Several of the tourists loudly said, "Yes!"

"Ah, good! That's what I like to hear—some enthusiasm at eight a.m. Yes, yes. Okay, we will be on the bus a little over an hour to Lake Pátzeuaro. We'll park in a lot at the edge of the lake. From there, we'll walk to get on the boat, and that ride over to the island will take us, oh, just about thirty minutes. You'll have the rest of the day on the island. The last boat back to shore leaves at six p.m. I recommend you don't wait for that one; it's always very full, and you will not be as comfortable coming back across. In fact, any boat that leaves between four o'clock and 5:30 would be good. There's a restaurant near the boat dock. When you return from the island, let's meet in there for dinner before we get on the bus for our overnight trip. Any questions?"

There was silence.

"Okay, good. We'll be there soon."

"Here we go," said Steven.

Eva smiled and asked, "What exactly is the Day of the Dead anyway? I mean, is it like our Halloween?"

"Not exactly," Steven replied. "It's about the same time of the year as Halloween. But it is not so much about kids dressing up and asking people for candy."

"Oh?"

"It's a time of year when deceased loved ones are honored. It's a time of celebration, rather than a time to scare people."

"And how do they celebrate and honor their loved ones?"

"There are many customs. I know we'll see evidence of those on the island. It'll be better to explain all the details when you can see the art and the other decorations used."

"I'm intrigued."

Eva and Steven peered out the window as the bus traveled down Mexico Highway 14 toward Lake Pátzeuaro. The scenery was a mix of farmland, and distant, dormant volcanic mountains, and mountain ridges miles away. They passed a large area that was thick with growth as the highway wove around to the location of the small village of Revolucíon Pátzeuaro. The streets were fairly narrow, and the bus negotiated each turn carefully until they reached the area where they would depart the bus and walk to the boat launch.

"We are here," said Adrián. "If you look out this side of the bus, you'll see the place we'll meet for dinner. And if you look out this way," he said and pointed in the opposite direction, "you'll see the boat loading area. Is everyone ready? If you need a quick break, go into the restaurant, and they'll allow you to use their facilities. Let's go."

The bus door opened, and the passengers poured out in to the street. They arrived near the boat dock.

"Look. In the distance," Steven said. "That's the statue in the center of the island. You can just make it out."

"I see it. It looks pretty far out there."

Steven and Eva stepped off the concrete walkway and onto the dock. They filed in to the covered, colorful boat along with the others in their tour group.

As the boat leisurely sputtered away from the dock through a marshy channel, Eva relaxed. She had never been a fan of boat rides; but sitting here next to Steven, she felt more at ease. She felt safe.

The boat made a smooth crossing over to the island. A small boy on the other side assisted the passengers off the boat. The landing area, a dock with a covered building, had a vendor inside selling snacks. The passengers meandered out to a walkway. They explored the uphill sidewalk. A series of steps led them to a higher level.

"Look out there," Eva said. "You can see across the lake. And the rows of houses built on these hillsides . . . quite something to see."

"It is. I didn't know the island was so steep. Looks like we will be walking up for some time just to see the statue," Stephen said.

"And what are those men doing out on the lake? What are they holding?" Eva asked. She watched several men in shallow flat-bottom boats waving large, oblong nets over the water and then into the water.

"Oh, those are butterfly fishing nets. Famous way to fish in Mexico," he replied.

They continued upward on a walkway that had white-painted rock walls on each side, trimmed with red, lining the top of the walls. They reached a section of multiple vendor booths. Blue tarps were strung across the sidewalk for shade. Beneath many of the tarps, multicolored banners were hanging. The banners were small, rectangular, colored paper flags strung together above the walkway.

"What are these flags?" Eva asked.

"They're called *papel picado*. It's a paper cutout and a common Mexican decoration," Steven said.

"*Papel picado*," she repeated. "I've seen them in restaurants, but never this many. It provides a vibrant atmosphere."

A slight breeze off the lake blew the rows of *papel picado* gently, but the breeze was not enough to cool the air. Eva looked at the trinkets, clothing, and jewelry, and noted the prevalent theme of skulls and dancing skeletons in colorful attire.

"So, these are the Day of the Dead decorations?"

"Yes, and you see these? These, on this shelf, are actually candy. During the festival, there are many sugar skulls."

"Fascinating," Eva said. "And these?" She pointed to small, decorated tin boxes with candle holders on the bottom of some of them.

"Those are *nichos*."

"They look a little like shadow boxes," Eva remarked.

"But these are like an altar or a little shrine to honor and remember your loved one. These are made to put a picture of your loved one right here, see? And over here, there are some decorated *nichos* with women or *catrinas* inside. On this table, there are bride and groom skeletons, skeletons riding motorcycles, a skeleton walking a skeleton dog—"

"A skeleton for every possible scenario," she said and laughed. "So, exactly what is the ceremony like?"

"It's believed during the end of October and the first of November, the dead come back to visit the living. The end of October is when children who've died come back and visit with relatives. Others come in November. During that time, the whole island will be celebrating."

"And what happens when the deceased return?"

"Oh, that's where the food and family reunions happen. The people in the family work for days to get ready. They'll have an altar—not just the *nicho*, but often a larger altar—in honor of the loved one. These altars, or *ofrendas*, are elaborate. They decorate the altars with candles, the loved one's favorite foods and drinks, and always pictures of the loved one. When those who have died come and visit the family, their spirits are believed to eat and drink to restore their spirits and to enjoy spending time with the family. The family also decorate their graves to get ready for the celebration. And on the night of November first, the family members can spend the night in the cemetery where they believe their loved ones will visit. Of course, the graveside is decorated for that night, too."

"It sounds like quite an event."

"It's a big ceremony all over Mexico and especially here."

"But from what I understand about the Catholic faith, this doesn't seem to fit in with that religion," Eva said.

"It started out as an Aztec celebration, and since the Catholic church came to Mexico after the Aztec customs were in place, the two just kind of melded together."

"I see," Eva said.

"Let's walk down the sidewalk and look at other shops. Maybe you'll find a souvenir for your mother or sisters," Steven said.

Eva surveyed the walkway ahead. The steep walkway turned into a long stairway with houses and vendors encroaching on the path all the way to the top. The long, ascending walkway with twists and turns was lined with vendor after vendor. The colorful tarps and *papel picado* flags waved in the slight wind off the lake. Vendors had tarps covering the walkway in front of their shops and tables full of merchandise, hoping tourists would stop under their tarp to cool off and purchase their wares. For each vendor, at least one large section was dedicated to the Day of the Dead.

"This is amazing," said as she looked down at the steps descending with tarps and colorful *papel picado* banners at each flight of steps.

They followed a pathway to a cemetery with an open wrought iron gate. Above the gate, a bell was suspended from a stone archway. Stone steps led down to the graves, tombstones, and monuments.

"Let's go down," Steven said without hesitation.

Eva followed, noticing his broad shoulders as he walked ahead.

Steven read the names on some of the tombstones and pointed out some of the decorations that remained from the last Day of the Dead celebration.

"The family will come back and clean all of this up before the next celebration."

Some of the grave sites had altars and flowers on them. Most had a cross of some type. They continued walking on the steep sidewalk.

Eva asked, "What is that smell? Someone is cooking something that smells very tasty."

"Let's go over there and have a look."

A vendor was cooking very small fish and dishing them out into cups.

Steven asked, "What are those?"

"*Charales y salsa,*" replied the woman.

"And that's a fish?" Steven asked.

"Sí, sí. You try." She offered him a cup.

Steven gave the woman some pesos and got two cups full of the slender, fried delicacies. He handed one to Eva.

"They're, well, good. Kind of like a French fry. Crunchy. Like a fish French fry," Eva said laughing.

Steven ate a couple, then added the salsa. "The salsa is good, also. Try it." He placed one near to Eva's lips.

"Umm . . . " She took a small bite. "Yeah, that's good."

They strolled slowly, munching on their *charales,* and continued their climb to the statue. Reaching the top, they walked around the base of the statue. Up close, it looked as if it was covered with tiles, which could not be seen from a distance. Further inspection revealed the squares were not tiles but bricks that gave the statue its unusual appearance. They walked to the doorway and entered the statue.

"This is pretty cool," Eva said. "I didn't know it had an inside."

"It said in the brochure that if we climb the steps to the top, we can look out."

Eva groaned, rolled her eyes, and smiled as she said, "More steps. But I wouldn't want to miss it."

Spiraling balconies with murals on the walls engulfed the inside of the statue. Eva and Steven studied the paintings. Eventually, they arrived at the top and were able to peek through the openings out across the lake and the surrounding countryside.

"This was worth the climb," Eva said.

"I wonder how many miles out we can see from here. So many mountains over there, and the edge of the lake and beyond in that direction."

"The fishermen look tiny from up here."

They descended the towering steps slowly. Steven steadied Eva's arm as they walked. She was feeling tired and hungry, but Steven's reassuring hand made her smile.

"You know," Steven remarked, "I could go for a meal. It must be past time for lunch."

Eva smiled and said, "That's what I was thinking, too."

"We can find a restaurant down closer to the lower level where we board the boat."

Eva added, "So we don't have far to walk after we eat?"

Steven said, "Now that's what I was thinking."

They both laughed.

Over a late lunch of white fish, they talked about their home life, their jobs, and their countries.

"Tell me, Eva, what do you think about what is happening at the border?" he said gazing into her eyes.

"Well, I'm not sure I'm the best person to ask. I just moved to the border last week." She laughed, feeling embarrassed that she did not have a better answer.

"In your country, it seems the politicians don't want to allow any more Mexicans in," Steven said, trying to sound as if it did not concern him too much.

"We have many Hispanics in the area where I live. I can tell you this much—I'm one of the few Anglos in my apartment complex. In fact, I'm the minority anywhere along the border," she replied, thinking that was all she could offer for a response.

"I suppose that's true."

"I guess I'll learn more about how that all works when I get back and get settled into my new job at the university." Eva didn't know what to think about the immigration issues. She had been busy concentrating on her own studies for such a long time that she didn't pay much attention to current events.

Not wanting to start any conflict, Steven asked, "Do you want to shop now for your family? We have a couple of hours until we need to head for the boat."

"Sure."

Eva found Day of the Dead souvenirs for her mother and sisters. She would enjoy explaining the traditions to them when she went back to visit in Virginia. She didn't know if her description of the island would do it justice. It was a unique little corner of Mexico. They ambled down the walkway toward the boat and watched the butterfly net fishermen for several minutes.

"Ready to head for the boat?" Steven asked. It is four o'clock."

"Yes. This has been an experience to remember."

Steven nodded.

Eva and Steven rode the boat back to the dock and walked to the restaurant where the other tourists from the bus were gathered. The whole group looked fatigued.

"Hello, all," Adrián said. "You're all accounted for. Let's go inside and take our time for a relaxing meal. The owner of the restaurant has arranged for a local group to entertain us while we eat. They'll be performing music and dancing traditional folk dances from this region. We have two hours before we take off. Remember, we'll be on the bus overnight. Enjoy this last couple of hours before that long trek begins."

Adrián took his seat at a table with three tourists from the bus, and the show began. The dancers, wearing traditional white dresses with red and green trimmed ruffles, performed a spectacular dance that combined dance with theater. The mariachi played as the dancers performed.

Eva thoroughly enjoyed her dinner and the entertainment. She liked the company even more. She looked at his handsome face. She had good feelings about Steven and hoped they might continue to see each other after the trip. After all, they only lived a bridge apart.

CHAPTER THIRTEEN

DOLORES DIDN'T KNOW WHAT TO do. Either the mother of the infant didn't realize the infant was dead, or she knew it and didn't want to believe it. Dolores sat down a short distance away from the mother. Emilio and Ernesto caught up to Dolores.

"What's wrong with her?" Ernesto whispered.

"She said her baby girl is sick," Dolores answered. "But I think she's dead," she whispered very quietly.

"What should we do? Can we help her?" Ernesto whispered back.

Dolores said, "Let's go over there, so she won't hear us."

They moved a short distance away, and Ernesto asked, "Can we do anything?"

Emilio asked, "Yes, how can we help?"

"We can't leave her here. She needs help," Dolores said.

"But there isn't much we can do," Emilio argued. "And we might miss the train."

"Emilio," Dolores whispered. "Look at her," she urged as she glanced toward the woman.

Sitting in the weeds, the woman had her head down, staring at the dirt. She was rocking her dead baby.

"If we don't help her, someone will hurt her, and she won't be able to defend herself," Dolores argued.

"What do you want to do?" Ernesto asked.

"You two stay right here and let me talk to her. If I can help her to know her baby is in Heaven, we can bury the baby and then help her to get on the train if she wants to go."

The brothers nodded and stayed in their position.

"Miss, hello," Dolores said softly as she slowly approached the woman.

The mother kept rocking the limp baby and did not respond.

Dolores inched closer to her. "Miss," she said. "Miss."

Dolores moved closer still and gently put her hand on the mother's shoulder. The mother didn't answer, but she allowed Dolores to touch her. Dolores paused for a moment and then softly eased her arm around the mother's shoulder.

"It is okay. Your sweet, sweet baby. It's okay," Dolores said.

Dolores moved to hug the woman. The mother put her head on Dolores' shoulder and cried harder and harder.

"Your sweet baby is with the angels. The angels have her now. She's not sick now. The angels have her."

The mother, Dolores, and the dead baby sat for a long time, the three huddled up in a long hug. The mother sobbed even more. The train came and went.

As the sky darkened, Dolores and the mother sat, motionless. The mother, still crying, eventually pulled away from Dolores. She handed the dead baby to Dolores, who placed the baby gently on the ground.

"Ernesto, Emilio, can you help me please?"

"Yes," they said simultaneously.

"We must dig a small place for the baby," Dolores instructed.

Dolores, Emilio, and Ernesto used their hands to dig out a shallow, tiny grave. As they struggled with their bare hands, they could hear the music playing in the *zocalo* in the old part of Veracruz. They heard laughter, and the music played louder through the night. With hurting fingers, they dug a shallow grave.

"Okay," Dolores said to her brothers, "gather some stones. Stay out of sight from anyone else waiting for the train. And don't talk."

Dolores looked at the mother. She was sitting as if in a trance. The mother didn't look at Dolores but only stared at her baby lying on the hot, dry ground. Dolores fought the urge to cry. Her heart ached for the pain the mother must be feeling.

Ernesto and Emilio brought back several stones and smaller rocks. They went back into the field to look for more rocks.

Dolores placed her hand on the mother's shoulder again and said, "We'll put your baby here. And then we'll pray."

The mother did not talk. She didn't agree or disagree.

"Is that okay?" Dolores asked.

The mother looked in Dolores' eyes and gave a faint nod.

"You can help me," she told the mother.

Gently, Dolores and the mother lifted the baby and placed her inside the shallow grave. Emilio and Ernesto knelt behind their sister. Dolores took the mother's hands, and while both women were on their knees, Dolores prayed, "Father, we place this baby in the hands of Your angels. Help her journey to You. Please watch over the baby's mother. We place our lives in Your hands."

Both women made the sign of the cross on their chests. Dolores hugged the mother, who wept uncontrollably. She helped the mother move a little distance from the grave. Dolores, Ernesto, and Emilio covered the tiny baby with stones. Ernesto found two small branches and some twine and vines from the bushes. He fashioned a cross and nestled it between the rocks over the grave. He said a silent prayer and made the sign of the cross.

No one said anything. They sat in the blackness of the vacant field, listening to the music in the distance. They each found a spot near the grave and laid down. The mother laid alongside the grave. Daylight would come before they were ready.

* * *

The birds woke Dolores before dawn. She nudged Ernesto and Emilio. She looked over to wake the mother, but she wasn't there. The mother was nowhere in sight. Dolores stood up and scanned the railyard. No woman with a pink and red flowered blouse. She looked out in the other direction.

"Is she gone?" Ernesto asked as he sat up rubbing his eyes.

"Yes, and I'm worried about her. I hope she's okay."

Emilio was stretching and yawning. "I think I slept about two minutes." He looked over to the grave site.

"Where'd she go?" he asked.

"I don't know. She left when we were all sleeping. I know she's upset—"

Emilio interrupted. "Maybe she went to the railyard and is sleeping there."

"Maybe," Dolores said.

"Think we might find some food?" Ernesto asked.

"Let's walk over there." Dolores pointed to the end of the field. "Maybe there will be some bananas. I saw plenty of banana trees from the train yesterday."

The three walked over to the end of the field and found several kinds of trees, but no banana trees. They looked under the trees—nothing there. They walked around the outskirts of the field, near the street.

A tiny, elderly woman walked by with a cart.

"Young man," she said loudly to Emilio.

Fearing he was in trouble, he said, "I'm sorry, I was just looking for something to eat."

"Come here." She motioned for him to join her.

Emilio walked over to the woman. She opened up a metal container in the cart.

"I sell these to the tourists walking in the *zocalo*. They pay too much money for them," she said with a laugh. "Please, take one."

Emilio's eyes lit up. She handed him a fresh sweet tamal wrapped in a banana leaf and tied with a strand from a leaf.

"For your breakfast," she said.

"Thank you. Thank you so much. We haven't eaten since yesterday," he said to her.

"Here, take another one. You can share."

Emilio thanked her again and jogged over to his sister.

"Dolores, Ernesto, look."

"God is good," Dolores said.

They unwrapped the tamales and ate bites of each one, breaking off the pieces with their fingers.

"I am not sure I have ever had such a good sweet tamal," Dolores said. "How long since we had one with raisins? And cream? Delicious."

Their breakfast was consumed within minutes.

"Let's walk back toward the train tracks. I'm not sure when the train will come today," Dolores told her brothers. "We must be ready."

Dolores led her brothers as they walked back toward the train tracks and closer to the railyard. People were gathering again today. Other travelers remained near the railyard, but not in plain sight, wanting to remain undetected by the Mexican authorities.

Dolores scanned the railyard, looking for the mother who disappeared in the night. *What could have happened to her? Where did she go?*

"Let me know if either of you spot the mother. I'm afraid for her," Dolores said.

They walked around the railyard, scanning for Mexican authorities and for the mother of the dead baby. Seeing neither, they found a place in the shade against the wall of an old building. The mosquitoes were thick, and the air was as heavy as Dolores' heart.

Dolores thought about her family back home. She missed them so much. She wished she could tell her mother and grandmother about the baby they buried. She wanted to feel her mother's arms around her, comforting her. She wished she could go to her church and talk to her priest about what had happened and ask if she could have done more for the mother.

"When do you think a train will come?" Emilio asked.

"I don't know. We'll have to wait here with the mosquitoes until the train arrives." Dolores swatted at a swarm.

Hours passed and finally Emilio said, "That tamal seems like a long time ago."

Dolores agreed. "Yes, but remember how delicious it was?"

"And now," Ernesto said, "I am hungry for Grandma's pork tamales."

"Remember how tasty those are?" Emilio said. "Just the right amount of spiciness!"

"I think if we keep talking about food, we'll be hungrier," Dolores added.

Emilio and Ernesto became sleepy sitting for such a long time. By late afternoon, they were both napping. Dolores kept watch so that no harm would come to them. A disturbance at the far side of the railyard got her attention.

Ernesto awoke. "Look," he said. "An officer."

"Yes. Watch and see what happens."

A man, waiting for the train, was arguing with the officer. The officer's voice got louder and louder.

"Show me your papers."

"I have no papers. Please. I'm poor. I'm from Honduras and trying to go to the United States. Please let me leave when the train comes."

"Give me your money, and I will let you go."

When the officer could not shake any money from the man, he said, "You're not going to the United States. You're coming with me. You're going back to Honduras."

The man reluctantly stood still. The officer took his arm and forced him to leave the train yard.

"We must be careful. The officer will be back," Dolores told Ernesto and Emilio.

They remained in their shady spot by the wall of the old building. The Mexican police officer returned and had another officer, a narcotics federal officer, with him. Dolores, Emilio, and Ernesto watched as he approached two men in gray, hooded jackets. The two men, holding plastic bags, stood at the end of the railyard trying to avoid eye contact with the officials.

"You two . . . " The narcotics officer pointed. "With me."

The two men walked to the officer. He looked in their bags, then put them on the ground and put a band around their wrists. The two officers took them away.

By nightfall, the three were losing hope that the train would arrive. Dolores looked at the sky. The moon was glowing as brightly as it had the night before. She could not think about last night. She put the horrible memories away for now.

At last, they heard the train's engine.

"Here it comes," Emilio said.

"You ready to get on?" Dolores asked.

"I know how to get on the train easily now," Emilio said.

"I don't think the ride will be too long." Then, trying to cheer up her brothers, Dolores said, "Maybe we can find a shelter again at our next stop."

The train whined as it advanced toward the group. It picked up speed as Ernesto got on the ladder and helped Dolores pull up. Emilio followed Dolores. They scanned the train car they were riding on. No one looked like trouble. Everyone on board appeared to be travelers going to the United States. But it was dark, which made it difficult to determine for certain.

Dolores looked ahead. She couldn't see much, but she knew they were moving toward the mountains. The track would take them through this part of Mexico and eventually to the frontier of flat plains, cacti, and mesquite trees. But for now, the train progressed through coastal southern Mexico.

Not far from the railyard, the train increased speed. Dolores looked behind her to see the outskirts of the city of Veracruz. She looked ahead and thought she spotted something out of place near the tracks.

"Dolores," Ernesto said. "Look, there is something up ahead."

Dolores stared hard and squinted her eyes in the dark to focus. The light of the train alerted her to something. "Is that—"

"It is her," Ernesto said. "The mother we helped last night."

Dolores made out the pink and red blouse. "She's too close to the tracks!" she yelled in panic.

The mother walked without being aware of her surroundings. She was in a trance of disbelief from the death of her baby.

The train did not slow down.

"You're too close!" Dolores yelled again.

A barely audible thump followed by a scream over the loud shrieking of the train told Dolores that it was too late. The train hit the woman.

"No!" Dolores screamed.

"No!" Emilio yelled.

Ernesto was in shock.

It couldn't have happened, thought Dolores. She looked back behind her. The woman was lying face down on the side of the tracks. Dolores wept.

"It's okay," Ernesto said to Dolores, trying to comfort her. "We did what we could," he added.

Dolores could not stop crying. Emilio and Ernesto attempted to comfort their sister. But Dolores wondered if there was something different that she could've done. What would her mother tell her now? How would her mother handle this? *I'm too young to know what to do,* she thought. *How I miss Mamá.*

"Dolores," Ernesto said, "she's with God and her baby now."

"Yes." She sniffed and wiped her eyes.

"Her baby is happy now, and so is she. Remember last night, you prayed that we would be in God's hands?" Ernesto asked.

"Yes," she replied, still sniffling.

"God knew the mother could not go on without her baby," Ernesto said.

Ernesto, so young and so wise, Dolores thought.

Emilio scooted over to his older sister and put his arm around her. "We're in God's hands. You know we have been since we left Honduras. You've told us many times on this trip that God watches us. He watched the mother, too."

Dolores held both of her brothers' hands and calmed herself down. She thought back to the day they left Honduras and how they'd argued about her staying home. Now, she was glad to be so close to her brothers. She said a prayer to thank God for the love she had for them and the love they had for her.

The loud noise of the train was irritating to Dolores at this moment. She wanted quietness and rest.

Emilio looked up at the sky. "Do you think Mamá and Papá and Grandma are looking at the sky tonight?"

Dolores knew that her family often sat in their yard and looked at the heavens and prayed together.

"Yes," she said. "I think they're probably doing just that."

"Then we're all together. We're all looking at the sky tonight and praying, just like at home," Emilio said.

Ernesto asked, "Do you suppose they can hear Mr. Martinez's loud music and awful singing down the road?"

They all laughed. Mr. Martinez sometimes had too much *guaro* (sugar cane liquor) and played his guitar and sang too loud. The other problem was that Mr. Martinez couldn't really sing. He was always off-key.

"Maybe they can hear him." Dolores smiled.

Then Emilio said, "Shhhh . . . I think I can hear him all the way up here! Oh! He is hurting my ears!"

"Now, that's funny, Emilio!" Dolores said and smiled again.

Dolores, Ernesto, and Emilio did not talk anymore. Dolores looked into the sky and wondered about the risks that tomorrow might bring.

CHAPTER FOURTEEN

THE EVENING MEAL AND MARIACHI music in the restaurant were over. Eva and Steven entered the bus and took their seats. They sat together near the back.

Adrián said, "Everyone, make yourselves comfortable. We have about an eight-to-nine-hour drive ahead of us. Put your chairs back and relax. I'll not be disturbing you throughout the night. We'll be making a couple of stops for fuel; and if you need a snack at that time, you can find something at the stops. We'll be in Veracruz for breakfast. You'll have your eggs and chorizo by the Gulf of Mexico."

Once all the passengers were seated, the bus driver dimmed the interior lights.

Eva found her travel pillow and blanket and settled in. She wanted to be comfortable for the long ride.

"You came prepared," Steven said.

"Creature comforts," Eva said.

Steven smiled.

A couple of nights ago, Eva had slept on the bus all night from Monterrey to Dolores Hidalgo, and yet it seemed like months had passed. She had seen so much, learned so much, and probably had eaten too much unfamiliar food. And, most unexpectedly, she met Steven. She smiled.

"Looks like we'll have a smooth trip. The route we are going includes some toll roads, which is good," Steven said.

"Oh?" Eva asked.

"Yes. The speed limit will be faster, and the toll roads are better protected, safer."

"That's a good thing," Eva said.

"Yes."

They rode along in an awkward silence for several minutes. Eva hoped Steven would start another conversation. Then Steven asked, "Have you spoken with your family since you've been on the trip?"

"Yes. I've talked with my mother a couple of times, and I called my sisters."

"And is everything okay back home?"

"Back in Virginia? Yes, it's fine. Every time I speak with Mom, she tells me over and over how dangerous it is in Mexico."

"You know she's telling you the truth, right?" Steven asked with candor.

"I know there are some bad people in Mexico, like everywhere else in the world," she replied.

Steven hesitated a minute and then said, "Yes, but in most of the world, police and government officers are legitimate."

"But what about the police in Morelia?" Eva asked.

"Think about it. The police in Morelia made the news because they do things right. It is what the police are expected to do in other countries. But here in Mexico, that is the exception, not the rule. It was a headline story."

"You have a point."

"Anyway, give your mother credit. She's right. In Mexico, whether it is the police or anyone walking down the street, you never know whom you can trust."

Eva thought about what Steven said. Then she made a remark that may have been misunderstood. "I guess I need to be careful then about whom I trust."

The silence now was even more awkward. She did not want Steven to think she didn't trust him. It was like a contest to see who would make some benign comment to restore the carefree conversation they had earlier in the evening. At last, Eva thought of something to say.

"Tell me about Veracruz. What do you know about the city?"

"Oh. Let's see . . . first of all, it's humid and hot there. There will be many mosquitoes. You know, it's right on the coast of the Gulf of Mexico."

"We will get to the beach at some point?" Eva asked.

"Yes, it's on the itinerary." Then he added, "Now, here's a Spanish quiz for you."

"Okay. I'll try. What's the quiz?"

"What do you think Veracruz means?"

"Clueless. Give me a hint," she said, feeling the blood rushing to her face.

"Well, the Spanish word for truth is *verdad*."

"Okay. Still got nothing. Ah . . . true something or other," Eva said, laughing self-consciously.

"The Spanish word *cruz* means 'cross.'"

"Truth about the cross?" she asked, laughing.

"True cross," he said.

"Learned something there," she said still laughing. "And what else can you tell me about Veracruz?"

"It has its share of tourist industry," Steven said.

"Will it be crowded there?"

"Where we will be going, probably. I imagine we'll stay around the tourist area."

"And what might we see there?" she asked.

"Colonial buildings, restaurants, music, dancing, and, of course, the beaches near the area," he said. "There are some of the best restaurants and clubs there in the historic center of town. I've heard the old historic plaza is much like the one in Havana, Cuba, although I haven't been to Cuba to find out."

"But you have been to Veracruz before?"

"Yes, many times. Usually on business. I don't get to see the tourist side of the city, you know, the attractions," he said.

"I understand. Hard to enjoy the beach when you have to work. What other things are going on in Veracruz besides the tourist industry?" Eva asked.

"Well, the state of Veracruz has a lot of agricultural business."

"What do they grow there? Plantains?"

Steven laughed. "They grow bananas, coffee, vanilla beans, coconuts, and other vegetables."

"Interesting. So, we will have some great food there?" Eva asked.

"Yes. And of course, you will find plenty of seafood. When I've been to Veracruz before, I was limited by time, so I didn't try many restaurants. In fact, although I stayed in the city, I didn't get to see much of it."

"This time, you will," she said, smiling.

Steven put his hand on hers and said, "Yes, this will be a good visit to Veracruz."

She hoped Steven would keep his hand on hers through the night. She looked out the window at the blackness. She could make out the stars through the speckled clouds, but generally she couldn't see anything else. She reasoned that she was in the countryside of Mexico.

Steven tilted his head on the headrest of the seat. Eva looked closely at him and determined he was already asleep. His hand slowly released hers. Her mind wandered in the tranquil atmosphere. What exactly did Steven do for a living? What did a manager of a *maquiladora* entail? She would ask him.

She couldn't help but gaze at his sleeping face. He was quite attractive. Dark hair, eyes, irresistible smile. He was also very polite and thoughtful. He was very knowledgeable. She enjoyed their conversations and spending time with him. She wondered how he felt about her.

As the bus progressed on the route to Veracruz, Eva felt sleep taking over. She fluffed her pillow and tucked her blanket around her legs and feet. She found the most comfortable position she could in the reclined back seat and dozed off. She awakened when the bus slowed down for a fuel stop. She realized Steven's head was on her shoulder. It felt good there, and she didn't want to disturb him. The bus driver opened the door to step outside. The noise disturbed several of the passengers around her, but Steven slept, undisturbed. Eva closed her eyes and went back to sleep.

* * *

The emerging sunlight had not awakened Eva, but the sound of the opening bus door did. Steven was awake and looked forward out the front window. It was daylight, and most of the passengers were already talking.

"Good morning," Eva said.

"Good morning," he said.

Eva nodded and smiled at the other passengers and returned "Buenos días" to each one who spoke to her.

Eva looked out the window and discovered they were at a gas station with lush green vegetation and mountains not far from the road.

"Any idea where we are?"

"Yes. We are in the state of Veracruz about twenty miles away from the city of Veracruz."

"It looks like a jungle out there," she said.

"We are in the rain forest part of the state."

"Nice!" she said.

Adrián stood at the front of the bus and said, "Good morning! We are nearly to our destination city, Veracruz. I know some of you have been anxious for a cup of coffee. If you'd like to grab a cup before we head out, there's a nice little café attached to the gas station. They have fresh coffee from Veracruz, and I think you will like it. If you want to wait until we get in the city, our hotel has a nice restaurant, and there are other restaurants nearby."

Steven stood up, turned to Eva, and asked, "Would you like to get some coffee?"

"Sounds heavenly," she replied as she got up from her seat.

"Were you able to sleep?" Steven asked.

"Oh, yes. I think I was just tired enough to fall right to sleep."

Eva wondered if Steven knew he had slept with his head on her shoulder. She decided it might be best not to bring it up.

"What's that noise?" Eva asked as she stepped out of the bus. "So shrill."

Steven laughed. "The spider monkeys. Probably over that direction near the side of the mountain."

"Monkeys?"

"Yep. There are other animals over there, but we probably won't hear or see them. Most of the other animals that we have in Mexico, you have in Texas, too."

"Seriously? Like what?"

"Wild boars, ocelots, coyotes, pumas—to name a few."

Steven opened the door for her as they went inside to get coffee. The coffee was steaming hot and full of flavor.

"I think I've found my new favorite coffee. I never knew Mexican coffee was so rich."

"It's good," he said.

Back on the bus, Eva and Steven looked out the window at the rain forest scenery. The land became flatter but still lush with growth as they neared the coast. Buildings and city traffic emerged. The bus traveled along the main road beside the coastline. The cabin full of tourists on the bus suddenly came alive with chatter and "oohs" and "ahs" as they viewed the water. The dark blue waves were lapping up onto the sand and rocks. Seagulls, humidity, and salt filled the air. The bus rolled on around the bend of the coastline to the Gran Hotel Diligencias and parked.

The weary but excited passengers disembarked the bus and looked at the nearby famous main *zocalo*. The hotel was situated at the perfect location on the main *zocalo* close to the water.

Eva retrieved her bag. She and Steven followed the others into the lobby of the classic hotel. Chandeliers hung from the tall ceilings, and the lobby and restaurant had large, decorative archway windows. A large, white column in the lobby displayed white palm leaves at the top appearing to hold up the ceiling. The décor included plenty of tropical plants and flowers against the backdrop of creamy yellow walls. The restaurant was well-appointed, and the lounge looked comfortable. By far, the most elegant hotel on the trip.

"Well, this is something," Steven said, looking up to the chandeliers.

"A change from our other hotels," Eva agreed.

Adrián signaled the group to gather around.

"Welcome to the city of Veracruz. You'll have all day today and tomorrow to see the city or go to the beach. As you might have noticed, we are at the historic, central *zocalo* and very near the old fort, San Juan de Ulúa. You don't want to miss either one. I have a list of excursions here; and if you want to go out to the beach excursion, you will travel about fourteen miles from here. If you are interested, you need to sign up today. This particular beach, Anton Lizardo Beach, has several protected reefs, which makes it a great spot for snorkeling. If you want to reserve a snorkeling trip, they will furnish the gear and a guide. Otherwise, there are many things to see in the historic district, like the famous square. As you probably already know, Veracruz is known for its night life—like clubs, dancing, and wonderful restaurants. Just check in with me if you are interested in the beach excursion."

"Are you a snorkeler?" Steven asked.

"Not really, are you? I mean, I'd be willing to try it," Eva responded.

"Sure. I haven't had much time to snorkel lately, but I want to go while I am here. The reefs are supposed to be pretty good."

"Okay. I'll try it."

Steven and Eva met with Adrián to sign up for the snorkeling excursion.

"Glad you are going. Just fill out this paperwork here and then sign here. Be ready to leave on the bus tomorrow at ten a.m."

"Thank you," Eva said.

"Ready to go see the city?" Steven asked.

"Yes. Meet back in the lobby in a few minutes?" Eva asked.

"Okay."

Eva and Steven met in the lobby for a quick breakfast at the hotel restaurant.

Steven placed his knife across his plate as he finished and asked, "What do you want to see? I feel like I'm one hundred percent tourist today. I want to see everything!"

"Let's see, the beach is tomorrow, so what about the historic area? The square? I think there are shops and restaurants," Eva suggested.

"Sounds good. Maybe after lunch, we can head to the fort? We can take a walking tour, or if you want, we can visit the historical museums," Steven said.

Not really the museum or the old fort tour type, Eva smiled and said, "Sure, the fort tour sounds great." *Anything is better than another museum,* she thought.

They set off to see the *zocalo.* Like their hotel, it was the prettiest *zocalo* they had seen on the trip. Vendors and shops lined the walkways into and all around the *zocalo.* The architecture was magnificent with large archways and tile and stone floors and patio. Large palm trees all around swayed in the warm, humid breeze. Other tropical trees and plants were neatly landscaped around the *zocalo.*

Eva and Steven shopped in several of the stores on the main square. Eva found a long, white, cotton skirt with brightly colored Mexican flowers embroidered all around the bottom edge and a matching white blouse with tiny Mexican flowers around the neckline.

"I like those," Steven remarked.

"Thanks. I think I just might buy them. I can wear these to teach class."

Steven smiled as Eva turned to find the clerk. She bargained with the clerk, and in the end, paid nearly the full price, anyway. But she was pleased that she knew enough Spanish to bargain. She liked the outfit and hoped she would get a chance to wear it on the trip.

After shopping, Eva and Steven visited the cathedral on the square and went inside. They spent a good deal of time studying the sanctuary. Once again, Eva felt the reverence of being in a house of worship. She just couldn't quite put her finger on the feeling she had within the church. They left the cathedral and walked around the *zocalo*, peeking in every shop and venue.

"I am ready for lunch," Steven said. "How about you?"

Eva nodded.

They found a café amongst the multicolored umbrellas on the walkway and ate lunch. Eva ate nearly every bite of her seafood tacos and tried the variety of salsas.

"How far is the fort from here?" Eva asked.

"Let me ask our waiter. Sir, sir," he said as he held up his hand, getting the waiter's attention.

"How far is it to the fort from here?"

"About five or six miles by car," he said. "Would you like a taxi?"

"Yes, please."

Eva walked through the fort with Steven, but her heart was not in it. The guide discussed the details of the fort in Spanish, but Steven translated for her. She surprisingly understood a great deal of what the guide said, but she was thankful Steven interpreted to fill in the gaps. Nevertheless, she was anxious to see the rest of Veracruz and spend more time visiting with Steven. Steven intently listened to the guide, taking in every single word he said and studying every crack or stone of the fort. Steven, enamored by all of the historic facts, was concentrating on the fort, while Eva was aching to be back outside in the sea breeze. After nearly two hours, Steven was ready to leave.

"I was thinking," he said as he lightly touched her hand, "would you be up for dinner and dancing at the *zocalo*? It is famous for dancing La Bamba."

"I'd like to, but I must warn you, I have no idea how to do that dance," she said, already feeling worried about her clumsiness.

"I'll teach you," he said, flashing that smile of complete confidence.

"Okay, but no laughing," Eva said sternly.

"Promise," he winked.

They returned to the hotel a few minutes before five o'clock.

"Will you be ready to leave for dinner at six?"

"That would be perfect," she said. "I'll have time to give my mom a quick call."

"See you at six," he said.

Back in her room, Eva showered and dressed for the evening. She put on her new matching white skirt and blouse with the Mexican flowers. She looked in the mirror. "I like it," she whispered to herself.

She called her mother. It took several rings before her mother answered.

"Mom? You okay?

"Of course, I'm okay. I'm in the United States. The question is, are you okay?"

"Yes. Just checking in. Are you busy?"

"No. What would I be busy doing, for goodness' sake? I'm retired."

"You just didn't answer the phone right away. So, I was worried."

"Oh, I was in the other room. Don't worry about me at all. How is Mexico? Have you seen the caravan yet?"

"Mexico is wonderful. And no, no caravan. I'm in Veracruz today and tomorrow."

"And where is that?"

"On the Gulf of Mexico, Mom."

"Well, don't go disappearing in the water or anything."

"I'm fine, Mom. Tell my sisters hello, and I'll call them once I'm back in Texas. I will call you again in a couple of days."

"Fine, and stay away from the caravans and the cartels, okay?"

"Yes, Mom."

Promptly at six, Eva and Steven met in the hotel lobby.

"Nice outfit. I like it even better on you. A good look for you," Steven said, admiring Eva's new skirt and blouse as he took her hand and led her out of the lobby.

"Well, thank you, sir," she replied.

The evening temperatures had not yet begun to drop, and Eva felt the stickiness of the sea air. A man approached Steven as they walked along the sidewalk. He was speaking Spanish so rapidly that Eva could not determine what he was saying. The man was insistent about something, and Steven shook his head several times, disagreeing with the man. The discussion became heated. Both Steven and the other man raised their voices and talked for several minutes. Finally, the man turned and walked away.

"That was strange," Eva said.

"Uh, yeah," Steven said. He hesitated, knowing that Eva expected an explanation, and then he added, "He thought I was someone else." For a few moments, Steven seemed agitated and preoccupied.

Then he said, "Let's not let it spoil our evening." He took Eva's hand and led her to the restaurant.

CHAPTER FIFTEEN

INTERMITTENT SLEEP WAS THE BEST Dolores could hope for on the train. The clanging and shaking of the train as it meandered from Veracruz to Orizaba was not the culprit of her insomnia. She couldn't stop thinking about the events of the past twenty-four hours. She couldn't get the images out of her mind—the mother rocking a lifeless baby, putting the baby in the shallow grave, and then the mother lying on the side of the train track.

Dolores looked at her brothers. They were so young to be living these disturbing incidents. She was proud of how they had each supported and helped her. Their new life in the United States would be their reward for enduring these horrible experiences.

The train jostled over a narrow bridge and roused Ernesto. He scooted over to Dolores. He put his arm around her.

"How are you doing, Sis?"

"I'm fine."

They sat in silence. Dolores let Emilio sleep. She was concerned that her two younger brothers were not getting the rest and food they needed.

The blackness of the night began to turn into a murky gray. Dolores anticipated the coming sunrise. She liked watching the sunrise at home; however, these days on the train, the emerging light marked the beginning of another day of the unknown.

"Do you think we'll be at a stop soon?"

"I'm not sure, but we've been riding for a while. I heard another rider talking about a shelter somewhere. I hope there's one in Orizaba."

"It would be nice. The shelter we went in before was wonderful. I could use some food."

Dolores patted his knee. "I know, brother."

The train screeched as it slowed down.

"Emilio, wake up. We need to get off the train," Dolores said.

The three scampered down the ladder just as the train was approaching the town of Orizaba. They walked toward the railyard, keeping some distance away from the track. Other travelers walked with them in silence.

"It is much cooler here," Ernesto whispered.

"Yes, it is. We need jackets," Emilio said.

"It'll be warm soon. The sun will heat us," said Dolores.

They walked to the city. Dolores scanned to see if there might be a shelter in sight, but there was none.

"Let's look for food," said Dolores.

The sun rising over the majestic mountains that embraced the city in the valley below gave Dolores a sense of optimism. Sunrises always caused Dolores to feel hope for the coming day. She said a silent prayer, thanking God for showing her this beautiful sunrise. The tragic events of the day before made her appreciate the magnificence of the sunrise even more.

"Are you getting warmer?" Dolores asked her brothers.

"Yes. Walking helps," Ernesto said.

The three walked for some distance and reached the train yard. The train was leaving already, and there was no chance they would be able to catch it.

"That was a quick stop," Emilio noted.

"It was," said Dolores, "but now we'll have time to find some food."

Dolores inspected the train yard and the people sitting around it. It looked safe. She didn't see any sign of a shelter or food nearby.

The travelers were finding places to sit or sleep right around the railyard.

"Do you want to stay and rest here?" Dolores asked.

"I want to look for food. I didn't see any banana trees as we walked in. Maybe it's too cold here to grow bananas. We might need to look for something else to eat," Ernesto said.

In silence, they walked around the railyard. They expanded their search area, always keeping the train yard in view. They had no luck.

"I think if there was any fruit growing around here, it's been taken already," Emilio said.

"Let's expand out from the track a little more and search. God will help us," Dolores said as she prayed silently.

Walking another block over from the train yard, they saw a small church. Dolores wanted to go inside. Maybe they could rest in the warm church for just a few minutes.

"Should we go in?" Emilio asked.

Dolores nodded.

Inside the small stucco church, there was an altar with a few candles burning. They sat on a pew near the back. They remained very quiet.

Dolores was happy to be in a church. She wanted to have a conversation with God about their journey to the United States and pray for safety and guidance.

Near the front of the church, a door opened. The priest dressed in a white robe entered the room and smiled at Dolores, Ernesto, and Emilio.

"Good morning!" the priest cheerfully said.

The priest walked to the back near the pew where they sat.

"How are you today? You look like you are just passing through our city of Orizaba."

"Yes, Father," Dolores said.

"Then my guess is that you're hungry. If you come with me, you can help yourselves to some coffee and a few sweet rolls."

The tears rolled down Dolores' face. She could not stop the tears no matter how hard she tried. She managed to mumble a soft "Thank you" in a hushed voice. She knew she was crying more about the tragedies of this journey, but she was also crying because she was happy to have food again and to feel safe—if only for a little while.

"Come, children," he said as he led them to a door on the side of the church.

A table was set in the front of a small room with chairs in the back. A coffee pot sat on one side of the table, and a platter of sweet breads and tortillas sat on the other side of the table.

"Please, help yourselves. Have a little breakfast."

The aroma of the sweet breads and the coffee filled the air of the small room. Dolores, Emilio, and Ernesto each took one of the sweet rolls, a tortilla, and a cup of coffee. They rolled up the tortillas and put them in their pockets. They sat in the chairs in the back of the room.

"We get many travelers through here," the priest said.

Dolores finished her first bite of the sweet roll and asked, "Is there a shelter nearby?"

"No, my child. We don't have one. But there are occasional visitors, such as yourselves, who might wander by the church, and we try to help all we can."

"We're so blessed that you are here. We're grateful for our breakfast," Dolores said.

Ernesto and Emilio didn't join the conversation. They were occupied, eating their rolls and drinking their coffee.

"We have some facilities over there," he said, gesturing, "if you need them. Feel free to use them. You can wash up a little.

"Tell me, where are you from?"

"Honduras, "Dolores replied.

"Ah, Honduras. I've met many travelers from Honduras. You must be careful here in Orizaba. There are people here, much like in Honduras, who want to take money and hurt people."

"Yes, Father," Dolores said.

"And these two are your brothers, I am guessing?"

Dolores, Emilio, and Ernesto nodded.

"You must all take care of each other. Now, let's pray for your protection."

The priest said a prayer, asking for God to protect them. Then he added, "You feel free to stay as long as you like. Mass is about to begin. You may join us there, too. And don't forget to take some of these bottles of water with you when you leave," he said as he gestured to boxes of bottled water next to a wall.

"Thank you, Father," Dolores said.

Dolores, Emilio, and Ernesto took turns in the washroom.

After they washed up, Dolores said, "Let's go in to mass. It would be good for us to do so."

Ernesto and Emilio agreed and followed Dolores into the sanctuary.

They sat in the back of the church. Dolores was grateful that she was able to find this church and to sit in the warmth and participate in mass. For just a moment, she felt no anxiety. She felt protected and loved. She thanked God for the gifts He had given.

* * *

Dolores, Ernesto, and Emilio exited the church and walked toward the train yard. The happiness remained in Dolores' heart as they walked three more blocks to the tracks. She was nourished and refreshed.

"Do you suppose we will find a good church in the United States?" Ernesto asked.

"They have many churches there. We'll find a good one. I'm sure of it," Dolores replied.

Nearing the railyard, Dolores saw something that looked like trouble.

"Do you see them?" Ernesto asked.

"Looks dangerous," Emilio said.

"Yes. I see them," Dolores acknowledged.

"Shouldn't we try to help her?" Emilio asked as he moved rapidly toward the scene.

"No, Emilio, wait," Dolores pleaded. "They might take us."

Dolores was torn between wanting to help the young girl and protecting her younger brothers. She didn't think she and her brothers were strong enough to fight these evil men. In her heart, she knew she must protect her brothers and pray that God would help the young girl.

Ahead, four men dressed in dark clothing walked around the train yard. They weren't travelers on the train. They surrounded a teenage girl sitting on the ground. She began screaming. Two of the men grabbed her arms and pulled her up. The other two men walked down the street and to a van. They opened the van, got in, and drove to the spot where the other two men were holding the girl. The two men took the girl to the door and shoved her in the van. The door slammed, and the van drove away.

"I wish we could've helped her," Ernesto said.

"I feel such sadness for her," Emilio said. "Will she be taken to a brothel somewhere, like Lola?"

"I feel sad for her, too. There is no way to know what will happen to her," Dolores answered. "We must remember her in our prayers and ask that God will help her."

"Do you think there will be a time when Mexico is safe for everyone?" Ernesto asked.

Dolores thought for several minutes and responded, "Evil exists everywhere. We must try to stay safe and ask that God watch us."

"Do you think it's safe in the United States?" Ernesto asked. "Will we be safe there?"

"There will be protection from the gangs and other evil men. But we'll have to watch out for the police. Just like in Mexico, if you're in a country without permission, they can send you back to your country," Dolores said.

"Then we'll have to be very careful," Ernesto said. "Once we have enough money, we can go back home."

"Yes. Do you miss home?"

"Yes," Ernesto said. "I miss Mamá and Papá and Grandma."

"Me, too," Emilio said. "When we talked about going to the United States, before we left Honduras, I thought the trip would be fun."

"And now?" Dolores asked.

"It's not like I thought. I enjoy seeing all of the countryside. I don't like being scared and hungry and tired," Emilio said.

"I feel the same," Ernesto said.

"Let's look for a place to wait and stay out of view from the people who would cause us trouble," Dolores warned.

They walked around the train yard but stayed some distance away. They found a field with trees and bushes.

"How about over there?" Ernesto asked.

Dolores agreed.

Dolores found a nice smooth spot under a thick bush. It looked like others had slept there before. Emilio found a spot under a nearby tree, and Ernesto found a place beside a large rock under another bush.

"Let's sleep as long as we can," Ernesto said. "It won't matter if we take a later train. We need to rest."

"Yes. Rest would be good," Dolores said.

The sun had warmed the air enough to be quite comfortable. They all fell asleep in the warm sun within a matter of minutes.

Dolores didn't know how much time had passed when she heard Emilio screaming.

"No! No!" Emilio screamed as he ran.

Dolores and Ernesto sat straight up and saw a man with a machete was chasing Emilio down the street, swinging the machete and yelling. The man chased Emilio down the street screaming.

"Give me your money!" he yelled at Emilio.

Emilio ran so far that Dolores and Ernesto couldn't see him.

"Please, God, help him," Dolores prayed.

"Where is he?" Ernesto asked.

Dolores was crying. "I can't see him or that horrible man."

Both Ernesto and Dolores knew that Emilio was a faster runner than most of the boys his age.

Ernesto said, "He'll run faster than the wind. He can get away from him."

"We must go look," Dolores said.

They walked in the direction that Emilio ran. They looked in buildings, behind buildings, in the field. They didn't see him anywhere. They searched for a long while.

"Where could they have gone?" Ernesto asked.

They walked further and scanned the area. No sight of the man or Emilio. Dolores cried. She didn't know what she would do if Emilio was taken somewhere, or worse, killed. She prayed silently over and over.

Dolores and Ernesto walked so far and such a long time that they feared the worst. If he had been taken somewhere, it might be too far for them to find him on foot.

"I'm hopeful," Ernesto said.

They walked in silence. Dolores wept softly. She felt more sorrow with each step. My baby brother, she kept thinking. My poor, sweet, baby brother.

"Wait," Ernesto whispered.

"What? Do you see him?" Dolores asked.

"Shhh . . . I thought I heard something."

"There it is," Ernesto said.

Dolores listened intently. A weak moaning sound could be heard.

"Where's it coming from?" Dolores asked.

"I think . . . this way."

The two walked together, pausing to listen every few steps. Dolores' toe bumped something and nearly tripped her. She looked down.

"Emilio!" she screamed with sorrow in her voice.

At her feet in the weeds lay Emilio. Blood was oozing from his shirt.

"He cut me here," Emilio whispered.

Dolores peeled back Emilio's shirt and saw a long gash across his side. He was bleeding. She was worried the cut would get worse.

"Dolores, don't be mad. He took my money," Emilio choked out with tears running down his face.

"It's fine. Don't worry about that, little brother. I'm thankful you had money to give him, so you're still living," she said hugging her brother. "We don't need the money."

Ernesto opened a water bottle and poured the water on Emilio's cut. There was nothing else to use to treat him.

"Dolores," Ernesto said, "do you think the priest would help us?"

"He might. But we need to get Emilio over there without anyone seeing us. And pray he'll help us."

The walk back to the church was not a long distance, but Emilio was very weak. The three walked a few feet, and then they needed to set Emilio down for a brief rest. It took them over an hour to make the short walk back.

"You wait here with Emilio," Dolores said. "I'll go find the priest and see if we can bring Emilio inside."

"Okay," Ernesto said.

By now, Emilio was pale and very quiet.

Dolores found the priest inside the room with the coffee pot.

"My child, you've returned. Trouble?" asked the priest.

Dolores nodded and said, "My brother is hurt."

"Where is he?"

"Outside," she said.

The priest ran quickly behind Dolores. He saw Emilio on the ground with Ernesto.

"Okay, son. Let's get you inside," he said.

They helped Emilio inside. The priest took them into another room off of the sanctuary. He got a cot from the closet.

"We keep these here for emergencies. Let's lay him here. Then we can get him cleaned up."

The priest worked with Dolores to clean up the wound, and then he brought some bandages and antibiotic ointment from the cabinet.

"These should help," the priest said.

Emilio fell asleep as soon as he was cleaned up. The priest called Ernesto and Dolores out of the room.

"I think his wound isn't too deep. I've seen much worse. God was with him today. He'll need to rest a day or two until the wound begins to heal. You can stay here in the room with him. We'll tend to his wound, and you can all rest. I have only the one cot. You can sleep on the floor. I will give you some blankets to use."

"Thank you, Father," Dolores said.

"Yes, Father. Thank you."

"Now, let's say a prayer for your brother."

They bowed their heads as the priest said a prayer asking for healing.

Dolores and Ernesto spread the blankets on the floor. It was more comfortable than the ground or the train. They all slept for several wonderful hours.

Dolores woke before Ernesto. They sat in silence, hoping Emilio would sleep a little longer.

When Emilio awoke, he asked, "Where are we?" as he rubbed his eyes.

"You don't remember?" asked Ernesto.

"No."

"We are at the church. The priest said we can stay here until you can travel. How do you feel?"

"Hungry," he said.

As if the priest heard Emilio from the other room, he entered with a tray of tortillas, rice, and beans.

"Anyone want to eat?"

For the moment, Dolores felt safe. She was warm; she had food; and her brothers were safe.

CHAPTER SIXTEEN

EVA AND STEVEN WALKED HAND in hand across the *zocalo* and down a tile walkway. Eva was curious to know where they were going to eat. All Steven said was, "You'll see. I think you'll like it."

They walked about halfway around the *zocalo* in the warm coastal air.

"Here it is." Steven pointed to a small yet upscale restaurant.

They went in, and Steven spoke to the maître d'. The maître d' looked on the list and said, "Ah, yes. Right this way, senorita and señor."

They followed him to a waiter station, where the maître d' presented their waiter. "This is José. He will be your head waiter for the evening and will be assisted by two others. José, I present Eva and Steven."

"Hello," Steven said and then turned to the maître d' and said, "Thank you."

The waiter led Steven and Eva to their table and lit a small candle in the center. All of the tables had white linen tablecloths and were set with silver place settings and white linen napkins.

"This is very nice," Eva said. She examined the room. The Spanish colonial style was obvious. The Spanish influence was mixed with just the perfect amount of glitz.

"Yes. The concierge at our hotel recommended it. I selected this particular place hoping you might allow me to buy your dinner."

"Oh, I couldn't possibly." Eva was flabbergasted and more than touched. Inside, she hoped that Steven would insist on paying for her meal, like on a date.

"Honestly, I would be more than honored to do so. Please, allow me."

Eva could not take her eyes off his enchanting smile and had to admit something to herself that night: she was smitten.

"Well, thank you. You are sweet to do so," she said as her heart quickened a bit.

The waiter brought the menu and told them of the specials. The problem was, the entrées were so unique that Eva could not understand much of the Spanish the waiter used to describe each one. She thought she heard tidbits here and there, like "cooked with onion," "baked in the oven in white wine sauce," and "stuffed with crab," but she wasn't sure her interpretations were completely correct. It seemed that the people of Veracruz had a slightly different dialect than she heard in Texas and northern Mexico.

When the waiter finished providing the detailed information about the long list of specials and the general menu, Eva turned to Steven with a lost look in her eyes. She didn't want to order something that she wouldn't like or, worse, something that would be too awkward to eat on a date, assuming this was a real date.

Steven placed his hand on hers, looked her in the eyes, and speaking slowly in Spanish said, "The food ranges from beef and chicken to all kinds of seafood, including lobster, oysters, shrimp, squid, octopus, and all kinds of soups and salads."

"That is quite the selection," she replied in English.

Steven squeezed her hand tighter and turned to the waiter. "You have given us a great number of choices. Can you give us a minute?"

Eva's heart melted. Steven was being her protector and cared enough for her to help her out of a tricky and embarrassing situation.

The waiter nodded and walked away.

"Any ideas? Do you like fish, lobster, shrimp?" Steven asked in Spanish.

"The shrimp sounds good," she replied in broken Spanish and then, in English, she asked, "Did he say how it's prepared?"

Steven took his time and responded first in Spanish and then explained each sentence in English to help her. "They prepare it in several ways. You can have shrimp enchiladas in a white wine sauce with garlic, like a shrimp scampi, or spicy shrimp, or a combination shrimp sampler if you want to try a couple of different kinds. Actually, it says here the combination is three types of shrimp. You can pick which three of the seven shrimp items on the menu you want to try."

Eva attempted to answer in Spanish, even though some of the words were not quite right. "That sounds good. I can have a taste of each one," she said. Steven smiled and squeezed her hand again. Then she switched back to English, "And thank you for helping me with the interpretations. I had it just about figured out but got tripped up on some of the cooking methods," she said.

"No worries. I can help you whenever you need it, but you are doing quite well." Steven signaled for the waiter to return.

Eva decided on shrimp cocktail, the spicy shrimp diablo, and the shrimp scampi for her combination plate, and Steven ordered ahi tuna.

A small group of people dressed in traditional Mexican attire began to play music, but it was not the typical mariachi music. This sound seemed more Caribbean.

Steven asked, "Do you like this music?"

Eva said, "Yes, it's different than the music we heard earlier on the trip."

"It is called Son Jarocho, and it comes from this area of Mexico. It's unusual. The rhythms are different, and so are the instruments."

"But . . . a harp? I would never have associated that with music from Mexico. When I think of harps, I think of church or Christmas or something."

Steven laughed. "And tonight, you will learn to dance to this music."

"Wow. Let me just go ahead and apologize now," she said, blushing.

"For what?" he asked.

"For embarrassing you on the dance floor."

Steven laughed and put his arm around her. "It'll be fun."

Watching the harp player, Eva said, "Look at her fingers plucking the strings so carefully, picking each separate note. She's amazing."

The waiter and his two assistants brought their food to the table. He quickly served the specific items as the assistants handed each to him.

"Thank you," Steven said as the waiter completed his task.

"*Buen provecho*," the waiter replied.

Steven and Eva lingered over dinner, clearly enjoying each other's company.

"Now, Steven, tell me more about a *maquiladora*," Eva requested.

"Sure. *Maquiladoras* became popular in Mexico when companies of the United States realized that Mexican labor is cheaper. But not only the U.S., but other countries as well. So, what they discovered is that paying cheaper wages and less tax to operate factories in Mexico contributes to the industry's bottom line."

"Uh-huh. Now that sounded like a business analyst on the news or something," she laughed. Steven smiled and winked. *Oh, that smile,* she thought to herself.

The waiter and the assistants were very vigilant. The water and tea glasses were never empty. The bread basket was refilled as needed. The service was impeccable and added to the nearly magical evening.

He continued, "The *maquiladoras* helped the companies make more money. And now, there are some companies that want to relocate back to the U.S. and hire more American workers. I think the tax environment is better now for the big corporations."

"And what type of work do you do in your factory? I mean, what's made at the factory?"

"We did make parts for televisions and computers. We subcontracted out with several different companies to make the parts."

"Did? As in the past?" she asked.

"Yes. The business slowed because some of the companies are looking elsewhere, like the U.S. and other places. As new technologies develop, the Mexican workers may not have all of the skills needed. It depends on the product and the level of training needed for the employee."

"Interesting."

"Yes, except now, we are closing some of our warehouses, and they sit empty."

"That's a shame."

"Hey," Steven said smiling, "I'm on vacation! Enough talk about work. I'm thinking we need dessert."

"That sounds good. What unique desserts do they have in Veracruz?" Eva asked.

"My favorite from the ones listed on the menu is the Empanadas de Guayaba," he said.

"That sounds exotic. What is it exactly?"

"Think of it as a small, fried fruit pie," he said.

"Hmmm, okay, I'll try that."

"Sir," Steven called the waiter.

"Two Empanadas de Guayaba, please."

"Very good, sir. Right away, sir."

Eva and Steven remained in deep conversation, oblivious to everyone else in the room, until the waiter brought their desserts. Steven held her hand, making her heart melt a little more by the minute.

"This looks interesting," Eva said as she cut into her empanada. She took a bite.

"What do you think?" he asked.

"Very good. Delicious!" she said.

Eva knew she had eaten too much. *I will need to dance this off*, she thought.

Steven finished dessert, asked the waiter for the check, and said, "I think we have a dance to attend."

Steven paid for dinner, and Eva thanked him. She smoothed her long, white skirt trimmed in brightly colored Mexican flowers as she stood up. Steven held out his hand, took Eva's hand, and led her out to the *zocalo.*

* * *

Eva felt like she was gliding with Steven as they walked across the *zocalo.* He led her to a table on the side near the band.

"We'll sit here, so you can listen to the music first and watch the dancers," Steven said. "Then, we'll give it a try."

Eva nodded.

Steven put his hand on hers and watched the dancers. The first song the band played was slow. Couples floated out on the stone tile dance floor and moved in a synchronous rhythm Eva had never seen before. The couples looked like one entity moving to the music. The white flowing dresses and colorful skirts of the women swayed along with each strum of the guitar.

The dance floor was surrounded by tall palm trees that moved along with the melody. Something amazing was blooming nearby, and the scent filled the warm, humid air. The scene was hypnotizing. Eva felt transformed, like she would be able to move effortlessly alongside her partner.

The slow music ended, and a faster-paced Son Jarocho song began. The dancers' steps on the open-air dance floor gave the appearance that each one was flirting with their own partner. It was a game of enticing cat and mouse to music. Some of the women used fans as part of the dance. With a flip of the wrist, the fans opened with an airy flutter as the women directed a provocative look toward their dance partners. The women moved their hips gently to the rhythm, and then men held the hand of their partner and stepped gently alongside them. Every once in a while, the men twirled their partners. It was a beautiful and seductive dance.

"What do you think?" Steven asked.

"I think I should've bought one of those fans at the shop when I bought this skirt," she said, laughing.

Steven laughed. "Are you ready to try it?"

"Umm . . ." she replied hesitantly.

"I'll help you. I can guide you along. Come on," he said, holding out his hand.

Not wanting to miss the opportunity to learn this dance, Eva nodded and stood up.

Steven took her hand, and they found a spot on the dancefloor. Steven held her hand out and placed his other hand on the small of her back, moving her along smoothly to the music.

"There, you see," he said.

"Not so hard," she agreed.

They danced one dance after another, moving as if they were one. Eva enjoyed both the slow and the fast dances to this new music. She smiled. Gliding along with Steven, she was having one of the best times of her life. After so much turmoil and hard work, she was at long last enjoying herself. She felt she had arrived at "the good life." An independent, self-sufficient, highly accomplished woman having the time of her life. Things couldn't be better.

Steven stopped dancing abruptly. A man had tapped him on the shoulder. Steven turned so that Eva couldn't see his face or make out the words he was saying. Again, it sounded as if Steven and the man were disagreeing about something. She couldn't quite make out the words, but she thought the other man was talking about moving people somewhere? She didn't understand enough Spanish to even ask Steven to explain what the man said. Steven spoke with him for quite some time. Eva didn't know if she should go back to the table. She felt awkward standing there while Steven was enthralled in some type of argument. The man finally walked away.

Steven, looking like he was not sure how to explain the situation, at last said, "I must really look like that person."

"I couldn't figure out what he was saying about people. You mean, that guy also mistakenly thought you were someone else?"

"Oh, yes. Strange, huh? I don't know what he was talking about. The guy I look like must live in Veracruz," Steven said as he nervously cleared his throat. "Let's not let that stop your dancing. You're doing very well."

"I have a good teacher," she flirted.

They continued dancing, but Steven appeared preoccupied for several minutes. He gradually began to relax and seemed to enjoy the evening again.

The palms moved along slowly with the sea breeze to the rhythm of the music playing in the *zocalo*. The moon poured its soft glow all over Veracruz. They continued dancing for several other songs. Eva thoroughly enjoyed this type of dancing; but she needed a short break, and Steven likely did, too.

"Say," she said, "want to go for some coffee?"

"Terrific idea," he said.

Steven was more watchful and apprehensive as they moved down the walkway. They found a small café as they strolled through the old part of town. They went in, and Steven ordered two café con leches. Eva liked watching the waiter make this drink. The waiter placed the milk in the cup first, set it on the table, then poured the coffee from about shoulder height but never missing his target. It was a common way to serve coffee in Veracruz.

"This place is intriguing," Eva said.

"This café?" Steven asked.

"No, the city. It has so much charm and character."

"I agree. It is fascinating. Maybe we can walk through a little more of the town before we return to the hotel."

"Okay. Plenty of moonlight shining over Veracruz to light our way."

"Excuse me just a minute. I need to get this work call." He walked a few feet away as he spoke.

"Okay . . . "

He returned a short while later. "So much for vacation time. I asked not to be bothered this week. Maybe that will be the last of it."

"I hope so. Hard to relax when they call unexpectedly," she said.

"Exactly. Shall we go for that walk?"

They strolled block after block, still listening to the Son Jarocho music playing loudly in the *zocalo*. Steven tutored Eva in her Spanish and even made her practice saying certain phrases and words.

"The whole verb conjugation thing. It gets me all tangled up."

"Well, when you are listening, the most important thing is that you know the actual verb. You can usually figure out who is talking to whom in the context of the moment."

"Good to know," she said.

"I have to say, though, you've been making much more progress in Spanish than I expected. You're a very good student. Guess all your professor brains help you." He laughed.

"Maybe so." She laughed at the thought.

The evening passed as they admired the Spanish influence of the architecture along the narrow streets. They were at the end of a block near the last buildings and a field.

"Well," Steven said, "it looks like we're at the end of the charming part and at the beginning of the "I'm not so sure about this neighborhood" part. Shall we turn around?"

Eva, feeling a bit anxious about the surroundings, said, "That's fine with me."

Eva saw something that caught her attention past the last building. "What is that? What are they doing over there?" she asked.

"It looks like the police are there. I think they are putting yellow tape around a spot by the side of that train track."

"Hmmm. How strange."

"Yes, it is. It seems they are examining something on the ground there. It almost looks like a body. It looks like it might be a woman on the ground. You never know what goes on down by the train yard. This doesn't look like the best part of town. We should walk a little faster. No need to tempt anyone," Steven said.

Eva began to feel uneasy. If Steven thought it was an unsafe neighborhood, it likely was. He was certainly familiar with the various indications of unsafe areas and crime in Mexico.

Steven took her hand. Their pace quickened as they walked. Within minutes, they were near the hotel and the *zocalo*. They entered the hotel lobby.

"Thank you for going dancing with me," Steven said.

"And thank you so much for taking me, and thanks again for dinner, "Eva said.

"It was my pleasure. We have our snorkeling adventure tomorrow. Want to meet in the lobby and go to breakfast first?"

"Yes. And get some more of the wonderful coffee."

"You really do like the coffee, don't you?"

"Yes, I do," she replied with a grin. "I like a lot of things about Mexico."

Steven smiled and winked. "Let's meet in the hotel restaurant at nine."

"See you then."

With that, Steven gave her a quick kiss on the forehead and walked to the elevator.

Eva walked down the first-floor hallway to her room, still smiling.

CHAPTER SEVENTEEN

DOLORES WAS AWAKENED WHEN THE priest opened the door the next morning. She slept so long that she felt stiff when she moved her legs.

"Well, good morning," the priest said, smiling from ear to ear.

"Father, did we sleep all through the night?"

"Yes, you all did. You needed the rest."

Ernesto sat up and looked at Emilio on the cot. Emilio was just opening his eyes and looked disoriented.

Ernesto stood up and began folding the blankets. "Hey, Emilio," he said, "How are you feeling now?"

"I'm a little better," he said. Emilio remained on the cot. He looked weak. He lifted the bandage a bit to look at the injury.

"Father," Dolores said.

"Yes, child?"

"What's your name, sir?"

"You can call me Father Francisco."

"Thank you. Father Francisco, what time is it?"

"It's almost ten in the morning."

"Why did we sleep so long?"

Father Francisco answered Dolores' question with a question. "When was the last time you slept all night? Not on the train but when you felt safe?"

"We were in a shelter several days ago, and we slept then. But not very long."

"I see. Your bodies are very tired," he said.

Father Francisco walked over to Emilio and said, "Let me take a look at that cut, young man."

Emilio sat up and lifted his shirt and peeled the bandage off.

"That looks better. You're lucky. That machete just grazed you. It is not a deep cut. Now, if you will stay here just one more day, you should feel strong enough to go on your way. You're welcome to stay longer, but my sense is that you three are on a mission to get to the United States as soon as you can."

Dolores replied, "Yes, Father. We'd like to get on another train soon."

"I'll fix you some breakfast, and you can tell me your story. I would like to hear about it."

Dolores went to the washroom and cleaned up her face and hands. The water was refreshing. She was elated to get the dirt and dust off her face. Ernesto took a turn freshening up.

"Wow," Dolores said, "you look like a new person all cleaned up."

Ernesto smiled.

"Emilio, let me help you wash off that cut," Dolores said. She got the ointment and bandages and took a cloth and washed the cut. She put new ointment on it and then carefully put on a large clean bandage.

"There you go. Can you get up?"

"Yes," he replied.

"Okay. Go into the washroom and get cleaned up. You'll feel better," she said as she messed up his hair.

"Awe, you used to do that to me when I was only this tall," Emilio said as he held his hand out to toddler height.

"You are still my little brother," she said and gave him a hug. She was relieved to see he was recuperating from the attack as he limped to the bathroom to wash up.

"Come to the table and eat breakfast, my children," the priest said as Emilio re-emerged.

On the table, there were hot tortillas, beans, eggs, and potatoes.

"This is a feast!" Emilio said.

"It will help you get well," Father Francisco said.

The father said a blessing, and they ate. Dolores couldn't remember the last time she had an egg. She *did* remember the last time the three of them sat at a table for a real breakfast. They were in Honduras with her family. Perhaps it was the week before the trip. She remembered the chickens laid eggs, and her grandmother made a stack of hot tortillas and a pot of beans. That wonderful meal was topped off with their favorite local fruits and hot coffee. She turned her thoughts back to her current situation.

"Father," Dolores said, "Do you know when the train runs through town?"

"Ah, La Bestia. It runs only every two or three days. It was here yesterday so it will not come until tomorrow or the day after that."

"Thank you. We'll be ready to go by then. We don't want to cause you any trouble or be a burden."

"No, no. But, as long as you are here, we have mass again this morning."

Dolores was thrilled to hear that she could go to mass two days in a row. She missed church. She looked at Ernesto. He was also smiling at the news of mass. Emilio continued eating as if no one had said anything.

The priest turned to Dolores and said, "And after mass, if you like, you can go with me to the market. I need to pick up a few things and stop by a woman's house. She is old and can't go to mass. I told her I would come by."

"I'd like that," Dolores said. She thought it would be good to do something more normal. It would help her keep things in perspective, and her brothers could rest.

"I will stay with Emilio," Ernesto said.

Dolores and Ernesto helped Father Francisco clean up the dishes.

"Now, before we go to mass, come with me, Ernesto and Dolores. I want to get something."

They followed Father Francisco down a small flight of stairs. In the storage room down below the church, there were boxes stacked up.

"Now, let's see," he said. "Ah, this one." He pulled a box down and opened it up. "Yes, it is the one."

Then he crossed the room and got another box. He looked inside. "Yes. This will do. Will you help me carry these two boxes upstairs?"

Dolores took one box, and Ernesto took the other. They walked up the stairs to the room where Emilio was resting.

"Set them down here please."

Father Francisco opened the first box. He pulled out a ladies' blouse and pants. "Dolores, try these on."

"They are beautiful. Look Ernesto, Emilio." She smiled as she held the blouse up for him to see.

Then Father Francisco opened the second box and gave a shirt and pants to Ernesto and another set to Emilio.

"Now, I know these aren't new, and they're not fancy, but you may have them. Ernesto and Dolores, put yours on for mass. Emilio, you can wait and put yours on tomorrow if you are well enough to get on the train."

Dolores was beside herself. Not only were these the nicest clothes she had ever owned, they were warmer and more durable than the clothes she had been wearing since she left Honduras.

Dolores asked, "Father Francisco, may I have one of our old shirts back? And do you have sewing instruments? I'd like to make inside secret pockets on our new clothes to hide our money."

"Good idea. Yes, I'll get the things you need," he replied.

Once Dolores finished the pockets, she and Ernesto divided up their remaining funds so that Emilio would have money also.

"I'm sorry I lost the money," Emilio said again.

"Don't worry. We have plenty," Dolores said and gave Emilio a hug.

Ernesto looked older and more sophisticated in his new clothes. He smiled when he put them on. He did not look like he was so poor anymore.

"Okay, children, mass will begin in about five minutes. Emilio, you get some rest."

Dolores and Ernesto went to mass. Dolores got on her knees and prayed prayers of thanks for Father Francisco. She prayed it over and over. She felt so blessed to be in his care. After mass, Dolores accompanied Father Francisco to the market. Father Francisco let Dolores pick out the vegetables and fruit for dinner.

"These vegetables look like the ones we grow at home on the farm," Dolores said. "We used to have many vegetables and fruit. We could sell them when we had extras. But after the drought, we didn't have enough to eat."

Father Francisco asked her to tell him everything about their home land. Then he asked her if they had any trouble on the train. As they walked through the market, she told him about Lola being kidnapped. She told him about the two Zetas who robbed people, about the younger one who fell off the train, and about the older brother who jumped off the train after the younger brother fell. She told him about the dead baby and the mother who was hit by the train. She told him how Emilio was attacked not far from the church.

"Dolores, you're no longer a child. God has helped you with these experiences to become an adult. Now, you can take better care of your brothers and, someday, your own family. You understand now how important it is to be safe. God watches you. You and your brothers could have had worse outcomes. Now, you'll have to keep the strength to help them make the journey. You will draw your strength from God. You must ask Him each day to keep you strong and keep you safe."

"Thank you, Father," she said.

"You'll find staying safe is the most important thing you have to do on your journey."

Father Francisco paid the market for the fruits and vegetables, and they stopped to visit the old lady who was homebound. She reminded Dolores of an older version of her own grandmother.

"You're reminding me of home and my grandmother," Dolores said.

"Poor child," the old woman said. "You miss your family?"

"Yes."

"But you are traveling far away for your family. They are in your heart, and you are in theirs. Bless you, child. Every grandmother wishes for a granddaughter like you."

"Thank you," Dolores said.

They left the old woman's house and walked back to the church. Father Francisco enjoyed the company of Dolores, Ernesto, and Emilio and prepared wonderful food for them. And for thirty-six hours, Dolores and her brothers were safe, well-fed, and rested.

* * *

The next day, after a late breakfast, Father Francisco gave each of them bottles of water, fruit, and tortillas for their journey. Dolores, Ernesto, and Emilio said their goodbyes to Father Francisco. Dolores felt the tears flooding her eyes as she walked away from the church. She couldn't help but give the priest an extra-long hug. She had only known the priest a short time, but she felt so safe and loved in his presence. The unknown lay ahead. Now she would have to muster her courage and strength once again to fight off the rest of the world. Her brothers required her watchful eye and care.

"Before we get to the train yard, let's check our money in our pockets and be sure we have divided it up," she said.

Ernesto nodded, took his bills out of his secret pocket, and handed them to Dolores. She counted the money and handed each of her brothers an equal amount.

"We've been so blessed to save our money so far. We didn't need to use any money for food. Since Father Francisco gave us so much to eat, we can get by for a day or longer and not worry about eating yet."

Emilio and Ernesto agreed.

They arrived near the railyard and examined the area for any sign of trouble. Father Francisco warned them the man with the machete might stalk the railyard looking for people who were waiting on the train. He told Dolores to be sure and hide and to check the surroundings closely.

Dolores said, "We can hide over there, in that empty building, and watch for the train. Remember, the train doesn't stay here long. When we hear it, we should be prepared to go."

"Okay," Ernesto said.

"Emilio, since you can't run as fast as usual, you go first this time when the train is moving slow," Dolores said. "After Emilio, I will go, since you, Ernesto, run faster than I do, and you come right after me."

"That's a good plan," Ernesto said.

"Let's pray we don't have to wait long today. If the train comes soon, we'll be away from trouble," Dolores said.

Dolores examined the railyard. A great number of other travelers were sitting under the bushes and next to the walls of the buildings waiting for the train. She didn't see any signs of Emilio's attacker or any Mexican officials.

They entered the empty building after inspecting the inside first. It was dark inside, and spider webs covered a good portion of the corners, windows, and the tops of the doors.

"Looks like no one has been here for a while," Ernesto said.

They found a position with a good view of the railyard. Emilio carefully sat down, and Ernesto and Dolores watched for the train. They waited most of the day.

"Listen," Dolores said.

"I hear it. Far away but coming," Ernesto said.

"Emilio, do you need help to get up?" Dolores asked.

"I think I can get over to the door."

They stood by the door and watched. As the train stopped, they moved toward the track. They weren't sure how long the train would remain stopped, but they knew that with Emilio's injury, they needed to be ready the moment the train eased toward them.

"As it starts to roll, Emilio will get on," Dolores reminded them.

The train began to move. Emilio struggled to take the first hop up the ladder, but he succeeded. Dolores and Ernesto followed. When they were all on top, Dolores hugged her brothers.

"We did it!" she said. Then she asked Emilio, "Did it hurt for you to catch the ladder and pull up?"

"Just a little. I don't feel very strong. I thought you might have to push me up," he laughed.

"We're all here now," Ernesto said.

They looked at the cars behind them. People were scrambling to climb aboard.

"There are more people than any of the other trains we have been on before," Ernesto said.

"Perhaps as we get closer to the United States, more people want to get on," Emilio said with a smile. "We're getting closer with each train ride!"

Dolores nodded.

The loudness of the train was more noticeable after being in the quiet environment of Father Francisco's church.

Dolores watched the sun set behind the mountains. She watched over her brothers. The train shuddered and squealed through the night. The night air in the strong breeze of the moving train was chilling. Dolores was appreciative of the warmer clothing from Father Francisco that she and her brothers were wearing. She stretched out and closed her eyes for a few moments. Tomorrow, they would be in San Luis Potosí. She prayed their stop in that place would be uneventful.

CHAPTER EIGHTEEN

EVA WOKE UP FEELING LIKE she was on top of the world. The night before had been absolutely perfect. The whole evening was like a dream. The meal was outstanding. Dancing under the moon with the palm trees swaying was incredible. And the Son Jarocho music playing in the background added an air of romance when she and Steven walked through old town Veracruz.

Eva dressed and was in the lobby in plenty of time for breakfast. Thinking about how things were going with Steven brought a smile to her face. In her excitement, she was ready ahead of schedule. She waited in the restaurant for Steven to appear.

"Is anyone joining you this morning?" asked the waiter.

"Yes, there will be two of us," Eva said and smiled.

"Perfect. Can I bring you a drink while you wait?"

"Yes. Coffee, please, with milk," she said.

"One café con leche."

Eva sipped her coffee and watched for Steven. To her surprise, she saw him coming in the front door of the hotel. He looked around as if he was checking to make sure no one had seen him enter the lobby. He seemed nervous as he looked from side to side. She thought it was curious that he was out so early. She thought there had been several unpredictable events for Steven here in Veracruz. Maybe it was nothing. Perhaps he wanted to talk to the bus driver or the tour guide about the snorkeling trip. If he wanted her to know what he had been doing outside the hotel before breakfast, he would tell her.

Steven had not seen Eva in the restaurant. He stood in the lobby waiting to meet her.

Eva went to the door of the restaurant and waved at Steven.

"Ah, you are early," he said.

"Yes," she said. "I'm excited about snorkeling today."

"Me, too," he agreed and squeezed her hand. He offered no explanation about why he was outside the hotel so early.

The waiter returned with two menus and took Steven's drink order.

"I heard that we'll see a good variety of fish on the snorkeling trip. They hang out in the reef area where we'll be swimming."

"That sounds intriguing," Eva said.

Steven continued, "There are puffer fish, shrimp, lobsters, all kinds of colorful fish. And, there are a number of sunken ships in that area of the Gulf."

"Now I'm really excited. Maybe we will find a treasure chest," she said and laughed.

"That would be a possibility if we were doing some deep-water diving. My guess is that anything worth value where we are going was taken a long time ago," he said.

"Good point," she said.

They ate their breakfast speedily and were outside near the bus when the driver came. He opened the doors to the bus and let them in. Eva and Steven were the first ones on the bus and remained the only ones for nearly thirty minutes.

Adrián joined them and said, "Good morning, early birds."

"Are we the only ones who signed up for the trip?" Steven asked.

"No, here they come," Adrián replied, looking out the door.

Another couple and a few other people came on the bus.

"I was beginning to think we were the only ones going," Steven said.

"Me, too," Eva said.

Eva whispered to Steven, "Of course, if we were the only ones, no one else would have seen us discover the hidden treasure."

"Yes. Now I guess our secret will be out when we bring the treasure chest on board the bus." He laughed and gave her that wink that made her heart skip a beat.

As the other tourists got on the bus, Adrián greeted each one.

Another couple sat in the seats across the aisle from Eva and Steven. The man asked, "Have you been snorkeling before?"

"Yes," Steven said.

"Not me," Eva replied.

"Me either," said the woman. She introduced herself and her husband.

Steven and the man continued chatting about snorkeling and their favorite places to snorkel. Eva and the other woman talked about their inexperience snorkeling.

Adrián interrupted the chatter. "Hello and good morning to you all. We're going to take about twenty minutes to reach our destination. Once we're there, if you signed up for snorkeling, your guide will have the equipment ready for you."

Adrián continued, "We'll be there for approximately three hours. If you get hungry, there is a concession stand in the middle of the park. Enjoy yourselves at the beach."

The bus exited the parking lot and started down the road to leave the city.

"What is going on over there?" Eva asked as she pointed out the window.

"I'm not sure. It looks like a group of people going toward the train yard. They may be hoping to get on board," Steven said.

"But it looks like a freight train parked over there. I don't see a passenger train," she remarked.

"No. They climb up to the top of the train and ride up there."

"That looks like it would be difficult. Do you think that whole group will be trying to get on the top of that train?"

"Probably."

"I've never seen such a thing. What an adventure that would be! Is it dangerous?" she asked.

"I've seen the train many times with people sitting on the top. It can be dangerous," Steven said.

The bus drove out of the city a few miles. It progressed down the coastline road by the water. The route provided a clear view of the beach and the pristine water.

Eva, looking out the window, said, "The water is an amazing color here. Kind of a mix between a royal blue and aquamarine."

"Wait until you swim in it. It's very clear."

The bus driver parked the bus in a designated parking area for tourist buses. It was early in the day, so it was not too crowded.

Most of the people on the bus opted only to go swimming on the beach. A few people signed up to snorkel. Steven and Eva checked in with the guide and were each given the gear for the dive. The guide gave a few instructions about how to use the equipment and the boundaries of the snorkeling area. The guide also warned the group that they were not to take anything from the reef.

"Well, shoot," Eva said. "Guess we'll have to leave the treasure here."

Steven laughed. "I guess so."

Eva followed Steven down the pier to the entry for the dive near the reef. She felt both excitement and fear about going snorkeling. She had no experience in open water swimming.

Steven took her hand as she entered the warm, clear water and took her first few breaths. She had her first glimpses of the reef while she was near the pier. The colors of the fish were amazing: yellows and purples, black spots on shiny silver, brilliant blues. The reef and the grasses and underwater ferns were intriguing. Eva enjoyed every minute.

Steven touched Eva's arm and signaled to swim toward a different part of the reef. He pointed down to a partial boat sitting on the bottom. They swam further and saw sea urchins and starfish below. Before Eva realized it, it was time to return to the bus.

The bus ride back to the hotel was relaxing. Eva thought the snorkeling was amazing and exhausting. Steven pulled her closer, and she rested her head on his shoulder. She felt like she was on fire with a sunburn. She thought it might be a good day to go to bed early.

Adrián talked with the group before they exited the bus.

"Tomorrow, we have an early drive up to Puebla. As you know, Veracruz is the most southern point on our tour. That means tomorrow we will be working our way back north. We will be in Puebla tomorrow night, which will be our last night of the tour.

"Let's be on the bus by ten o'clock tomorrow morning. That will give you time for breakfast and to check out of the hotel. We'll arrive in Puebla for a late lunch."

Steven walked Eva into the lobby of the hotel. He looked exhausted, too.

"What do you say we have an early dinner? Maybe go listen to some music afterward for just a bit?" Steven asked.

"That will be fine. I could use an early night."

"Me, too. I'll meet you in the lobby at five?"

"See you then."

Eva returned to her room exhausted. She showered and then collapsed on the bed. Just a short nap, she thought.

She didn't know what woke her, but she was startled. She grabbed her phone in a panic and checked the time. "Four-fifteen!" she yelled to no one.

Eva scampered around the hotel room and pulled her outfit together. Her makeup went on in record time. She was out the door by two minutes before five.

"Good evening," Steven said.

"Hi," Eva replied.

"I asked about some decent smaller cafés for dinner. The concierge suggested that we walk down one of the streets beside the *zocalo*. He said there are three or four cafés we can consider, depending on what you would like to eat. We can look at the menus posted outside each one and see what you think. It'll give you a chance to practice more Spanish."

"Sounds like just what I need," Eva said.

"As I said last night, your Spanish is amazing for a beginner. Just keep practicing. You already know enough to get around, order food, and ask questions. I can tell you are determined."

Eva had been working hard on her Spanish, and she felt very good hearing this from Steven. She believed she was going to meet her goal for the trip of increasing her knowledge and use of Spanish.

They walked down the specific street suggested by the concierge. The choices of food included Italian, seafood, Mexican, traditional Veracruz, and a café with a little bit of everything. They read each menu. As they stood out in front of the traditional Veracruz café, they heard music inside.

Eva commented, "Oh, if we go in there, we can listen to music and eat at the same time."

"Great idea," he said.

They enjoyed their dinner. It wasn't as glamorous as the night before, but they were both tired. Eva enjoyed visiting with Steven, but she felt like she needed to call it a day. Eva's sunburn was hurting even more. They listened to the music after dinner and had a cup of coffee. Once again, Steven gave her a short kiss as they said goodnight.

In her room later that evening, Eva called her mother.

"Hello?" her mother said.

"Hi, Mom. How are you?"

"I am safely in the United States. How are you?"

"I am safe in Mexico," Eva replied.

"When are you coming back in to your own country?"

"Day after tomorrow, Mom.

"Okay, good. Have you seen the caravan?"

"No, Mom."

"How about the cartel? Have you seen any of those criminals?"

"No, Mom. I'm fine. And I'm learning Spanish. In fact, I'm getting pretty good at it."

"Well, you'd better be for the risk you are taking. You're risking your life to be down there learning Spanish. It makes no sense to me whatsoever."

"Anything new going on with you, Mom?" Eva asked.

"Not really. We had a new lady come to our prayer group this morning. She's going to send me a recipe for a chocolate cake she brought to the meeting. It was delicious, and the icing was wonderful. I want to make it for your sister's birthday. Back to you, now. Are you sure you are fine?" her mother asked.

"Yes, Mom. I'm fine. Just wanted to check in. I'm having fun and learning a lot. I'll call you when I get back home."

"Just keep your eyes open for those people in the caravan. There are thousands of them."

"Yes, thousands. Goodbye, Mom."

* * *

Adrián stepped up to the bus promptly at ten a.m. and began to address the group. "Our route today will be different. We will be going through a mountain pass and to a town called Orizaba. We'll take a short break there for you to purchase a snack if you like. We won't be there long, but you'll get to see some beautiful scenery on this route. We'll go through part of the rain forest and then into the mountains, where it will be a little bit cooler. You may want to take your jacket when you get off the bus because the forecast is to be in the upper sixties. After spending so much time in the heat and the sun, it may feel cool to you. This road will be very curvy in some places, so we'll be cruising a little slower than normal. Enjoy yourselves."

"This should be exciting. A curvy bus ride—are you ready for that?" Steven asked.

"Sure. I'm game. Hey, I understood nearly every word that Adrián said. I don't think I could say every word that he said, but I understood it!"

"See? You just have to come to the country to learn the language," he teased her and winked.

Eva's heart was touched every time he winked. There was no way around it. She couldn't help herself.

The town of Orizaba was in the elevated valley area between mountains. Eva looked out the window at the sides of the mountains as they drove through. Once the bus neared Orizaba, it slowed down and meandered through a series of narrow streets.

As Eva gazed at the outskirts of the city, she grabbed Steven's arm and said, "Look, that guy is waving a machete at that kid."

Steven saw the flash of the blade, and then the two disappeared from view.

"Well, there you have it," he said. "That is the mark of the cartel. Now you can say you have seen it in action."

"Oh, my goodness! I've never seen anything like that. Well, maybe in the movies. That was horrible. Why was that guy chasing him? Did he catch him?"

"No way to know. Probably wanted to rob him, recruit him, or kidnap him," Steven replied.

"I am thinking I don't want to get off this bus in Orizaba," Eva said.

"We won't stop right here. Let's wait and see what it looks like when we stop. It is likely more tourist-friendly."

The bus turned the corner and drove up several more blocks. The town itself was quaint and had the traditional Spanish-colonial design. The bus parked near a *zocalo*.

Adrián announced, "All right. Here we are for those who want to get off the bus for a minute. Be back here in forty-five minutes. That'll give you enough time to get a snack or peek into the Cathedral de San Miguel Arcangel just down the street to your right."

Eva and Steven remained seated for a moment and then decided to run over to the cathedral. It was impressive. The yellow and red outside walls and towers of the cathedral were spectacular. The dome in the altar area of the sanctuary, the circular pendant lights, and the large, multiple arches all accented in gold, added to the splendor. They walked up to the front of the cathedral to see the detailed work. Eva couldn't explain it, but something about visiting these churches tapped into the feelings she had as a child, the feelings of being in a place where God was present. She didn't know how to put it into words. She thought she might talk to Steven about it someday. They walked quickly back to the bus.

They traveled through the curvy mountain road talking about the differences in climates in Mexico and the regions of the rain forest and the fruits and vegetables of Mexico. Steven and Eva passed the afternoon chatting about Eva's expectations of her new job. She knew the tour was coming to a close soon, and her new job would begin in just a few days. In no time, they were at the hotel in Puebla.

Adrián took a moment to talk to the group before they disembarked to check into the hotel.

"Welcome to Puebla. You all survived the winding road, and we are now in a great, historic city. This time, we are going to go even further back in history. There are at least two things you'll want to see in Puebla. One is the Aztec Cholula pyramid that is very large. Within it is a series of tunnels that can be very confusing. As part of your tour, we've arranged a guide to take you up there and through the tunnels tomorrow morning. That excursion will depart the hotel at ten a.m. The other thing not to miss is the church on top of the pyramid. You'll end up right at the church after your tour of the pyramid, so you should take the opportunity to see it before you come back to the bus. If you're lucky enough to have a clear sky tomorrow, you will be able to see the volcano Popocatepetl once you are on top of the pyramid. The van back to the hotel will leave the pyramid at three p.m. This excursion requires walking and climbing up stairs and slopes. Wear comfortable shoes.

"As for the rest of the day today, feel free to go to the *zocalo* and shop and eat. There are some cool places to eat there, including one that has little balconies, and you can sit out there and eat and look out over the square. Remember, we leave Puebla tomorrow night at nine p.m., and we'll be on the road all night tomorrow night. But for now, enjoy Puebla, your last city on the tour. Have fun!"

"Oh, my. I wanted to see a pyramid on this trip," Eva said.

"Yes. This tour has focused on the Spanish colonial period more than anything else, and of course, independence. But the Aztec pyramid is a good addition."

Then Steven asked, "Want to find that restaurant he mentioned for dinner?"

"The one that overlooks the *zocalo*?"

"Yes."

"I'd like that."

After settling their things in the rooms, Eva met Steven in the lobby, and they walked to the *zocalo*. It was easy to spot the restaurant with the balconies the guide had mentioned. Another couple from the tour bus was at the restaurant, too. They waved at each other as Eva and Steven were being seated. They were fortunate to get seated at a balcony table. The view was wonderful, and the weather was perfect.

Looking out over the balcony at the park, Steven asked Eva, "Are you looking forward to getting back to Texas?"

"Yes, I am. Next week, I'll have meetings before classes begin. That will give me opportunity to meet more faculty and learn about the university."

"I'm sure you'll be busy, but I'm curious. I wanted to ask you something. Do you think you will want to get together again once you are back in Texas?"

Eva was thrilled he asked. It was something that had been on her mind for several days.

"I'd like that very much."

"Me, too," Steven said and held her hand tighter.

CHAPTER NINETEEN

DOLORES SLEPT IN INTERMITTENT SPURTS on the long ride to San Luis Potosí. Her brothers had no trouble sleeping. They were fortunate to be on a car that had high grid grates on the top that served as side rails. They were less likely to roll off the train as they slept. Dolores was especially pleased that Emilio was resting. She prayed he would regain his strength before the next stop.

The sun peeked through low-lying clouds giving off an incredibly beautiful appearance, projecting orange, pink, and yellow streaks. She reminisced about the sun rises she witnessed at her farm in Honduras, and a twinge of sadness pierced through her. *I must be strong for my brothers; I must not be sad*, she thought. Remembering Father Francisco's words, she said a silent prayer and asked for strength.

The train slowed in the middle of nowhere. Without warning, a host of cars with lights and sirens stopped the train. The riders began scrambling off the tops of the cars and running far into the fields. Officials bolted from their cars and talked calmly with the engineers in the front cars.

"Ernesto, Emilio, wake up!" Dolores yelled. "We must get off the train. The Mexican officials have stopped the train!"

Ernesto slid down the ladder quickly. Dolores helped Emilio climb down. He descended carefully and walked as quickly as possible and found Ernesto. Dolores followed Emilio.

"Hurry, hurry," Dolores whispered to her brothers. "Over there is a spot."

They hid in the fields in the tall grass and bushes not far from the tracks. They watched to see what was happening in the first cars.

"Dolores," Ernesto said. "Look. They're not searching for the people in the cars back here. They're not stopping the people who are running away from the train. They're taking large bags off the train."

"Drugs?" Emilio asked.

"That would be my guess," Dolores said.

A large unmarked truck drove up beside the train. Two men in regular street clothes got out of the truck and loaded the bags into the back. The officials jumped back in their cars and sped away.

The travelers gradually began getting back on the train cars. The train started up. Dolores, Ernesto, and Emilio climbed back onto their car.

"What do you suppose that was about?" Ernesto asked. "The officials didn't care about catching any of us riding on top of the train."

"They weren't real officials, or they were officials who help transport drugs," Dolores said.

"You mean like the cartel?" Emilio asked.

"Yes, probably," she said. "How are you feeling, Emilio?"

"Other than being startled when you woke me up, I'm fine," he said.

"Sorry that I had to do that. You were sleeping soundly."

The other people on the train were all talking now. A lady sitting beside Dolores introduced herself.

"I'm Lupita. From El Salvador," she said.

"Nice to meet you. I'm Dolores, and we," she motioned to her brothers, "are from Honduras."

"You saw the police unload a lot of bags and put them on that truck?" Lupita asked.

"I'm wondering if they were real police," Dolores said.

"No. I can tell you they weren't. The same thing happens in El Salvador. People you think are authorities stop trucks, cars, and anything that can be used to transport drugs. Everyone thinks it's a traffic stop or that someone is in trouble and the officers are there to help. But it's a drug transport. It's hard to know who to trust."

"It's sad people can't trust the authorities," Eva said.

Lupita looked out over the countryside. She didn't talk further.

"Dolores," Ernesto said quietly.

"Yes?"

"I just remembered what Father Francisco gave us when we left," Ernesto said with a smile.

Emilio smiled and reached into his pocket. He hastily ate his tortilla, then started on his fruit. Ernesto did the same. Dolores took her tortilla out of her pocket and tapped Lupita on the shoulder.

"Would you like some?"

Lupita's eyes opened wide, and she smiled. When Lupita smiled, she did so with her whole face. It made Dolores happy to see a smile so big.

Dolores tore the tortilla in half and handed half to Lupita. She gave Lupita a piece of her fruit.

The day seemed more hopeful with something to eat.

"Lupita," Dolores said, "You know anything about where we're going to stop next?"

"You mean San Luis Potosí?"

"Yes," Dolores replied. "Do you know anything about the town?"

"Some men in the train yard said it was a large city. We'll have to get off the train before the city, walk to the other side of the train yard, and then get back on the train. You're going to Texas, too?" asked Lupita.

"Yes, we are."

"I heard San Luis Potosí can be dangerous. You can be stopped and asked for papers. But it's such a large city that it's easy to be unnoticed."

"Do you know if it's easy to make it from one part of the train yard to the other part where we have to climb back on? Is it a very large train yard?"

"I didn't hear anyone talk about the size of the railyard. We can try to make it back out on the same day," Lupita said.

Ernesto and Emilio listened as Lupita and Dolores talked about the city. Dolores asked, "Emilio, are you feeling stronger today?"

"Yes. I can make it. I won't hold us up," he said.

"Emilio, if you are tired, don't worry. We'll just catch the next train. It's okay. We'll get to the United States soon," Dolores said.

"No. I'm fine. We can get on the train again," he said.

They looked out at the countryside that began to show signs of being nearer to a city. More houses and small buildings appeared. The train followed a curve around to the right, and then they saw the view of the large city.

"Look," Lupita said. "There it is."

Dolores had never seen so many tall buildings in one place. The highways were full of cars, and the roads went in every direction. Some roads went up above other roads.

"We're here," she told Emilio and Ernesto. "We must be ready to climb off the train when it slows. We'll follow the tracks to the other side of the train yard. Let's walk in the city like we know where we are going. We'll act like we live there." Her brothers nodded their heads.

"It might be easier and quicker to split up and travel alone," Lupita said. "Thank you for the food. Maybe I'll see you on the train after we get back on. Be careful."

"Be careful," Dolores said. "We'll look for you."

The train began to slow. Since the city was so large, Dolores waited to get off the train until it was almost completely stopped. The other riders had departed. She didn't want Emilio to walk too far.

"Now," she said.

The train was going so slow, it took little effort to climb off. They walked through the street next to the track. In the new clothes that Father Francisco had given to them, they no longer looked like travelers from Honduras riding a train. Dolores said another thank you prayer for Father Francisco as they walked toward the end of the train yard.

"Dolores," Ernesto said, "when we get on the next train, will it end at Texas?"

"No, I don't think so. The map in the shelter showed the next stop for us will be in Monterrey."

* * *

Their walk through the city to the other side of the train yard went smoothly. In their new clothing from Father Francisco, Dolores, Emilio, and Ernesto looked like they were residents of San Luis Potosi. No one asked them any questions or looked at them curiously. Dolores felt proud of her brothers. *They are such nice young men,* she thought.

They reached a sidewalk and sat on a curb. It would be easy to climb on the train from this area just on the other side of the train yard. Then they saw a train was already ahead of them. Were they too late? Would they have to wait for another day? Dolores looked distraught. One of the workers of the railyard saw them walking near the yard.

"Are you going north?" he yelled.

"Yes," Dolores said. "We're on our way to the United States."

"What town?"

"Brownsville, Texas."

"Don't worry. The trains going north come through here every hour or so. This is a very busy train yard. Another train will be here soon. There's a water fountain over on the side of that building," he gestured. "Go get you a drink. And remember to get on the train that runs on this track," he pointed to a specific track on one side of the train yard. "Not those over there. Those trains go to California. You'll catch the train here that goes to Monterrey, then Reynosa, a city on the border that is near where you want to go. You'll then walk to the east to Brownsville."

Dolores smiled. "Thank you, sir," she said.

They walked over to the fountain.

"The water is cold," Ernesto said. "It is nice," he said, taking another drink.

"And the train will be here soon," Emilio said.

They walked back to the place on the curb where they could wait near the tracks. Within minutes, the train came into the yard.

"There it is," Emilio said.

Just as the train pulled beside Emilio, he hopped on, followed by Dolores and Ernesto. They took their places on the car. Dolores scanned the other riders. The people on the car looked to be travelers who were making their way north. Dolores did not see Lupita.

"Dolores," Emilio said, "look at the mountains all around."

"Yes. It's something to see."

"Do you think about home?" Emilio asked.

"Of course," she replied. "Do you?"

"Yes. I didn't think about it too much at first, until Orizaba."

"When that man attacked you?"

"Yes."

"What did you think about after you were hurt?" she asked.

"I was afraid I wouldn't see Mamá and Papá and Grandma again. I was afraid they'd be upset that I was in a place where that man got me and that I had to give him all of my money that they worked hard to give me. I wished that I was home so Mamá and Grandma could take care of me. You know, those kinds of things."

"Emilio, you couldn't help what happened. That wasn't your fault."

"I know. But I'm sorry it happened and cost us those extra days."

"Emilio, I'm sorry it happened, too. But if it hadn't happened, we wouldn't have spent time with Father Francisco. He's such a wonderful man. And he helped us all to feel better. We all had food and rest, and you got well again."

"Yes. It turned out the best way it could have. I'm thankful for that time with Father Francisco, too."

"Do you think anything else about home?" Dolores asked.

"Well . . . I hope we get to see Mamá and Papá and Grandma again. I mean Papá is not well, and Grandma is getting older. And Mamá has it hard taking care of Papá and the farm."

"And that's why we are going north. We'll help them. As soon as we can make enough money, we can go back home and help them even more. But first, we'll send money back. That will help them, too."

"Yes. I know. We'll be able to help them. That's why we are going so far away," Emilio said with sadness in his voice.

"And we are almost there," Dolores said, trying to cheer him. "We've come such a long way to get where we are now. This train ride and one more. Just one more train ride after this."

"Yes, just one more," Emilio said.

It was that moment that Dolores realized how much older Emilio seemed than he did in Honduras. In just a short time, he had experienced things that caused him to lose his youth. He was now maturing as a young man, before he was supposed to. He was older in his spirit and heart than he'd been just two weeks earlier. She was proud of him, but she was also sad for him.

Dolores, Ernesto, and Emilio watched the sun set again. Another night riding through a country that was not their own to reach another country that was not their own. Not knowing what the future would bring and not knowing how difficult it would be were the thoughts in their minds each night and each day.

The train rapidly moved through the cold night air. Dolores scooted over to Emilio and Ernesto. They huddled together down low on the car. The heat from each other helped them to sleep a while. The noise from the train woke them every hour or so. Nights of disrupted sleep were typical on the train. When dawn came, they didn't feel rested, but they did feel optimistic. They made it through another night and another train ride.

"Ernesto, Emilio," Dolores whispered. "Wake up. We're getting close to Monterrey."

Emilio and Ernesto rubbed their eyes and sat up.

"Look at the mountains. And the city ahead," Ernesto said.

"Only one more train to catch," Emilio said with a smile.

"Yes." Ernesto agreed.

"Listen," Dolores said. "We must watch carefully. We're getting close to the border. You remember what it was like traveling into Mexico from Guatemala? When we crossed that border?"

"More officials and criminals," Ernesto replied.

"Yes. There'll be more Mexican officials and, as we get nearer to the United States, we'll be watching for officials from the United States. The cartels are very bad in the cities on the border. We'll need to stay out of sight and be quiet."

Her brothers agreed.

The train slowed as it approached the railyard in Monterrey. Dolores had no knowledge of this city or this train yard. She was unsure of how long it would take them to get back on a train.

"Maybe we can find food," Emilio said.

"We can look. Try to find some water to drink. But we must always worry about safety."

They were able to hop off the train without difficulty. They walked closely together without talking. They didn't walk with the other travelers who had departed the train. But up ahead, Dolores saw Lupita making her way toward the train yard.

Dolores and her brothers moved a block over from the track. Lupita was on the same street. They continued walking block after block, following Lupita. They passed the area of the train yard and traveled another block up.

Lupita stopped when she found a place to sit and watch for the train. Dolores and her brothers caught up with her.

"That wasn't bad," Dolores said to Lupita.

"Oh, hello," she replied with her huge, memorable smile. "Yes, so far that was the easiest walk through the city on my trip."

"I hope we don't have to wait long for the train," Dolores said.

"Me, too. Are you going to Reynosa?" Lupita asked.

"Yes, and then to Brownsville."

"You'll have to walk or get a ride east from Reynosa. I have family in McAllen, Texas. That's just on the other side of Reynosa."

"That's good you have family there. We don't," Dolores said.

"Where will you go in Brownsville?"

"I don't know. We will look for a family who will let us stay with them until we can find work."

"I'll ask my cousins. They might know someone there to help you. I'll tell you their telephone number, and you can call me," Lupita offered.

"That would be helpful," Dolores said.

Ernesto and Emilio nodded. They were both smiling.

"That is a relief to us," Ernesto said to Lupita. "Thank you."

Lupita told them the telephone number and made each one repeat the number several times.

"Now, you know it? Tell me again," Lupita said. Then she waited several minutes and asked each one again to tell her the number, and they all laughed as they said the number.

Emilio said, "Do you think there's any food around here?"

"Ah, little brother, look at this city. Tall buildings. Busy streets. There are no banana trees or other fruit trees or plants nearby. I'm sorry. I'm hungry, too. We'll look when we get to Reynosa," she said.

"Listen," Ernesto said.

They all heard the train wheels slowly rolling.

"Are we ready?" Dolores asked.

Her brothers smiled and nodded.

CHAPTER TWENTY

EVA AND STEVEN MET FOR breakfast in the hotel on the last morning of the tour. They joined the group for the fifteen-minute ride to the Pyramid of Cholula and to the church on top, La Iglesia de los Remedios. Eva and Steven sat together and observed the city of Puebla on the way. It was a mix of traditional, Spanish-colonial, and new upscale buildings. They stepped off the bus on the street some distance from the pyramid, and the church on top of the pyramid could be easily seen. It appeared to be significantly higher than the level of the street.

"Are you ready for this?" Steven asked.

"Sure. Looks like quite a climb," Eva said, gesturing toward the pyramid.

Eva and Steven walked the long stone and brick walkway to the entry level of the pyramid. The incline began early in the walk and continued for the walk to the pyramid. It was understandable why it took a while to discover this pyramid. The amount of ground it covered was massive, yet it had the appearance of a large hill. Grass covered the exterior, but large stone walls and tops of walls protruded through the grass. It was quite tall.

Steven took Eva's hand and helped her with the steep slopes and steps.

"Doing all right?" he asked.

"Yes. I have to admit I am a little winded."

Steven agreed, "This is a little more strenuous than it looked from the bus."

Eva, Steven, and the other tourists from the bus met the pyramid tour guide. The church bells were chiming loudly from the top of the hill and were likely audible to the whole city.

They handed their tickets to the guide, and he told the group a few facts about the pyramid and the church. The guide informed the group of the history of the pyramid, which is the largest known pyramid in the world. He informed them of the Spanish origin of the church on the top. He took the group around the outside of the pyramid before they entered the tunnels and reminded them to stay with him and not wander off. "You'll be within a tunnel system that is more than five miles long," he said.

"Five miles?" Eva asked Steven.

"You understood what he said about the tunnels?"

"Yes. I think I understood what he said about the history of the church and the pyramid. I was surprised to know that there is an active archeological dig on the premises. That is interesting."

Steven smiled and said, "Before long, I'll only talk to you in Spanish!"

Eva said, "That'll be helpful for me. But speaking it is still difficult for me."

"You'll get the hang of it. Just keep trying. Since you understand so much of it now, speaking will become easier."

"Hope you're right."

The guide said, "The walls were built in 300 B.C. So, you see, they are very sturdily built. And this area is believed to be an altar that was used for sacrifices."

Eva and Steven followed the guide into the long, triangular-shaped tunnels. Sections of the tunnel included steps from one level up to another one. The tunnel inclines were gradual and long, and Eva was winded for most of the tour. She hadn't anticipated the inclines, steps, and steepness. She was thankful the tunnels were lighted, and she was thankful for Steven's hand guiding her along the way. They completed the tour of the pyramid and were at the top, near the church.

The guide said, "You have an hour to spend here on the top of the pyramid. Look inside and outside the church. In an hour, meet me back at this very spot. And, look, today the volcano is visible."

"Oh, my goodness!" Eva said. "Look at that!"

The volcano appeared in the distance and had a small plume of smoke rising from the top.

"That's spectacular," Steven said. "And so is the view of Puebla," Steven said, placing his arm around Eva.

"Yes, it's breathtaking."

They walked up to the level of the church. The church was a mustard yellow with white trim and ornate details within the trim in contrasting dark red. Inside the church, Eva once again sensed the nearness of God. She noted a large altar was in the front. The walls were cream-colored with gold trim, and gold-colored columns were behind the altar. A massive chandelier hung above the altar area.

The church was filled with music and people. Eva felt the music added to the sentiment of holiness. Flowers were interspersed around the altar, and candles were burning in different places within the church. Her heart felt warmth in this church. Like the other churches she had visited in Mexico, she felt a sense of peace when she was inside.

"Another impressive church," Eva whispered.

Steven nodded.

Eva and Steven left the church and walked around the top of the hill, looking at the city of Puebla again. When they were away from the rest of the group, Steven took Eva's hand and said, "This has been a memorable tour. But when I look back on the week, my fondest memory is meeting you."

Eva blushed and said, "It's been a wonderful week. I'm sorry it is nearly over, but since I know we'll see each other after the tour, I won't be sad."

Steven smiled, took her hand, and said, "Me either. Seeing you will give me something to look forward to when I return. We should start back down the hill."

* * *

On the way back to the hotel after the tour of the pyramid, Adrián said, "The bus leaves tonight at nine p.m. We'll be driving all night to get to Monterrey in the morning. You have time to get some dinner, maybe do some shopping on the last night of your tour."

Eva and Steven agreed to return to the Puebla *zocalo* for dinner. They would explore first and check out the nearby shops.

"Do you mind if I go to the room and freshen up before we leave?" Eva asked.

"No problem. I'll get packed. Meet in thirty minutes?"

"Great."

Eva packed her bag and freshened up. She didn't want to think about the tour ending, but she knew her new job was waiting; and the fact she would continue to see Steven made her smile. A quick comb-out of her long, brown hair and a refresh of her lip gloss, and she was ready.

As they left the hotel, Steven asked, "Are you looking for anything special on our shopping exploration?"

"I want to look for something to remember the trip. Something that is from Mexico, like a silver ring or bracelet, that I can wear to work and be reminded of this week."

"That should be easy. There's plenty of silver in Mexico."

The two walked down the street to the *zocalo* and ducked in every store on the square. Eva examined several pieces of jewelry at different stores. She was careful to compare prices, and in Spanish, she negotiated the price.

"Look at you!" Steven said. "You are speaking the language well. You said you couldn't, but you are."

"When it comes to bargaining, I need to know those words," she laughed.

Eva picked out two items, a simple silver ring and a silver bracelet with small, blue topaz stones. The work on the bracelet was intricate, and the gemstones increased the price. After negotiating, she decided on the ring because it didn't cost as much. Remembering how much she spent to come on the trip, she thought she should save her money.

"Let's see it," Steven said.

She showed him the ring.

"Very nice," he said.

They left the jewelry store and strolled around the *zocalo* one last time. A small café on the main square looked inviting.

"Shall we?" Steven asked.

"Of course."

The menu was unique, offering a variety of wild game, steak, soups, salads, and specialty Mexican entrees.

"For my last night in Mexico, I'll have the specialty Mexican Cornish hen," Eva said.

"Oh, the Veracruz style? That sounds good. Think I'm going for the quail," Steven said.

After they ordered, Steven excused himself to make a work call. "The reception is not very good in here," he said as he stepped outside.

"Sorry," he said when he returned. "Starting back to work next week will be hard to do."

"I can imagine," she said.

A man playing the guitar in the small café provided a wonderful atmosphere. Their meal was outstanding. And too soon, it was time to go back to the hotel, retrieve their luggage, and board the bus.

Eva and Steven took the seats they had been in for most of the week, next to each other toward the back of the bus. Eva checked her documents to be certain she had her pass for the bus from the travel agency back to the central bus station in Monterrey and the subsequent pass from Monterrey to Brownsville. It would take all night to get to Monterrey and all day tomorrow to get back to Brownsville. She took out her travel blanket and pillow. She wasn't looking forward to the long bus ride, but she wanted to get back to her apartment and prepare for her new job.

The bus rolled along on the highway in the clear night. Eva looked out the window at thousands of stars. Steven sat without talking. She wondered what was on his mind. She thought he might be as exhausted as she was. It had been a whirlwind tour. So many towns, churches, Spanish-colonial buildings, *zocalos*, music, dancing, and entirely too much food. *Hope I can fit into my work clothes*, she thought.

Steven took Eva's hand. The other tourists were sleeping. The bus had been on the road for two hours. They sat in the silence.

Then Steven said, "Eva," and he reached into his pocket. "I know you bought your ring to remember the trip. But I want to give you this so you will think about me, you know, when you are at work."

From his pocket, he pulled out and opened a small, velvet jewelry bag. Inside was the silver and blue topaz bracelet she had picked out.

"Oh," she gasped quietly. "When did you . . . ? How did you get this without me seeing you? I love it so much."

He put the bracelet on her and said, "The phone call at dinner earlier this evening was a way to leave the café for a few minutes."

"You are so sneaky!" she said and gave him a quick kiss. "Thank you. I'll certainly think of you each time I look at it. And I'll definitely wear it to work."

"I'm so thankful that I met you. I want you to remember what you said, that we will see each other again once we are back in our own lives."

"Of course. We'll work out a way to see each other." Eva stared at the bracelet.

"Good," he said, kissing her on the cheek. "I come across the bridge frequently for business. We'll not have trouble getting together," he said.

The two held hands as the bus moved steadily down the road. An hour later, they were both sleeping soundly. Steven had his head on Eva's shoulder, and she leaned against him.

The sound of the bus door opening awakened the passengers on the bus. It was dawn, and the bus was parked at a gas station.

Adrián stood in the front of the bus and said, "Good morning. We are here for petrol and breakfast. We will be here about thirty minutes. If you would like coffee and something to eat, feel free to go inside."

"Coffee?" Steven asked.

"You know me well."

They departed the bus and entered the gas station with a small breakfast café. They ordered coffee and a breakfast taco. This time, Eva ordered in Spanish.

"You continue to impress," Steven said.

"Thank you."

She sipped her coffee and then asked, "What are your plans for today, when you get home?"

"Unpack, check the status of my house, and probably go to the market. I am out of a few necessities. Then I'll just rest up for work tomorrow. You?"

"By the time I get home, I won't have time for anything but unpacking and going to bed."

"Oh, it will be late when you get home," Steven said.

"When do you have to be in Matamoros again?" Eva asked.

"A week or two. Depends on what is going on. Since we aren't operating in all of the facilities there, I spend more time in Monterrey."

"That makes sense," she said.

"If I can make it up to Matamoros and cross in to Texas sooner, I will call you."

"I'll keep my fingers crossed," Eva said.

They returned to the bus and settled back in their seats. Holding hands, they watched the scenery out of the window knowing they only had another hour or so until they went their separate ways.

It seemed like only minutes had passed when the bus turned into the parking lot of the travel agency. The passengers left the bus at a much slower pace than they had entered the week before. Everyone was tired. A few family members met some of the passengers and took them home. Others got in their cars and drove away.

Eva and Steven had a short kiss, squeeze of hands, and a "See you soon," as they departed the bus. Steven took a taxi back to his home. Eva rolled her suitcase to the sidewalk and entered the city bus. This time, she spoke to the bus driver in Spanish.

She hopped off the city bus at the Monterrey central bus station and went inside to the main lobby. It did not seem so overwhelming this time. At the information desk, Eva asked where the bus to Reynosa boarded. Eva understood the directions to the correct terminal. Walking out into the terminal area of the bus station, she felt no fear. Her independence had been reaffirmed. She easily found the bus and boarded. She would be back to the border in a few short hours.

CHAPTER TWENTY-ONE

EMILIO TOOK HOLD OF THE ladder first and pulled himself onto the freight car. Dolores and Ernesto followed. Lupita climbed on the next car. Their final train ride was underway, and Dolores felt immense relief. The journey was coming to an end, and their new lives would begin.

Dolores and her brothers laughed and joked as they pointed out different aspects of the desert land between Monterrey and Reynosa.

"That cactus looks like it is walking to the United States!" Emilio said.

"And that one is crawling over there. It's thirsty," Ernesto said and then followed with a hearty laugh.

They were excited to be so close to the end of their journey. They felt as if the purpose for their travel would be realized.

For some reason, this part of the train ride seemed to be taking forever. Dolores was eager to reach Reynosa, and she was hungry and knew her brothers were, too. Surveying the land along the way, Dolores determined it did not hold much promise for food. Even the cactus looked dried up.

They bumped and shook all the way of the last trek. This train seemed louder and older than the others. The air was the driest and hottest it had been on the entire trip. They neared the edge of Reynosa.

"Look," Emilio said, nudging Dolores.

At a distance, six Mexican police cars were positioned to stop the train.

"What should we do?" Ernesto panicked. "If they stop us, what should we do?"

"We are very close to the border. This time, these police may be attempting to catch us, so we won't make it across the border. If the train slows down like it is going to stop, we should get off and not get back on. We'll walk the rest of the way," Dolores determined.

Emilio and Ernesto agreed.

The train began to slow and was not quite slow enough that would allow them to jump off easily.

"Ready?" Dolores asked.

"Yes," her brothers said.

"Okay, we'll jump off and head for some kind of cover."

"Got it."

Dolores jumped off first, followed by her brothers. The train was moving a little faster than they liked for jumping down, but they were able to leap to the ground without injury. They ran to a small cluster of cacti and mesquite trees and hid. Watching ahead, they saw the police chasing and catching some of the other riders from the train.

"We'll stay here until they leave," Dolores said.

They watched as the police chased Lupita. They caught her and took her to a large truck with the others they captured. The truck was full of train riders. The police weren't able to catch the remaining riders. The last few riders ran far and hid well. An officer closed up the back of the truck, and the truck and police cars left.

"I hope Lupita is okay," Ernesto said.

"We'll call her cousins when we get to a phone and let them know. Maybe they can help her somehow."

"She was so close to making it to Reynosa," Emilio said.

The police had stopped the train only a few miles from the city. Dolores was thankful they didn't have to walk far to the edge of the town. The three began the weary, hot, dry walk to Reynosa.

As they approached the city, a man working on his house as they passed by loudly said, "Hey."

"Sir?" Dolores said.

"You look thirsty. Would you like water?"

"Yes, sir," Dolores said.

The man went inside his house. As the man entered, a small boy came out the front door.

"Hi," said the boy as he waved hello.

"Well, hello," Dolores said.

"Hi," Emilio said.

They walked over to the house. The man came outside with three plastic cups filled to the top.

"You thirsty?" the boy asked.

Emilio and Ernesto nodded as they drank the water.

"Would you like more?" the man asked.

"Please, sir," Ernesto said.

They handed the man their empty cups, and he returned with full cups once again.

"Thank you, sir. You're a blessing to us," Dolores said.

They finished their water, and Ernesto asked, "How much further to Reynosa?"

"About two miles. Are you going there to meet someone?" the man asked.

"No, we are going there, then to Matamoros," Dolores replied.

"No need to walk all the way to town. You can turn on that road up ahead on the right. It will take you to Matamoros. But it will be a long walk for you."

"How far away is Matamoros?" Dolores asked.

"If you had a car, it would take over an hour. But on foot, probably two or three days, maybe more in this heat."

Dolores was despondent to hear the length of time it would take them to walk. They had no food or water.

"Sir, is there a place we might buy some water to take with us?" Dolores asked.

"You can take these cups. And about a mile on that road, you will see a gas station. They have water there."

"Thank you," she said.

The little boy yelled bye through the door as they left.

Dolores, Ernesto, and Emilio walked toward the road as the man had instructed.

"We have to walk three more days," Ernesto complained.

"But think of it. In a couple of days, we can be in the United States," Dolores said, hoping to make him smile.

"Yes, a couple of days," Emilio said with a smile.

They trudged on to the road, then turned right. Once they rounded the corner, they saw the gas station far in the distance.

With one foot in front of the other, they plodded to the gas station. They sipped on the remaining water in the plastic cups the man had provided them.

"Perhaps we should buy a little food to keep for the next two days," Dolores suggested.

"Should we buy some to eat now, too?" Emilio asked.

"Yes, of course," Dolores said. "Let's take a little money from our inside pockets and put it in our pants pockets and save the rest."

They all agreed and took out a few bills each, hiding the rest in their secret pockets. Inside the gas station, there were packages of foods Dolores had never seen before. She smelled some food cooking in the back. She looked at the menu posted above the food and coffee display. The menu listed several types of tacos. On the counter was a basket of apples, bananas, and oranges.

"Those tacos sound delicious," Emilio said as he smiled.

"That's what I want," Ernesto said.

"Okay, let's get fruit to take with us and each of us get a large bottle of water," Dolores said.

They asked the clerk for their tacos and fruit. She handed each one a large taco stuffed with meat, cheese, and beans. Ernesto picked out three large bottles of water from the cooler. They paid for their food and went outside. In a shady spot on the side of the building, they sat down to eat and drink.

The clerk came out and asked, "Where are you going?"

"Brownsville," Dolores said.

"You are headed in the right direction. Up the road about fifteen miles or so, you will see a long line of mesquite trees. Those trees line the river. You can follow the river until you get there," she said. "The river will take you to the bridge in Brownsville. It might save you some time."

"Thank you," they said in unison.

"Watch out as you travel. It can be dangerous," she said. And then she added, "Fill up those water bottles with the hose over there before you leave."

"Thank you, Miss," Dolores said.

* * *

The sky was completely clear, giving the sun ample opportunity to beat down on them. Dolores felt the sweat rolling all over her body and soaking her shirt. She and her brothers walked many miles without shade. The clothing provided by Father Francisco had kept them warm in the cool mountain air but were too heavy for the blistering heat of northern Mexico. Finally, they spotted a clump of mesquite trees just off the road that might give off enough shade.

"Let's sit there and cool off," she told her brothers.

They cut through the tall, brushy grass to a flat, sandy surface that was speckled with cacti.

"Shhh . . . " Ernesto said. He stopped dead in his tracks.

"What?" Emilio asked. "What is that?"

Ernesto pointed toward the mesquite trees. Then Dolores and Emilio heard it also. They walked a little further to determine what was making the noise.

"Emilio! Look out!" Ernesto shouted.

On the right side of the mesquite tree, a very large rattlesnake was winding its way toward Emilio. Emilio jumped back quickly. The snake struck at Emilio but missed by inches.

"That was close! We'll walk over this way, away from the snake," Dolores said and pointed. "We should watch where we step. There could be more snakes out here."

Hot and tired, they continued without a break. Dolores knew her face was baking in the sun. Her lips were cracking. Ernesto and Emilio were suffering the same consequences from being in the sun for so many hours.

"I never thought I'd say this," Emilio said, "but I am missing the breeze we had on the train."

Ernesto laughed and said, "Are you missing the shaking, jostling, and loud noises?"

Emilio laughed. "I can't say that."

Their exhaustion slowed the pace of their travel. They rationed their water by taking small sips intermittently. It was taking so long to walk to the line of trees by the river that they all became discouraged. Dolores held the thought in her mind that soon their journey would be over.

"Look, over there," Emilio pointed.

A small, abandoned, rundown shack stood by the side of the road.

"Can we stop there and rest for a while?" Ernesto asked.

"Of course. If there are no rattlesnakes," Dolores said.

They walked carefully to the shack. There were no snakes. They inspected the outside and the inside to be sure no one was there or nearby.

"It looks clear," Ernesto said.

"Except for this guy," Emilio said.

Emilio stood staring at a full-sized skeleton lying in the dirt.

"Wonder what happened to him," Ernesto said. "Look, here's another one. His arms are tied together behind him with a plastic band."

Dolores said a silent prayer for the souls of the people there and prayed they had not suffered. As she finished praying, she heard Emilio.

"Oh, I see. Look at this one's head," Emilio said.

Ernesto looked closer. "He has a hole, like he was shot in the head. Isn't that what the cartel killers do to their victims?"

"I'm not sure," Dolores said. "We shouldn't talk about such things." Dolores knew that both of the people had likely been murdered or executed by the cartel. She felt unsettled in this desert full of snakes, cacti, and skeletons. She longed to feel safe again.

They sat down on the other side of the shack and drank sparingly from their water bottles. Occasionally, an old car or truck would muddle down the road. No one passing by seemed to care that three strangers from Honduras were walking through the flat, hot, dusty countryside.

"How far do you think we have walked since we got off the train?" Ernesto asked Dolores.

"I am not sure. We've been walking all day. The sun will be going down soon. We can walk a little in the dark, but it might be better to rest."

"I agree," Ernesto said. "We do not know the exact direction. We only know that we are looking for the trees that line the river. It will be better to walk in the daytime. We can see the snakes during the day."

"Let's rest just a few more minutes and then walk until dark," Dolores suggested.

Her brothers agreed.

They walked without talking, each one lost in their own thoughts. Dolores was thinking of her pain. Her legs throbbed, and her feet ached. Her skin hurt from the sun. She attempted to put these thoughts out of her mind by shifting to her future. Dolores wondered what the United States would look like on the other side of the river. This part of Mexico was not very habitable. Rattlesnakes were one of the very few living things that could survive in this environment.

"Ah," Dolores said, "the sun was beginning to sink below the horizon. Let's find a place to stay for the night. Look for something that would provide a little cover from the road."

All three scanned the road ahead. It was flat, and there was no sign of anything that would offer protection of any type. Even the cacti were short and scattered about the ground, providing no cover.

"Let's walk and keep looking. We'll be careful," Ernesto said.

At dusk, there was still no sign of a place to sleep. One by one, stars emerged in the sky. Slowly, a half moon was visible as it ascended.

"The moon will give us a little light," Emilio said.

"Do you think it'd be okay to walk just a few feet over in that direction? If it looks clear, and there are no snakes, can we lie down for a couple of hours?" Ernesto asked. "My feet are starting to get blisters again."

"Yes. We need to rest. We've walked a very long time today. We can eat a piece of fruit and rest. Let's go over there," Dolores said as she gestured.

Off the road in the light of the half moon, they saw an area with more cactus plants. At first, the tall barrel cacti and the saguaro cactus trees were mistakenly thought to be human figures walking through the night. Every few minutes, when they came upon a new cactus, it would give them a scare. They investigated a patch of flat dirt several yards from the road. There was not much cover, except for the brushy grass that was less than one foot high and several small barrel cactus plants. They sat down next to each other and took out their pieces of fruit to eat.

Sitting under the stars, it was quiet and hot. A slight breeze came every few minutes. It was just enough to make them wish for more to cool the air. Somewhere from a distance, the breeze carried the music from some small house in this almost-barren land.

"What is that kind of music?" Emilio asked.

"I'm not sure," Dolores said. "It's different."

"One of the other riders on the train talked about it. It's called Tejano, and it's a mix of Mexican and Texan music. Kind of like Mexican cowboy music."

"That's unusual," Dolores said.

As the breeze ended for the night, so did the music. Emilio and Ernesto fell asleep quickly. Dolores stayed awake as long as she could to watch over her brothers. When she could fight the sleep no longer, she laid down and closed her eyes.

All three were abruptly awakened by the sound of coyotes howling all around them.

"Do you think we are safe here?" Ernesto asked Dolores.

"I think they sound closer to us than they are. Let's stay quiet and see if they stop."

The howls of the coyotes became screams and crying as the animals circled their prey in the night as they fought amongst themselves.

"I think they're now fighting over their dinner," Ernesto said.

The howls and screams ceased.

"We can rest again," Dolores said. "They have stopped."

They resumed their positions on the ground. Ernesto and Emilio quickly fell back to sleep. Dolores listened a while longer, but sleep soon overtook her.

The brightness of the sun in the wide, open sky woke Dolores. She wondered what the time was. They had many miles yet to cover. They hadn't yet seen the line of trees along the river. She squinted and looked ahead. Still no trees. *Will we ever get there?* she asked herself. She saw a scorpion with babies on her back scamper by a barrel cactus.

"Ernesto, Emilio. Wake up. We need to get moving. It's morning."

Both of her brothers groaned and yawned loudly.

"Are you sure we have to wake up now?" Emilio asked.

"Yes, little brother. Wake up," Dolores said. "We need to find those trees and go to the river. You know, the river by the United States?"

Emilio could not help but smile when Dolores said the magical words "United States." He bounced up off the dirt.

"Let's go!" he said.

Another day of walking. Another day closer. Another day of praying for safety as they continued to go east. They would soon be in the safe arms of the United States.

Today, there was no breeze, and the air heated up within minutes. Dolores felt the heat from the sun and the heat radiating from the dry, sandy soil. She started sweating and slowed down her pace. Ernesto and Emilio slowed their pace to stay with Dolores. Dolores looked at the ground, surveying for snakes and any other dangers.

"Dolores," Emilio said after walking some distance.

"Yes?"

"Look, is that the tree line of the river?"

Dolores and Ernesto both looked closely at what they assumed were the tops of the mesquite trees in the distance.

"Yes! I think you're right. We're almost there!" she said.

CHAPTER TWENTY-TWO

EVA LOOKED OUT AT THE countryside of Mexico. She was in the state of Nuevo León and would be entering Tamaulipas in less than an hour. The land was sparsely dotted with cacti, yucca plants, and mesquite trees.

In her mind, she ventured back to the days she spent with Steven on the trip. She was looking forward to seeing him again, even though they had just left each other's side. She missed him sitting beside her on the bus. A sleeping woman sat in the seat next to her. Eva was thankful for the quiet. At some level, she still couldn't believe she had taken a weeklong trip to another country. She was proud that she had learned so much Spanish in that amount of time. And the best part of her trip, she had met Steven. She smiled and felt such affection for him.

The bus slowed as it entered the terminal at Reynosa. One more short jaunt to Matamoros, then Brownsville, and then her own apartment.

Thinking of the apartment reminded her of her new job starting on Monday. Her classes didn't begin for another week, but she had orientation meetings and general faculty meetings to attend. At once, her mind shifted from the daydreaming of Steven to the anticipation of her new job. She raced through scenarios of possible interactions at work. She met the dean and the department chair during her interview. She didn't know anything about them. She would ask Maria, the faculty member whom she connected with easily, to tell her about the administrators.

Eva's bus to Reynosa continued on to Matamoros. She didn't have to depart at the Reynosa terminal to find another bus. All of the other passengers left the bus. Eva waited in the empty bus for nearly fifteen minutes before a few other passengers entered. No one sat beside her. *Just as well*, she told herself. *I can stay in my own world and think about my past week and my future.*

The bus driver entered and closed the doors. The bus traveled through the city of Reynosa and on to the highway to Matamoros. Eva looked out the window and decided that Reynosa was still not exactly quaint or inviting. Not like the many Spanish colonial towns and cities she had seen. Reynosa wasn't a good representation of the rest of the beautiful country.

The scenery between Reynosa and Matamoros was not enthralling. It was barren in some places. Dry, hot, dusty, uninviting.

Seeing the outskirts of Matamoros gave her a sense of relief. She would soon be in her own home. She could think of nothing but a nice, long, hot shower and early bedtime. She only had one more day until she reported to her first faculty orientation meeting. She'd spend that day resting.

The bus turned in to the bus terminal in Matamoros. Most of the passengers exited. A few others entered the bus. And finally, the bus headed toward the International Bridge in Brownsville. The bus stopped just short of the bridge. Once again, the passengers were all required to leave the bus and show their papers. All of the luggage was searched and put back on the bus. Then, a short ride across the bridge and to the bus terminal in Brownsville.

Eva mustered up the energy to get her suitcase to the taxi area and find a taxi. The driver addressed her in Spanish, and she replied. *That was easy,* she thought. She felt she had learned enough Spanish to get around and speak in common, everyday situations. She might not sound very good, but she could do it.

The ride to her apartment seemed longer than she remembered. The sun was setting. She was exhausted. She entered her front door and smiled. "Home."

Eva kicked off her shoes and unpacked her suitcase, taking special care of the new white skirt and blouse she had purchased in Veracruz. She would wear it again to dance with Steven someday soon. She started her laundry, took a shower, and dressed for bed. She called her mother to let her know she was home.

"Hi, Mom."

"Eva, I have been worried sick about you. Have you seen the news? A caravan is getting closer to the United States."

"No, Mom. I just walked into my apartment, and I wanted to let you know I'm home."

"Back in the United States?" she asked.

"Yes, Mom."

"Well, thank goodness!" she said in an exaggerated tone of voice. "Don't go down to Mexico again. Listen to your mother! You had me worried sick!"

"I'm back, and I am fine. The trip was wonderful. I learned quite a bit of Spanish."

"When do you go to work?"

"Monday."

"Good. Then you won't have time to be prancing down to Mexico again. Do you think you will be rested up by Monday?" her mother asked.

"Yes. I'll rest all day tomorrow."

"Good. I'm sure you'll need to rest after that trip."

"Okay, Mom. I have to go. I'm finishing up some laundry. But I want to tell you all about my trip someday. Right now, I need to get my laundry finished and get organized for work on Monday. I'm going to bed early, so I'll wait to call my sisters tomorrow."

"Well, glad you're home. Call me soon," her mother said.

"I will. Goodnight."

"Goodnight sweetie."

Eva switched out her laundry and turned on the TV. She got some fruit from the refrigerator. She examined it. "Still good," she said to herself. She took the label off a mango and noticed that is said "product of Mexico." *Excellent,* she thought. *It will be delicious.*

In an instant, Eva was back at the hotel the first morning, remembering how Steven had introduced all of the fruits from Mexico to her. I need to get some star fruit, she thought.

Her attention was drawn to the television as the local news began a story about a caravan.

"Local authorities and the U.S. Border Patrol will meet Monday to devise a plan for the anticipated caravan that is heading to Texas. In the regional State of the Border meeting, the new chief informed the local authorities of the steps being taken by the Border Patrol. In a coordinated effort, the local authorities all along the border are working hand-in-hand with the federal and state law enforcement."

Well, what do you know? Mom was right, she thought.

* * *

Eva spent Sunday finishing her laundry and organizing her clothes for work. She chatted with each of her sisters between doing laundry and unpacking the gifts she had purchased in Mexico. She was putting away her shoes when her phone rang.

"Hello," she answered.

"Hello, Eva?"

"Yes."

"Hi, this is Maria from the university."

"Oh, hello. How are you?"

"Doing well. I wanted to make sure you were in town and ready to go to the first faculty meeting tomorrow. Your orientation is at nine a.m."

"Yes, I got moved in to the apartment about ten days ago."

"Perfect. The orientation meeting will be in the main auditorium of the College of Education Building. If you come early, say 8:30, they serve breakfast."

"I would like that."

"Good, I'll meet you there. I have a committee meeting at nine, so I thought we could meet for a quick breakfast, and I can fill you in on what else you will be doing this week."

"That would be great, thank you."

Eva hung up the phone and sat on the sofa. *I'm really going to be a professor,* she thought, and a smile stretched across her face. She looked through her books and papers and organized what she would need to begin her classes the next week. This would be the best job she had ever had.

She spent the day jotting down outlines for her first classes. They were rough drafts, but it was a start. She knew the university required a particular format, and she would find out more about that tomorrow.

Eva bounced out of bed Monday eager to go to work. It took her no time to get ready, since she had laid out her clothes the night before. She was in a casual suit and open-toed, dressy sandals. Of course, she wore her new ring and bracelet. Maria assured her during the interview that the dress expectation at this university was casual. She explained to Eva it was more about dressing for the heat than trying to impress people.

The university was a short, five-minute drive from her apartment, including parking time. She turned in to the parking lot. The university campus was unique because it bordered Mexico. The wall of the parking lot—which was, in reality, a tall, reinforced fence, was the "wall" between Texas and Mexico. It wasn't very strong and could easily be breached if no one was watching. Eva smiled, knowing the meager fence was the only thing between her country and Steven's. She wished she could see him again. Maybe in the next week or two.

Steven had her phone number. He asked her for the information before they left the parking lot of the travel agency in Monterrey. Maybe he'd call today. But he was probably as busy getting back to work as she was. She turned her thoughts back to her own job as she locked her car and walked to the College of Education Building.

One of the things Eva loved about the campus was the architecture. It was pure Mexican design, right down to the fountains and the Talavera tiles decorating the doors and stairways. The patios and courtyards reminded her of so many she had seen in Mexico. The landscaping was carefully planned to include the beautiful plants native to Mexico.

Eva walked to the auditorium to meet Maria. Just outside the auditorium were large tables set with every possible kind of *pan dulce* and Mexican fruits just waiting for the faculty members to enjoy. Large coffee urns and pitchers of juice completed the breakfast.

"Eva! Good morning," Maria said as she gave Eva a hug. Maria had explained earlier that this culture was all about hugging. You hug everyone for any reason whatsoever, but especially upon greeting each other.

"Good morning," Eva replied.

"Come, let's have some breakfast before we go to our meetings."

Maria was about to explain to her the different types of exotic fruits when Eva told her about her recent trip.

"Oh, yes, I ate those last week in Mexico," Eva said.

"What in the world were you doing in Mexico last week?"

Eva told her about her reason for going and how she had learned a great deal of Spanish.

"Oh, Eva, your Spanish is probably better than mine! When I was growing up, we were not allowed to speak Spanish in school. So, my parents forced me to learn and only use English. They said it was to keep me from getting in trouble in school. So, when I got to high school, I took Spanish for three years. But my teacher was not a native Spanish speaker."

"That's wild," Eva said. "Who would have thought?"

"Right?" Maria looked at her watch. "We just have a few minutes before we start. I am going to a committee meeting about a federal grant. I wanted to know if you want to be on the committee with me?"

"That would be terrific. I need committee assignments for my tenure file."

"Yes, you do." Maria smiled.

"Maria, I wanted to ask you something, too. I wondered if you would be my faculty mentor?"

"I was hoping you would ask. Yes, I would be honored."

"Thank you," Eva said.

"Okay. Well, my meeting is about to start, and yours is, too. Do you want to meet for lunch? You should be finished by noon. It's hard to believe they talk to new faculty members for three hours, but it's a lot of information, so take good notes."

"Okay. Yes, on lunch. Should we meet back here?" Eva asked.

"Perfect," Maria said.

Eva learned a great deal of the history of the university in her meeting. She saw charts on the organization and leadership and heard about the mission statement and the five-year plan. She learned about the university accreditation study. She heard the emergency plan for hurricane season. She listened to heated discussions and presentations about the proposed wall between Mexico and Texas that marked the property of the university. At the end, the new faculty members were introduced by department. There were twenty new faculty members starting the same week. They were from all over the world. China, the Philippines, Brazil, Spain, Canada, and the United States. The faculty were then given an agenda for the week that included several optional meetings and a few mandatory ones. Eva decided she would go to both mandatory and optional meetings and learn about all of the committees and campus leadership activities.

The meeting ended, and they were dismissed for lunch. Eva went to the designated meeting area and saw Maria already there.

"How was it?" Maria asked.

"Interesting," Eva replied.

"Learned a lot?"

"Yes, I did. I had no idea there would be so many new faculty members from all over the world."

"Everybody wants to live in the United States. And this university administration prides itself on welcoming newcomers to the country."

"I see."

"For lunch, I thought we could go to a little place down the street. It's a taco place, but the owners are from Mexico, so it's good food. They came here last year when the cartels forced their restaurant to close in Matamoros."

"Wow, that's too bad. I thought Matamoros had a ghost-town appearance when I went through there."

"Yes. A lot of people have moved to other places in Mexico and here to get away from the violence. We should each take our own car to the restaurant because I'll need to get to another meeting across campus after lunch."

"Okay," Eva replied.

"You can follow me over there. It's a little hole in the wall but one of my favorite places to eat lunch."

Eva walked to her car. Opening the car door, her bracelet glistened with the sunlight. *Steven*, she thought as she sat down in the car. She missed him already.

Eva followed Maria to the parking lot of the restaurant. They walked in together. The menu was all in Spanish, and Eva easily ordered her meal.

"Nice job," Maria said, noticing Eva's ease of the language.

As they ate, Maria gave Eva some advice.

"Now, about tenure, I need to warn you about a few things. First, as an untenured faculty member, you can't really voice your opinion about a lot of things. Try to always listen and observe to determine where people stand on any issues, or plans for the university, or even politics."

"You don't have to worry about that. I am not crazy about politics."

"Good. But remember, this university is run by its politics. Be aware of everything you hear and don't be tempted to disagree with others who are tenured. You just don't want to make anyone mad that might end up on your tenure committee."

"But that is six years from now," Eva said.

"Yes, but they remember. You kind of have to walk on egg shells until you are tenured. And, of course, it's even worse when you are talking with an administrator. You wouldn't want to disagree with a department chair, dean, vice president, or any other administrator."

"Wow. That is a long time to be silent about things."

"Yes. But you can always talk to me. I can let you know where people stand."

"Thank you—and you were right, this food is delicious."

Maria smiled, then said, "Oh, I almost forgot. In my meeting this morning, I added your name to the committee for the grant. And the most exciting thing, we have a retreat on Saturday on the island."

"What? Really? That *is* cool."

"Yes. It's just for the day. We will meet in a hotel meeting room and then go to lunch at the café on the beach, The Palms Café. It overlooks the water. And it is an open-air restaurant, so you can enjoy the beach while we talk."

"Sounds wonderful. I am looking forward to it."

"Oh, I gotta run. See you tomorrow? I'll be in my office writing up my syllabi," Maria said.

"I need to do that, too. Can you share the format with me?"

"Will do. I'll be at the office tomorrow by ten o'clock, and I can show it to you then. Let me know if you need anything."

"Thanks."

CHAPTER TWENTY-THREE

DOLORES, ERNESTO, AND EMILIO WALKED toward the line of trees. The flat land of northern Mexico was beginning to heat up. Dolores could feel her skin burning again. She would like to jump in the river when they found it. It would cool her off. They walked through more dusty land covered with cacti and mesquite trees.

"Ernesto, how are your feet today?"

"Not as bad as my sunburn," he said.

"Me, too," Emilio said.

"Yes, I was thinking the river might feel pretty good," Dolores said. They moved closer to the river.

"Is that a person over there?" Ernesto asked.

"It looks like some kind of officer. He's looking around like he is patrolling," Emilio said.

"Let's go over there to the trees and watch," Dolores said.

On both sides of the river, extra patrol officers were walking through the trees and along the river bank. The Mexican side had local, state, and federal officials patrolling. On the United States side, there were Border Patrol agents, Texas State Troopers, local law enforcement agents, and the United States National Guard. They were talking loudly in both Spanish and English.

"They are everywhere," Emilio said.

"It's going to be more difficult than I thought it would be to cross the river," Ernesto said.

"What are they saying?" Emilio asked.

They listened quietly.

"Look over here," the officer yelled to another officer. "Stop anyone you see. They must show you their papers. Anyone could be traveling with the caravan."

Dolores said, "Let's think about this for a while. We'll find a way."

They watched the officers as they continued searching. Two men were captured on the other side of the river. They put plastic bands on their wrists and made the men get on the ground. The other officers continued looking for more people trying to enter without documentation.

"Well, one thing is clear—we have to find another way to get across. Let's walk back to the road and then follow it in to Matamoros," Dolores said.

"Oh, we are so close," Emilio pleaded.

"Yes, and if they find us, they'll send us back to Honduras. Let's go to the road," Ernesto said.

Discouraged but still determined, they walked back to the road. Their legs ached; their feet had blisters; the sun's heat was relentless; and their hearts were discouraged.

"Here comes a van," Emilio said.

"We should hide until we know it's okay," Dolores said. "It could be more patrol officers."

They ran off the road several yards on the opposite side from the river. A clump of cacti and mesquite trees provided a little cover. They sat down quickly and followed the movement of the van. It slowed down. The windows were rolled down, and they could see inside the van.

"The men inside, they look like trouble. Look, tattoos on their faces," Ernesto whispered.

"I see," Dolores said. "Let's remain here for a while until they are far away."

They sat in the slim shadow of a mesquite tree and watched large ants in a long trail scurry past them. Lizards and horned toads ran around the cacti. It was several minutes that seemed like hours of sitting under that skinny mesquite tree.

"Okay. I think the van is gone," Dolores said. "Let's wait a moment longer to be certain they don't circle back."

After a while, they emerged from their hiding place and walked back to the road.

"Ernesto, any idea how far we are from Matamoros?" Emilio asked.

"No idea at all. But so far, we haven't seen any buildings, and Matamoros is a large city. I think we have to walk all day," Ernesto said.

"I have only one piece of fruit left," Dolores said. "Do you have any?" she asked her brothers. They shook their heads no. "We can share this orange." Each took sections of the orange. They looked for food and water as they walked along, but nothing was available.

A stranger burst out from behind a clump of trees by the road.

"Hey, amigos," the man said. "You need a coyote? To get you across tonight?"

Dolores didn't like the looks of this man. He didn't look like he would be a trustworthy coyote. Why was he hiding in the trees? Would he just take their money and run like they heard others had?

Was he pretending to be a coyote to rob them or lead them to a place where others would mug them? She didn't like him.

Ernesto and Emilio looked to Dolores. They said nothing, but their expressions said, "No, not him."

"No, we don't need to go across. We're meeting someone in Matamoros." Dolores felt a twinge of guilt for lying.

"Oh, you look like Central American travelers," the coyote said insistently, "like the caravan people."

"No. We're from Mexico," Dolores said, feeling even guiltier about the lie.

"Where are you from?" he asked in an attempt to push the lie out into the open.

"San Luis Potosí," quickly popped out of Dolores' mouth. It was the only thing she could come up with quickly.

"Oh, is that a nice place?" he asked, still pushing the issue.

"Yes, if you like tall buildings and lots of highways and lots of traffic," she responded convincingly.

"Oh," he replied, giving up his interrogation. "Okay, if you know anyone in Matamoros who needs a coyote, send them to this road."

"Okay," she replied.

Dolores, Ernesto, and Emilio walked for nearly a mile without speaking. Finally, Emilio said, "That was a close call with that coyote. I think he was a crook."

"That's what I thought, too," Dolores said. "You both were very careful. You've learned about trust, how to tell if someone is trustworthy. It's an important thing to learn."

They continued in silence. The heat was increasing, and so were the size of the blisters on their feet. The road stretched out forever.

Two miles later, Ernesto asked, "Dolores, is that something on the side of the road?"

Emilio and Dolores stopped and focused ahead to see what Ernesto had seen.

"I think it's a gas station," Dolores said. "We must be getting closer to Matamoros."

The buildings and houses were coming into view.

When they reached the gas station, Emilio turned to Dolores and asked, "Can we buy another taco?"

"Yes. We have only had a little orange all day."

Inside the gas station, they walked straight to the counter and looked at the menu. There were many choices of tacos and other favorites. Part of the gas station was sectioned off by a wall with small tables and chairs. A few men were sitting at a table eating. Dolores and her brothers decided to purchase their food and water and sit inside out of the sun to eat. They walked around the wall, and Dolores noticed the men were the ones they had seen earlier in the van that passed by.

"This is a nice break," Ernesto said, not noticing the men.

"This the first time for us to sit at a table and eat together since Father Francisco's church," Emilio said, wiping his mouth with a napkin.

Dolores smiled. "Father Francisco was one of the nicest people I've ever met." She glanced over to the men at the other table and continued to talk with her brothers.

"He helped me to get well," Emilio said. "I'll never forget him."

"We've traveled far since then," Ernesto said.

Dolores sensed the men at the other table were listening. She wanted to change the subject. She didn't want the men to know they were from Honduras. She didn't know who to trust.

One of the men said, "Good afternoon, Miss" when he noticed Dolores.

She spoke quietly to her brothers. "We need to leave. It's getting late." She pretended she had not heard the man speaking to her.

They took their paper napkins and cups to the trash can by the door. Without talking, each picked up the extra bottle of water they had purchased.

On the street, Ernesto asked Dolores, "What's wrong? Did those men frighten you?"

"They didn't look trustworthy. Two of those men had many tattoos on their arms, and another had a tattoo on his face. I didn't want to take any chances. They may be the same men that passed us on the road earlier."

"Should we be worried?" Emilio asked.

"No, I think we're okay. I think we're close to Matamoros. We should walk faster."

They picked up their pace until they were well out of sight of the gas station.

"Ah, there is the sign that says Matamoros," Ernesto gestured. "We're by the city now."

The street curved into another street, and then several intersections were in view. They stopped and looked at the choices.

"I don't know which road we should follow, but the river should be that way," Dolores said.

They turned on the street and continued walking. The streets became wider, and some streets were elevated above other streets on overpasses.

"Matamoros is a large place," Emilio said.

They walked alongside one of the wide, busy streets. They approached a bridge where there was another street. It was elevated above the street they were walking on.

"Oh, no!" Dolores gasped and rapidly made the sign of the cross on her chest.

"What?" asked Ernesto.

She said nothing, only stared. Ernesto and Emilio followed her gaze to see a man hanging upside down from a bridge. His head was gone.

"Let us move quickly and cross this street," she said, walking forward.

Down the street from the hanging man, they saw few people. Store fronts were empty. Others had windows boarded up. Some had broken glass.

"This town has a great deal of trouble," Ernesto said.

"It looks that way. I don't feel safe here," Dolores said.

They walked in silence.

Wheels squealed as a van pulled up beside them. The men from the gas station were inside.

"See, I told you we could find them," one man said.

Dolores, Ernesto, and Emilio ran. The van followed. The doors quickly opened, and the men jumped out. Dolores screamed. Her brothers yelled. Each of the men had a gun. They grabbed all three and shoved them inside the back of the van. The men forced the siblings' hands behind their backs and tied plastic wristbands on them. Then the men covered their eyes with dark cloth. The van sped away.

Dolores was crying and asked, "Where are you taking us?"

"Shut up. Sit there and don't talk," yelled one of the men.

Dolores felt her heart pounding and her stomach churning. Did her brothers feel the same way? She wasn't certain how long they had been in the van. She couldn't determine which direction the van was going. She sensed bumps, potholes, and turns in the road. She heard the men talking in the front of the van. The music on the radio was playing so loudly, she couldn't understand what the men were saying.

The van stopped, and one of the men got out and talked to another man near Dolores' window. She could hear the conversation.

"Yes, two boys and a girl. I think they're in good shape. Young. The girl is nice-looking. They'll bring a good price," said the man from the van.

"Good. You're behind this week. Rico will be pleased with this catch. Go ahead. I will let them know you are coming. They'll let you in."

The man returned to the van and slammed the door. Dolores felt the van turn to the right. Based on their earlier route to the river, she tried to figure out which direction they were going. She thought they may have been going away from the river. She feared they were moving further from the United States.

The van traveled for such a long time, Dolores believed they were no longer in the city. She was hot, and her stomach was cramping. She wanted the van to stop moving. She leaned to the side in an attempt to see if her brother was next to her. She felt only a tire and some equipment.

The van slowed and turned. She heard the driver speaking into some kind of a radio, and then she heard a large gate or fence opening. The van moved forward.

The van stopped, and the men got out. They opened the doors and pulled Dolores, Ernesto, and Emilio out. The men didn't take off the blindfolds. They led Dolores and her brothers for some distance on a concrete sidewalk or parking lot. She heard the men talking to other men. Large doors opened. The men led the three inside and sat them on concrete against a wall.

"You sit here. Don't talk."

Dolores waited until she heard the footsteps of the man walking away from her. She leaned over and gently touched something with her shoulder on her right side. She whispered, "Emilio? Ernesto?"

"Me, Ernesto," he whispered back.

"And I'm beside him," Emilio said.

"Pray," she whispered. "Pray hard."

The echo that Dolores heard when they entered the room told her they were in a large room made of concrete. The room was hot and damp. At times, she sensed there might be other people in the room with her, but it was very quiet. She assumed the others in the room might be blindfolded and have their hands behind their backs. She thought there were probably more people in the room than the number of men who kidnapped them. But there was no way for the captured people to defend themselves or help each other. She didn't remember a time in her life when she felt this helpless. Tears began to fall down her face and onto her shirt.

The concrete was uncomfortable. Dolores didn't know how long she was sitting there. She couldn't tell if it was still day or if it had turned to night. Once in a while, she would lean next to Ernesto, and he would lean back as if to say, "Yes, I'm still here."

Later, Dolores heard the large door opening. She heard footsteps.

"You sit here. Don't talk," the man said. "And you sit here."

Dolores sensed that someone had been placed beside her and that at least two more people had been added to the collection of people held against their will. She hadn't been touched by anyone, but she thought she could feel the heat from someone else sitting close. Dolores didn't talk. She feared the kidnappers were still in the room.

Someone in the room was softly crying. Dolores prayed she and her brothers would be safe. She prayed for the safety of the others in the room.

The doors to the room opened again.

"Everybody, stand up!" a man's voice yelled.

CHAPTER TWENTY-FOUR

ON WEDNESDAY, EVA'S PHONE RANG as she maneuvered her car into the university parking lot.

"Hello," she said, not recognizing the long-distance number.

"Eva? It's Steven."

Her heart picked up the pace as she said, "Hello. Good to hear your voice."

"Good to hear your voice, too. I'm going to be on the island for a meeting Saturday. I wondered if you could meet me for dinner?"

"That would be terrific. It will be wonderful to see you," she replied.

"I want to see you, too. Can you meet between five and 5:30 at the Sea Ranch? The food is good, and I am anxious to spend time with you."

"I can. Spending time together again sounds great. I'll be in a meeting on the island that day, so I will head to the restaurant as soon as it's over."

"Perfect," he said.

Eva's first week at the university came to a close. She alternated meetings and lesson planning throughout each day. A few students dropped by to introduce themselves to her. She met many new faculty members. Her last meeting on Friday to assign the sections of the grant proposal for the retreat was brief. Eva was looking forward to collaborating with her colleagues on the grant. The retreat on the island would be a wonderful opportunity to work closer with the faculty members in her department. The meeting would be interesting, but she was more excited about her dinner plans on the island Saturday night.

Friday afternoon, Eva walked to the parking lot of the university at a fast pace. She heard someone walking behind her. She turned and saw Maria trying to catch up with her.

"Eva, do you want me to pick you up to go to the island tomorrow?" Maria yelled almost out of breath.

"Thank you, but I'll be staying late on the island."

"Okay. You know how to get there?"

"Yes. And I'll let my GPS find the hotel."

"Great. See you at ten a.m."

Eva spent her evening trying on various outfits for the next day. She needed something that would be casual for the retreat and dressy enough for an after-five dinner date. She tried the same outfits on at least three times. Nothing seemed to be working. She was about to give up. Then she had an idea. Put the blouse with the Mexican flowers on with a pair of white capris, rather than the skirt. She tried it on.

"Yes!" she said. "This will work."

Saturday morning, she awoke an hour too early. She turned on her coffee maker to make her favorite coffee. Mexican coffee was the only kind she drank now and always with a sprinkle of cinnamon. She sat down for a moment and thought about her day. What a wonderful day it would be.

Eva typically turned on the news to see if there was anything she needed to hear about local events. But today, she was too excited to turn it on. Her mind was speeding ahead to five o'clock when she would see Steven for an early dinner.

Eva checked the mirror once more. She fastened the bracelet Steven had given her, then picked up her briefcase. All the grant information was tucked inside. Locking the apartment door, she felt the strong sea breeze of warm, humid air. She checked her make-up one last time in her car mirror before leaving.

She set her GPS. The drive to the island was about thirty minutes. Eva had not yet ventured to the island, although everyone at work spoke about how much they liked it. She was anxious to see it.

Eva drove down Highway 48 to Port Isabel, past the Port of Brownsville, and turned right on Highway 100. She passed the small sea cottages and drove through the fishing town. Port Isabel was a small town, complete with a lighthouse and several tourist-type restaurants. It was well-known for having a replica of a pirate ship. For just a few dollars, parents and grandparents took their kids out on the pirate ship that was full of pirates who painted moustaches on kids' faces and taught them how to say "Argggh!" and "Ahoy Matey!" She smiled as she drove past the lighthouse. *Not long now,* she thought.

She drove across the two-and-a-half-mile causeway bridge that linked the island to the mainland. Eva was amazed at the aquamarine-colored water. She could not believe this island was only a few miles from her new home. The waves thrashed against the boulders that reinforced the fishing piers. She glanced at the pirate ship moored at the pier. She drove over the causeway, heeding the warning signs to slow down for pelicans.

Reaching the end of the causeway, she stopped for the first signal light. The palm trees were surrounding the intersection, and a large sign posting "South Padre Island, Texas" was decorated with large, colorful umbrellas.

"Guess this is it," she said to herself.

Following the GPS directions, she found the Isla Grand Hotel and parked her car. She was greeted by large blue and yellow McCaw parrots with bright yellow breasts saying "Hello" and "Hi, Baby" as she walked in the lobby. The lobby had almost as many tropical plants as the landscaped flower beds on the outside of the entrance.

"May I help you?" the clerk asked.

"I am looking for a meeting of people from the university."

"Of course. Take the elevator up to the second floor. When you reach the second floor, turn left from the elevator and walk down the hall. They have the meeting room all set up for you. There's a sign posted on the door."

"Thank you," she said.

Maria and the others arrived shortly after Eva. The coffee was set up along with Mexican pan dulce. Eva's mind leapt to Mexico and the mornings with Steven sipping coffee and eating sweet rolls.

"Let's get started," Maria said as she shuffled her papers.

Maria handed each faculty member a grant booklet and extra paper. Members of the committee discussed their section of the grant proposal. The conversations gradually moved from a proposal for the local school population to the high number of immigrants entering the schools unprepared. The grant did not specifically address immigrants, but it was designed for children who were unprepared and from low socioeconomic environments. As the discussion escalated, Eva felt torn. Some of the faculty members voiced their fear of criminals and others who were coming into the United States without going through proper channels. Maria and others voiced the opinion that the immigrants coming in were fleeing their home countries for safety reasons. The discussion became heated. It seemed the group of faculty members were equally divided about their opinions.

Inside, Eva felt that she was going to burst. She wanted to add her own experiences to the conversation. She had seen some evidence of criminals when she was in Mexico, and she had seen so many kind people who lived in Mexico. She kept thinking of how nice Steven was, and yet he was concerned about the safety issues in his own home country. Eva remembered Maria's advice earlier in the week about not voicing any opinions and especially about politics. She sat and politely nodded and listened with intense concern.

Finally, Maria said, "Let's think of how we are addressing poverty in the grant request, regardless of the cause."

Well done, Eva thought.

The meeting moved to the Palms Café on the beach for lunch. This was Eva's first up-close look at the water off the beach of South Padre. The café was a small, open-air building with a pergola roof. The café was actually on the beach and was attached to a boutique hotel. Tiki torches outlined the café all around. The committee selected a long table on the edge of the restaurant so that the view of the water was visible just beyond the sand dune. Eva was mesmerized by the rhythmic rush of the waves as each one rolled in. She stared at the water as a group of brown pelicans flew past in a V-formation. They swooped by and flew down to the other end of the beach, then circled back again. The gentle breeze came through the café, and Eva smelled the salty air.

As the waitress set the food on the table, Maria asked, "What do you think of the university after your first week of work?"

"It's exciting. The faculty members and students I met have been especially nice."

"You'll appreciate the students. They're very committed to their studies. Many students are from homes where no one else went to college. Some are from homes where no one finished high school. Their families are so proud of their children going to the university."

"This week will be challenging for me, meeting all of the new students and starting classes. I am fortunate to have only two classes a week."

"The dean structures the schedule that way for new faculty members. She thinks it's important to have just a couple of classes your first semester so you can have time to do research and to write. You need to get published as soon as possible. Do you have a topic yet to research?"

"Not yet. I'm exploring. I'd like to visit the local schools to see what is going on there and then select a research topic."

"Excellent plan," Maria said.

The committee was scheduled to work on the grant proposal at the hotel until 4:30. At 3:30, Maria interrupted their discussion. "I just had an alert on my phone. The weather station is tracking a new hurricane near the Yucatan. They have already named it León. One of the predictions is that it will head this way."

"And what are the other predictions?" Veronica, another faculty member, asked.

"The models for the paths are all over the place," Maria said. "Anyway, it will take several days, so we will have time to plan."

"Oh, those always turn and go east. Very rarely do they head this way," Veronica said. Then she turned to Eva and added, "Don't worry, Eva."

A hurricane so soon after I moved here? Eva thought. *That can't be.*

The committee broke up a few minutes after four. Eva went to the ladies' room to freshen up. In a matter of minutes, she would see Steven again. It had been a long week.

* * *

Eva had no trouble finding the Sea Ranch restaurant. It was close to the causeway. It was distinguishable by the large, wooden dolphin sculptures near the front door. She told the hostess she was meeting someone, and the waitress replied, "Oh, I think he's here. Are you Eva?"

"Yes."

"Right this way."

Eva walked past the large saltwater tank. The colorful coral and the saltwater fish reminded her of the snorkeling trip she had with Steven. The large dining area had windows overlooking a sizeable marina that displayed a host of striking yachts. The causeway was visible from one of the windows near the back of the room. The view was spectacular. Blue recessed lights in the ceiling gave a visual image similar to ocean water along the edges of the room. Large, wooden fish suspended from the soft blue tray ceilings appeared to be swimming near the top of the imaginary water portrayed by the blue ceiling and lights. White linen tablecloths were on every table, and lit candles finished off the perfect ambience.

Steven's eyes brightened as Eva approached the table. He stood up and pulled the chair out for her. He gave her a quick kiss as she sat down.

"Good to see you," he said.

"And good to see you, too."

"Nice blouse. Where did you get that?" he said as he laughed and winked.

"Why, thank you. I found it somewhere in Mexico." She laughed.

"And nice bracelet," he added.

"Yes, it is. A charming fellow gave this to me," she smiled.

The waiter handed each of them a menu and took their drink order.

"Do you come to this restaurant often?" Eva asked.

"I have been here a few times."

"Any recommendations?"

"Their specialty is the red snapper because it's the local fish. They have just about every type of seafood. And I know you like shrimp. They prepare that several ways, too."

Eva examined the menu. "I will go with the red snapper, pecan encrusted, I think. And salad and baked potato sound good."

"The blackened red snapper sounds good to me."

The waiter returned with their drinks and took their order.

"Tell me all about your first week at the new job. How did it go?"

Eva talked through the entire meal, telling Steven every conversation and meeting in detail. He was so engrossed in her descriptions of the students and the faculty that he didn't say a word about his own work that week. And Eva was so involved in telling him about her new job that she neglected to ask Steven about it.

"Look at that sunset," Steven said.

"Beautiful. Looks like it's setting just behind the causeway."

They sat for a few moments holding hands and looking out the window. The moment was interrupted by the waiter.

"Anybody care for dessert?"

"What are your choices?" Eva asked.

Then Steven asked, "Do you have any Empanadas de Guayaba?"

"Any what?"

Eva and Steven both laughed. In an instant, they were back in Veracruz having dessert before they danced in the *zocalo*.

"Let me bring the dessert tray out and show you our choices."

Steven looked Eva straight in the eye and said, "I have been thinking about the trip all week long. It was the best week I have had in many years."

"It was wonderful," Eva said.

Steven leaned back in his chair as if to change the subject quickly and asked, "How is the Spanish coming along?"

"Pretty good. I study each night after work. And I am watching the Spanish television channels. That helps."

"You're a good student," he said and winked.

The waiter brought the dessert tray. They ordered a piece of cheesecake to split.

"We talked all evening about my job. How was your week?" Eva asked.

"Let's say the week of our trip was so much better that I'd rather not talk about this past week at work."

"Oh?"

"Yes. The owners are going to repurpose the empty warehouses. They're more concerned about making money than anything else."

"I can understand that. They are business men."

"I'm curious to know what they decide," Steven said.

They shared their dessert and ordered a cup of coffee.

"And what do you have this coming week?" Steven asked.

"My first classes. I have to admit I'm a little nervous."

"You'll be tremendous. The students will have the best teacher they have ever had," Steven said.

"You are too sweet," she said, squeezing his hand.

Steven looked at his watch. "I'd better get back across the bridge. Saturday night can be rough getting back into Mexico."

"I understand." Eva was disappointed. She hoped to spend more time with Steven. She fanaticized they might take a walk on the beach. She also knew it would be difficult to get across the Brownsville International Bridge later at night, and driving through Matamoros could be sketchy.

Steven paid the check.

"Let me walk you to your car," he said.

Steven gave Eva a kiss on the cheek, said he would see her again soon, and opened her car door for her. She wondered if they'd ever progress to a more serious dating relationship. She knew there were many barriers to overcome if the relationship moved to the next level.

Eva turned on the local radio station as she drove from the island back to Brownsville. The station played some of her favorite Tejano music. Between songs, the radio announcer gave the weather forecast.

"There's an outside chance the Category 1 hurricane León near the Yucatán will continue to develop. However, it is expected to cross over the Yucatán, then dissipate and be downgraded to a tropical storm. Stay tuned to the storm-tracker station."

Good, no threat, she thought.

Eva unlocked her apartment door and got ready for bed. Her phone rang in her purse. Hoping it was Steven, she got it out quickly. The caller ID indicated it was her mother.

"Mom? Is everything okay?"

"Of course. But lands' sakes! I saw on the weather channel you are going to have a hurricane. It is right by you in the Gulf of Mexico!"

"Mom, the storm is near the Yucatán and nowhere near Texas."

"Are you sure? Aren't you evacuating?"

"Mom, don't worry. It's going to dissipate. That's the forecast. It was just on the news."

"Well, good. Now, has the caravan made it to Brownsville yet?"

"Oh, Mother. There's no caravan here."

"Okay. Work going okay? You said you had a meeting this week?"

"The meeting was amazing. I saw the island for the first time. It is beautiful. Very tropical."

"Of course, it is. You are next to the Gulf, after all." Her mother laughed, then said, "Well, glad you are okay. Call me soon."

"I will, Mom. I'll call in a few days after my classes get going."

"Bye now."

"Bye, Mom."

Eva's head was swimming. Hurricane, Steven, the grant meeting, her first week of classes day after tomorrow. She was exhausted. A hot shower and a good book to read would help her relax. She would rest all day tomorrow and be refreshed for her class meeting on Monday.

CHAPTER TWENTY-FIVE

DOLORES, ERNESTO, AND EMILIO HAD no idea what was happening. They remained blindfolded and handcuffed with plastic bands. Dolores was hungry, and she knew her brothers were, too. Men were shouting and telling them where to go as they led them out a door. The men sounded angry. Dolores thought they seemed panicky.

"You, over there," a man said as he pulled Dolores. "And those two, put with her," the man said to another man. Dolores hoped the other two were her brothers.

At once, she was put into another van. She felt someone being thrown in beside her. She whispered, "Ernesto? Emilio?"

"It's me, Ernesto," he said as he touched her with his shoulder.

"Is Emilio here?" she whispered.

No one answered. Had they been separated? She felt sick again.

Another door opened, and a driver got in the van, while another man climbed in on the passenger side. The van motor started and sped away.

"Taking them to the south safehouse?" the passenger asked the driver.

"That's what I was told to do."

The men didn't talk the rest of the way. After a short ride on a bumpy road, they were placed inside a small safehouse.

"You stay here," the man said, placing Dolores in a room next to someone else. She heard the man return.

"And you, sit down. Stay here. Don't talk to each other." Then the man left and closed and locked an outside door.

Long silence filled the room. No one talked, and there was no movement inside the house. The only noise was the increasing howling of the wind.

Dolores couldn't tolerate the silence and not knowing about her brothers.

"Hello?" she whispered. "Ernesto?" she asked.

"Yes. I'm here," Ernesto whispered.

"Emilio? Are you here?" Still no answer.

"My name is Lupita," a voice whispered.

"Lupita? We were on the train together. It's me, Dolores."

"Yes, you shared a tortilla with me. That's before they stopped the train and caught me and brought me here."

"Yes. We don't know where our brother Emilio is."

"I'm sorry. Maybe we can find him later. I'll look for him wherever they take me."

"Thank you. I hope they bring him here later. Maybe in another van," Dolores whispered.

A loud noise happened outside the safehouse.

"What was that?" Lupita whispered.

"I don't know," Dolores answered.

They all sat in the silence. Unable to move. Unable to see. Hungry, tired, and afraid.

The door opened again.

"Any of you need to take a break? You're going to be here a long time," the man said.

All three answered, "I do."

"Great," he said sarcastically. He took Lupita first and cut her wristband free. He didn't allow her to take off her blindfold. He guided her to the other room and closed the door.

Then he yelled back to her, "Tell me when you are ready to go back to the other room."

The man let each one take a turn. Then he put the wristbands back on each of them. Dolores was last. Once she was inside the restroom, she gently pulled her blindfold up to see the type of place she was in. It reminded her of an older home she might see in Honduras. It seemed small and run-down. She quickly pulled the blindfold back down and called the man to take her back.

Sitting beside each other in the room, they waited. The man was talking on the cell phone in another room.

"Yes. Yes. Okay. I'll come and pick them up now. Take them where? Okay, and then I'll return here? Yes. Okay."

The man came into the room with Dolores, Ernesto, and Lupita and said, "I'll return in a few minutes. Don't talk or try anything stupid. There's a guard outside watching the house."

He then went in the hallway and asked the other man, "Are you ready? Rico called us back."

"Okay."

They heard the men leave. The van sped away.

Dolores said, "Did either of you try to look around when your hands were free?"

Ernesto whispered, "Yes, and when I had the chance, I peeked through the crack in the door."

"I tried to look through the door, but I couldn't get my blindfold up enough," Lupita said.

"Ernesto, did you see anything?" Dolores asked.

"It's an old house and very run-down. It looks like it's about to fall apart."

"I thought so, too. Did you see a window?"

"Only in the restroom. And I looked through it. I saw the yard in the front of the house. There's no guard there."

"Do you think there's a guard somewhere else around the house?"

"We didn't hear him speak to anyone else except on the phone," Lupita said. "He didn't even talk to the other man who was in the van until it was time to leave."

"Good point," Dolores commented.

"How can we get out of these handcuffs?" Ernesto asked.

After a few minutes, Dolores asked, "Did either of you see anything in the bathroom that would work to cut these?"

"No," they said simultaneously.

"We must come up with something," Dolores said.

They sat in the silence.

After several minutes, Ernesto said, "Hey, I wonder if the bathroom window has glass in it. We could break the glass and use the broken glass to cut these."

"That's an idea," Dolores said, "but I'm not sure the glass would cut the plastic."

"Probably not," Lupita said.

"Maybe when they come back, they'll bring Emilio," Ernesto said.

"We can pray for him," Dolores said.

Hours passed. The three sat helpless.

"Dolores," Ernesto said.

"Yes?"

"Lean over here. I will pull your blindfold up with my teeth. Then you can look for something that might cut these off."

Dolores scooted over to Ernesto. He leaned forward and took Dolores' blindfold with his teeth. They tugged and worked the blindfold up so Dolores could see.

"There," she said. "I can see, Ernesto. I'll look around."

Dolores got up carefully and walked through the house. She peered into each room before she entered it. It appeared that this place was not used as a house. There was no furniture. There were no dishes in the tiny kitchen. She used her elbow to pry open a kitchen drawer. Everything was empty. She returned to the room and sat down beside Ernesto and Lupita.

"There's nothing. But there's no one here except us. There's no guard."

"Are you thinking what I'm thinking?" Ernesto asked.

"Yes. Come here, and I'll help you each with your blindfolds."

Soon, the three kidnapped victims could all see. Their hands were not free. But they could stand up, and they could see.

"Now, let's try to open a door," Lupita said.

Lupita turned her back to the front door and wiggled the latch with her hand.

"I've got it. We can leave; but if they find us, they will kill us," Lupita said.

"And if we stay, we'll be sold . . . or worse. I heard them talking about a good price we would bring. You know we'd end up in a brothel. I can't stay," Dolores said.

The three escaped out the front door and ran as fast as they were able. The wind was increasing; and because of the heavy cloud cover, there was no moonlight. They ran down a dark road and turned on a street of small houses. Inside a window, they saw a woman making tortillas.

"There," Dolores said.

They followed her.

Dolores knocked on the door with her elbow and quietly said, "Miss, miss, can you help us?"

"Oh, you poor child!" the woman said as she opened the door. "Come inside, all of you."

They explained to the woman what had happened to them as she was cutting their handcuffs off. They took their blindfolds completely off.

"Oh, those bad men. Cartel, you know. They're all over Matamoros. They've ruined the whole city. Here, sit. I'll give you food. I know you are hungry."

The woman closed the kitchen curtains so that no one could see inside.

"You can stay here as long as you need to stay, but we can't let the cartel know. We must keep the curtain and the door closed at all times," the woman said.

"Thank you," Dolores said. "I'm Dolores, and this is Ernesto and Lupita."

"Nice to meet you. I am Juanita," she said.

"Nice to meet you, Juanita," Dolores said.

Then Dolores added, "We're hungry. And we appreciate the food. But Ernesto and I are missing our brother. He was taken, too. He's younger. He'll be very scared. We can't stay too long. We must find him."

"Please, stay here to eat. And drink plenty of water."

Juanita gave each of them tortillas, grilled chicken, beans, and rice. She handed them a large bowl of fruit as she said, "Please, take some."

"Thank you." Dolores smiled.

"Oh, this chicken. So delicious," Lupita said.

"It's been a while since we had chicken. Thank you, Juanita," Dolores said.

They finished their plates. Dolores and Lupita helped Juanita clean up after the meal. Ernesto watched out a small crack in the curtains of the window for any signs of the van or the men.

"So far, all is quiet. No van, no men searching for us," Ernesto said.

"Good," Lupita said. "We should leave and walk while it is dark."

Dolores and Ernesto agreed.

Juanita said, "Before you go, let's say a prayer together. We'll pray that God protects you from these bad men and that you will find your little brother."

"Thank you," Dolores said.

Juanita said a beautiful prayer. They made the sign of the cross, and then Juanita hugged each of them and wished them well.

"And someday, if there's no more cartel, please find me again and let me know you are all doing well."

"We will," Dolores said. She gave Juanita another hug and said, "Thank you again for the wonderful meal."

The three escaped kidnapped victims hid between the houses and behind trees as they zigzagged through the southern part of Matamoros. The progress was slow. They stayed completely out of sight. Every time a car, truck, or van came down the street, they hid. If anyone walked down the street, they hid.

"Think we are out of range? Where they would not look for us?" Lupita asked.

"Before they took us, they had spotted us eating in a gas station on the outskirts of town. We traveled quite a distance away from the gas station, all the way into the main part of Matamoros, and they found us again. I'm not sure we are safe anywhere in Matamoros," Dolores said.

"That's scary," Lupita said.

"Yes."

The wind continued to increase. They ducked in between houses and bushes. They advanced further until they reached the buildings of Matamoros.

"Ernesto, this large building looks like the kind of place we might have been when they first kidnapped us," Dolores said.

"Maybe. I wish we could've seen it. But the building seemed pretty big, like this one."

"Yes."

Then Ernesto asked, "Should we try to get closer and look inside? If this is the building, Emilio could be there."

"I don't want to get taken again," Lupita said.

"What if I go by myself to look, and you and Ernesto stay here out of sight?"

"No!" Ernesto said. "You might be taken off again and leave me alone."

"Okay, we can wait here a while and watch this place. It may not be the same place. Watch for any vans going in and out of the parking lot."

They sat behind a small wall that was part of a large bed with tropical plants. They hid behind the plants, where they could see through and watch the parking lot.

Nothing happened for some time. Lights were on inside the building, but there were no vans on the outside. They waited.

A van pulled in to the parking lot. Men got out, but they weren't the men who had kidnapped them. These men had tattoos on their faces and were yelling loudly. One was on the cell phone yelling. They couldn't make out what was happening. In minutes, the men got back into the van and sped away.

Four police cars came racing by and chased the speeding van. Four other police cars, federal narcotics official cars, and police trucks pulled into the parking lot. A television news crew came in and jumped out to start filming.

"What's going on?" Lupita whispered.

"Looks like the kidnappers are being arrested." Ernesto smiled.

The police went inside the building and brought out a nicely dressed man with handcuffs. Other officers were loading scores of drugs into a truck. A few people walked out from the building in a line and were also arrested and put in a different truck. The television crew filmed the whole episode. The police put yellow tape around the parking lot and on all the doors. The police car with the man, the truck with the drugs, the truck with the people in the line, and all the other police cars left. The television crew returned to their truck and left the scene.

"Well, that was something. Those other people in the line, I'm not sure they were kidnapped," Ernesto said.

"I couldn't tell either, but we won't know now," Lupita said.

"No sign of Emilio." Dolores sighed.

Dolores was suddenly overcome with emotion. She could not stop the tears from coming. Ernesto put his arm around her.

"We'll find him," he said.

The wind began to increase dramatically, and it started to rain. The wind roared even more. Tree limbs broke. Trash and small objects were blowing down the street. The rain stopped, but the wind continued.

"This is a bad storm," Ernesto said. "Maybe we should go in an empty building until the storm is over."

"Let's look in that building next door. We can check for an open door or window," Dolores suggested.

The three walked around the small building.

"Nothing here. These doors and windows are all locked up," Lupita said.

They walked to another abandoned building. Some of the windows were broken out.

It started to rain harder.

"We can go inside," Ernesto said. He pulled on a wobbly door until it gave way. "Here we go," he said.

They entered the dark building. They went from room to room until they found a room with no leaky roof. The wind was howling inside through the broken windows.

"At least we are dry," Dolores said.

They waited in the dark. The storm got worse. Dolores prayed to keep them safe and to help them find Emilio.

CHAPTER TWENTY-SIX

EVA SLEPT SOUNDLY SATURDAY NIGHT. She slept late on Sunday morning. It was the first true night of heavy sleep she had in many months. She felt completely refreshed. She had no worries.

Tomorrow, her classes would begin. She was prepared. She could take it easy the entire day and be rested for tomorrow. She made her favorite coffee and sprinkled the cinnamon. Still in her robe and pajamas, she switched on the TV.

"And in an unexpected turn, Hurricane León has veered from the northwesterly track to more of a northern track, which changes the trajectory. Here are the possible paths. As you can see, there is still an outside chance that it will head toward Brownsville. But most of the models place it headed for the Houston/Galveston area. Stay tuned, and we'll update you after the National Hurricane Center flies the next scheduled reconnaissance plane out to collect more data. We're expecting another report by five this evening, so check back with us. Remember to keep your TV set to KRGV Channel 5 News."

Eva picked up her cell phone and called Maria.

"Hello, Maria?"

"Yes, hi, Eva. How are you today?"

"I'm doing well. I saw the weather forecast on TV and wondered about the chances of Hurricane León coming here."

"Oh, yes, I saw that it changed course, but that usually means it will head more easterly once it gets a little further north. Don't worry. If I hear anything else, I'll let you know. But there are no alerts yet from the university. Did you sign on for the university alert system?"

"No. I'm not sure how to do that."

"Go to our webpage, and you will see the instructions there. Once you add your cell phone number, you will get a text message if it looks like the hurricane will impact the university. Sometimes, they close the campus in case of flooding. They don't want the students to risk driving in flooded streets."

"That makes sense. Thanks. I'll sign up right now."

"Okay. I'll see you after your first class tomorrow. I want to see how things are going," Maria said.

"Thanks. Maybe we can go for coffee?"

"Perfect. Bye now."

That is a relief, Eva thought. *The university's got my back.*

Eva changed the TV to her Spanish novellas for a language refresher. When she studied Spanish, she felt closer to Steven somehow. She wondered if his trip across the bridge last night went smoothly and what he might be doing today.

She took out her laptop and found the university webpage. She signed up for the alert system.

Eva sipped her coffee as she prepared a quick brunch of *pan dulce*, mango, star fruit, and bananas. Her mind drifted back to Mexico. She had an interesting thought. She knew the university schedule included a four-day weekend in the middle of the fall semester. Maybe she could get away to Mexico for a short jaunt and meet Steven. Perhaps to Monterrey. It wasn't too far. She could ride the bus down to meet him. She would talk to him about the possibility when he called.

She ate her brunch and watched the Spanish novellas. She was able to follow most of the storyline and understood what the actors were saying. She watched two shows and got sleepy. Before long, she was dozing on the sofa.

The telephone ringing woke her. She looked at the ID.

"Mom?"

"What are you doing? You sound like you are asleep in the middle of the day. Why aren't you packing?"

"What are you talking about?"

"Hurricane León. The weatherman said it wasn't going across the Yucatan after all, and it is going to hit Texas."

"Texas is a big state, and that's still a couple of days away, Mom. I have class to teach tomorrow."

"Well, you can't teach if your building blows away in a hurricane!"

"Okay, Mom. Even if it comes to Texas, it may not come here. It is rare that hurricanes hit here. So, don't worry."

"But aren't you right next to Houston? They said it will probably hit Houston."

"Mom, Houston is a five-hour drive from here. Don't worry. I'm fine."

"You keep watching the weather. You hear me?"

"Of course, Mom. I will."

"And the caravan is almost to Texas. Are you watching? They say it is going to some place called Reynosa or Matamor-something-or-other, Matamo . . . "

"Matamoros. Mom, please turn off the television. Are you still doing your knitting?"

"I know you are trying to change the subject."

"Okay, Mom, look, I'll watch the news. I promise. Now, I need to do a few things to get ready for work tomorrow."

"Okay. Call me tomorrow, so I will not worry about you."

"Okay, Mom."

Out of her mother's concern, Eva turned the news back on. And there it was, a caravan of people from Central America heading northward. The reporter said the group was hoping to cross into the United States somewhere in Texas. The camera scanned the crowd. Some of the people looked dangerous—large groups of men, some with tattooed faces. Other people looked like families with children. There were many women with children. The news reporter then scanned back to show the state troopers, the National Guard, and Border Patrol. Maybe Mom was right, she thought. No wonder the faculty members have such heated discussions about the border.

She flipped the channel back to her Spanish novellas. "That's better," she whispered. She watched several episodes and practiced her Spanish.

Eva fixed herself a light dinner and changed the channel back to the local weather.

"The National Hurricane Center storm chasers have returned with the latest data. Hurricane León has not wavered from the course projected to hit between Houston and the Louisiana state line. León has now been upgraded to a Category 2. On the Saffir-Simpson Hurricane Wind Scale, that means the sustained winds are now at least ninety-six miles an hour. The data from the hurricane team indicate that the sustained wind was 104 miles per hour. This track will take it over the warm Gulf waters and could increase in strength. Hurricane warnings have been issued for the Houston/Galveston area all the way to Lake Charles, Louisiana. Please keep alert, and we will let you know of any changes."

Good, not coming this way. She finished her dinner and went upstairs to organize her clothing for the week. Her class started at 10:30 a.m. She planned to get to the university at least an hour early. Tomorrow would be a memorable day of her first class as a university professor.

* * *

Eva turned on the news the first thing Monday morning. She wanted to make certain there was no change in the forecast. The first story she heard was not about the weather, but about a cracked levee that was downstream from the Gateway International Bridge. The inspection was a routine one, but the timing was moved up due to the potential threat of tropical storm levels of rain that might spin off from Hurricane León. An earlier report indicated there were significant cracks near the university campus. The reporter was happy to inform the viewers that the inspection indicated the cracks in the levee were of no immediate danger.

"Well, that's good news," Eva whispered.

The weather report was the same as the night before. There'd be another hurricane plane this afternoon. Eva planned to not worry about the hurricane until she came home from work. She had other things on her mind, like preparing for classes.

She put on the pants suit she had purchased a few months ago. It would be perfect to wear to meet her students on the first day of class. She added her silver ring and Steven's bracelet and checked the mirror. *There, ready,* she thought. She was in the car and on her way by 8:30, earlier than she had planned. She would have plenty of time to review her notes and syllabus before the students arrived.

The students were sitting in the classroom before Eva walked through the door. They were so polite and respectful. She reviewed the course syllabus, noting all expected assignments and the dates of the exams. She engaged the students in a meaningful discussion and directed them to read particular chapters before they met again on Wednesday morning.

She felt on top of the world walking back to her office after class. Her class could not have gone better. She was thrilled. She poked her head into Maria's office.

"Coffee?"

Maria replied, "Yes. That would be lovely. Let's go to the faculty coffee shop."

They walked through the magnificent courtyard with the unique fountains and decorative Talavera tile. The weather was unusually warm and windy. The palm trees blew frantically in the hot wind. She and Maria walked across the footbridge over the resaca that separated the College of Education from the other main buildings on campus. They crossed the street and entered the coffee shop through the back door. With their coffees in hand, they sat on the protected back patio overlooking the Resaca.

"Tell me how your class went today," Maria said.

"It was superb. I don't think it could have gone any better. You were right about the students. They're polite and seem to be enthusiastic about being in class. They asked great questions, and we had a relevant discussion."

"How many were in your first class?"

"Twenty."

"Nice size. Just enough for good discussions, but not too many when it comes time to grade papers."

Eva laughed. She hadn't thought about grading yet, but it was a good point.

Maria looked at her watch. "Oh, I have class in fifteen minutes. I should go."

They scurried back to the College of Education building.

Eva worked in her office until well after five o'clock. She was gathering information about the school districts in an effort to come up with a research project. The building was almost empty when she walked to her car. The graduate students, who attended at night, were arriving as she left.

Driving to her apartment, the sky was completely cloudy. She entered her apartment. Immediately, she had a feeling of being "home." She turned on the news to see where Hurricane León was headed. She kicked off her shoes and went into the kitchen to make a salad. *What a great day*, she thought.

She sat down on the sofa with her salad and turned on the TV. She turned from the Spanish channel to the local news.

The bubbly female news anchor said, "And here is our Channel 5 weatherman."

"Good evening to everyone. We just received the latest data from the National Hurricane Center. The eye of Hurricane León indicates sustained winds have reached the top end of the Category 2 range, putting sustained winds at 110 miles per hour. Now, folks, this could reach the Category 3 level and become a major hurricane by morning. The other change in the data shows us that León has picked up speed. It's traveling more quickly than we anticipated yesterday. It's on track to come to the coast of Texas and now looks like it will hit the Houston area dead on. City officials are already issuing voluntary evacuation notices, and we expect this to become mandatory tomorrow if this course continues during the night. Hurricane warnings have been issued for this area in red. And the tropical storm warning has now been extended down to the Brownsville, Texas, area. So, folks, we might get a little rain and wind out of this one if it stays on track. As of this moment, we expect it will either stay on course or move more to the east as these systems that originate down by the Yucatan tend to do. All but one of the paths on our hurricane models indicate an eastern movement. So, stay tuned, and we'll update you after the next reconnaissance flight returns around ten p.m."

Eva ate her salad and checked her phone. No alert from the university, so all must be well. Just a little rain and wind if it stays on the present course.

Her phone rang before she could put it down.

"Hello, Mom."

"Well, it's going to hit Houston, and you're going to have a tropical storm."

"I saw that, Mom. They're predicting we might have a few inches of rain."

"Do you need to get out of your apartment? Will you get flooded?"

"Mom, a few inches, not feet."

"And did you see the caravan? It's definitely going to south Texas. You better be careful. Is the border near your work? Or your apartment?"

"Mom, just because they want to enter Texas does not mean they will. Anyway, they are still in Mexico."

"Are you sure?"

"Yes, Mom. Hey, my first class today went really well. I liked my students."

"Do they even speak English?"

"Oh, Mother. Of course, they speak English. Most live in the United States."

"Most? Well where do the rest live?"

"Across the border, Mom. They come across here to go to school."

"For goodness sakes!"

"Mom, I'd better go."

"All right. Call me tomorrow."

"Or you call me, Mom."

"Okay. Bye now."

"Bye."

Eva flipped to her Spanish channel. It was time for the news. She watched for a few minutes. The newscasters were talking about the hurricane in Spanish. It was interesting to hear the Spanish words for all of the weather terms. After the weather report, the anchor switched to local news stories.

"Oh, no!" Eva yelled. Her heart sank. She dropped her salad plate on the floor. On the screen was a video of Steven being arrested in Matamoros.

"No! No! It can't be. It's a mistake!"

She listened intently to try and learn why they were arresting him. The words she easily understood were *maquiladora* and "taken over by the Gulf Cartel." The reporter scanned the warehouses. Some of the warehouses were stacked high with what Eva thought looked like drugs. The reporter scanned to other empty warehouses and caught a brief image of a line of people, but she could not understand what the people had to do with the *maquiladora*.

Eva was in tears. What was going on? He couldn't have known the cartel was taking over. He wouldn't work for them. She knew he wouldn't. Why? Why did they arrest him?

Eva was shaking and sobbing uncontrollably. This couldn't be true. In an instant, her whole world was turned upside down.

CHAPTER TWENTY-SEVEN

DOLORES, ERNESTO, AND LUPITA HUDDLED in a corner of the old rundown building trying to stay dry. The night passed, and slowly, gray daylight appeared. The wind and rain continued. The water poured in through the doors.

"Let's go up those steps. We can wait upstairs," Lupita said.

They waded through the ankle-high water and reached the steps. Once upstairs, they were forced to jump between spaces of sturdy floor and spaces where the floor had fallen through.

"Here, this is a better section of the floor. We can stay here," Ernesto said.

"The wind. It sounds like a haunting devil," Dolores said.

"It's violent," Ernesto said.

They stayed in a huddle, covering their heads. Debris flew through the room. The ceiling crashed down around them. Their tiny corner of the room provided some shelter.

"Dolores!" Lupita shouted as she pointed. "The steps!"

The water began to creep up the stairs. It was gushing across the first floor and rising rapidly. Debris found its way inside the building.

Dolores prayed aloud. They held onto each other. There was so much wind, rain, and water, that it was hard to see any part of the building except the small patch of floor they were on. The rain stung their skin.

A section of a wooden plank fence floated inside the building. They watched as it floated up the open stairwell. The water gushing pushed the wood toward them.

"Ernesto, can you reach it?" Dolores asked.

"Got it," he said, "but I can't hold it."

Dolores and Lupita leaned over to help hold the wood. They were holding the piece of wooden fence when the wall behind them was pushed outside.

"Get on!" Dolores screamed.

They held on to the makeshift raft. The heavy rain pounded their skin. Debris flew past and bounced off them. They held onto the raft as it was pushed down the street of Matamoros by large waves of continuous brown water. The raft moved up and down with each large wave of water. There was no visibility. Water surrounded them, and their makeshift raft bumped into buildings and trees. It bumped into cement blocks. It hit metal. They passed cars floating, and other cars passed them. Bodies floated by. Other people were screaming and scrambling to try to reach the raft but couldn't grasp it. Dolores saw people go underwater and not come back up.

They held on as the river they were floating on pushed the raft into a larger body of water. They hit the cement side of the International Bridge, and the water pushed them further. They couldn't tell the direction they were going. More bodies surged by. Large pieces of buildings bobbled and spun as they were moved by the deep water. A jumbled pile of cars and trucks stuck together moved beside them like a slow-moving train.

"Ernesto," Dolores screamed, "you okay?"

"Yes. Just hold on."

Dolores raised her head to see her surroundings. She was afraid they were out to sea. Water was out as far as she could see. She didn't see any structures or trees. They were swept along for what felt like hours. Suddenly, the raft slammed into a large brick tower with blue tile on the dome. They were caught on what she thought was a wrought iron railing. She held onto the railing with one hand.

"Ernesto, Lupita, grab hold," she said.

They helped to steady the raft against the railing. They stayed in the same position, straining to hold on to the raft and the railing. Dolores' hands had splinters from the broken wooden fence.

Dolores was uncertain how long they stayed in the same spot. Gradually, the wind diminished. The rain slowed down, then returned again. Hours passed. The water receded slightly. They determined the railing was a balcony of some type of tower.

Stepping onto the balcony, they let their makeshift raft float away. They sat on the balcony in the slowing wind and rain. They couldn't see any standing houses but only parts of the brick buildings. There were no trees, except the ones floating in the water.

Dolores held Ernesto and sobbed. Lupita cried. Ernesto attempted to be strong, but he could not.

"God has spared us," Dolores said.

The rain didn't stop, but the wind subsided. They sat, exhausted, and the stormy sky changed to night. The rain finally stopped. They couldn't move. They stretched out, completely exhausted; and side by side, they slept.

The landscape was grim in the early light. Dolores sat up and looked over the balcony railing. The water had partially receded but remained at the ceiling level of the first floor of the building. She saw two bodies, face-down, floating like buoys at sea. Ernesto and Lupita were sleeping.

The clouds gave way, and the sun beat down on her. She wondered if Emilio was alive. She began to cry and could not stop. Her sobbing woke Ernesto. He sat beside her and put his arm around her.

"We are blessed. We'll find Emilio. I know we will," he said.

Lupita heard Ernesto and sat up. She said, "Dolores, let's think about this together and make a plan. What do you want to do now?"

Dolores began to weep. "I don't know." It wasn't like her to feel so helpless and to have no idea of what to do next. She was overwhelmed.

In the hot, steamy, wet air, they sat in silence. A sparsely dressed body drifted by the balcony. The woman's eyes were open. It was a horrid sight. Dolores cried again. She knew she should be strong. She thought about the words Father Francisco told her, to depend on God for strength. She prayed silently.

"Dolores, the water is going down a little at a time. Later today, we might be able to climb down and swim to look for help," Ernesto said.

"Maybe," she said, wiping her eyes. Problem-solving had been easy for her in the past. She believed she could think of something if she had energy.

"This is a pretty large building," Dolores said meekly. "There might be some food here, or in that other building over there," she pointed.

"I'll look," Ernesto said.

"How can you get off this balcony and go to the other building?" Lupita asked.

"The water is not flowing so strongly. I'll get into the water and swim," Ernesto said.

Ernesto climbed down the wrought iron balcony to a brick column and into the water. He swam around to the other side of the building. A broken window provided a way into the building, but there was not much light inside. It looked like an office. Water covered the first floor, and only the tops of the furnishings were visible. There was no food. He swam back to the side with the balcony and climbed back up.

"No luck," he said.

"We'll wait until we can walk through the water," Dolores said.

* * *

In the hot air, the smell from the water became overwhelming after the second day. The water receded to just-above-knee depth. Dolores, Ernesto, and Lupita climbed down from the balcony and waded away from the building. Debris, cars, pieces of houses, structures, and unknown objects were obstacles wherever they walked. They were tired, hungry, and devastated about their situation.

The bleak, unwelcoming world in which Dolores now found herself was unpromising. They plodded through the water and muck looking for someone who could help them. No one was in sight.

"What is that noise?" Ernesto asked.

They listened. The faint sound of some type of motor was somewhere in the distance.

"Someone is around here. Whatever that machine is, it has to be run by a person. Maybe a boat? Or a machine to clear away the mess?" Lupita said.

"Yes. Can you tell the direction?" Dolores asked.

"No. We'll keep listening as we walk. It might become louder," Ernesto said.

Far away, a dog barked. There was no sign of other survivors. Dolores felt things were impossible.

"I have decided something," Dolores said.

"Oh?" Ernesto asked.

"Each time I feel sad, I'm going to pray for strength. Just like Father Francisco told me."

"Who is Father Francisco?" Lupita asked.

"Oh, Father Francisco," Ernesto said and smiled. "He was amazing. Remember the breakfast he fed us? And the dinner after you and Father went to the market?"

"Oh, yes! If we had just one bite right now!" Dolores said with a smile.

"Tell me everything he fixed for you," Lupita said. "I want to dream," she said and laughed.

Ernesto described every dish and how it was prepared. Then he told Lupita how Father Francisco helped Emilio when he was cut by the man with a machete.

"Oh, Emilio." Dolores sighed.

"Yeah, Emilio," Ernesto said. "We'll find him."

The scenery became dotted with other partial remains of buildings. Roofs were torn off; walls were down; trees were leaning on buildings or floating in the murky water. They came upon a body stuck on the limb of a tree. Once in a while, they heard a motor or clanging noises or a dog. They heard no voices and hadn't seen any sign of life.

"Should we rest a while?" Dolores asked.

They nodded and found a broken wall of a building and climbed up and sat down. As Ernesto climbed up, he found a flat place to stand on top of the cement. He stood up and looked out as far as he could see.

"Dolores, way over there." He pointed. "It looks like there are people moving."

"Can you tell what they are doing?"

"No. It looks like several people. It's like a large group."

"Let's watch. Are they coming this way?"

"Yes. I think they are."

Dolores, Lupita, and Ernesto sat on the concrete as the group got closer. As the group neared, Ernesto said, "We might have a problem."

"What?" Dolores asked.

"Uh, I think—no, I am sure. They are the Salvadorian gang."

"No!" Lupita said. "Are you positive?"

"If we sit here a little longer, you'll see their tattooed faces," Ernesto said.

"I can tell now that you've pointed it out," Dolores said.

"What can we do?" Lupita asked.

"We can't stay here. I don't trust them. They're survivors. They look strong. But they'll be as desperate as we are. I don't know what they might do," Dolores said.

The three scrambled off the cement and moved through the water as quickly as they could. The Salvadorians seemed to be following them. Dolores, Ernesto, and Lupita traveled through the water at a much faster pace than before. They spent the remainder of the day looking for a hiding place and keeping a distance from the Salvadorians. They reached an area of several broken-down flooded buildings.

"We can go there. Let's hide or go out the other side of the buildings and see what we can find," Dolores said.

Inside one of the buildings, they found a stairway to three levels. Not all of the walls were intact. They climbed up the stairs and ran through what was left of the second floor and through another hallway to a separate wing. They went through the wing of the second floor and found a different set of stairs going down. They followed the stairs and went to the other side of the next building.

"I think we lost them. I don't see or hear them," Dolores said.

They walked up to the second floor inside of another partial building.

"We can sleep here. It's getting dark. Tomorrow, we'll look for food," Dolores said.

"That sounds good to me," Lupita said. "There's plenty of space here. I'll sleep in this corner."

"Dolores and I can sleep on this side. Tomorrow, we'll find food; I'm positive," Ernesto said as he closed his eyes.

A scream pierced through the night and awakened Dolores and Ernesto. They sat up and saw two men taking Lupita in the darkness. The men pulled her down the stairs and took her away. Down below, two other men were waiting. She was screaming and kicking as hard as she could to free herself from the four men.

Dolores grabbed Ernesto's arm and said, "Shhh." She took his arm and led him down the other hallway, out the other stairs, and out of the building. Lupita was making so much noise, the men did not hear Dolores and Ernesto as they quickly waded away from the commotion. They heard the men tell Lupita to shut up, or they would put her head under the water. She screamed, and they dunked her under and raised her up by her hair.

"Now, will you shut up? Or will I have to do it again?" one of the men asked.

The men took Lupita with them.

Dolores and Ernesto continued muddling through the water in the darkness. Dolores was shivering from fright. Ernesto held Dolores' arm and pulled her so they would move more quickly. When the sun appeared on the horizon, they were still walking quickly through the water.

"I think we are away from them," Ernesto said.

"Ernesto, look around."

There were partial houses on each side of a street. They stared for a moment at the street signs that were in English.

"Are we . . . " Ernesto asked.

"Yes. We're in the United States," Dolores said.

"There's nothing left," Ernesto said.

"We'll find people and food. And we'll find Emilio."

The water had receded a little more, and the wading was slightly easier.

"I feel bad for Lupita," Ernesto said.

"There was nothing we could do. They took her in the night. They would have taken us, too, if they had seen us. We should pray for her. She came the whole way to the United States."

"Those evil men came here to the United States," Ernesto said.

"There was nothing to stop them," Dolores said. "There were no officials posted and no barrier left after the storm."

Dolores and Ernesto walked through the street with rows of partial structures that at one time were beautiful homes. There were no people.

"Maybe some of these houses still have food inside?"

"We'll look if no one is there."

They found a house that had some partial rooms standing and went inside.

"Hello?" Dolores walked through the door. "Hello?"

They waded to a kitchen and opened the cabinets.

"Look at these nice dishes and things," Dolores said. She had never seen anything like it.

"Oh, look. Here is a cabinet with some food. Some boxes of things. Look. I'm not sure what these are, but they look good."

They opened a box of crackers, chocolate cookies, and potato chips.

"Look!" Ernesto said. He pulled out bottles of water.

Dolores knew the food wasn't the best for them, but they were too hungry and needed something.

They sat on the counter, out of the murky water, and ate the crackers and drank the bottled water. As they sat inside, they looked down the street.

"Oh, no," Dolores whispered.

Ernesto scooted beside Dolores and looked.

A few houses further and across the street, five men, who were similar to the cartel members they had seen in Matamoros, were taking things out of a house.

"What should we do?" he whispered.

"Let's see what they are doing."

"It looks like they are stealing something," Ernesto whispered.

"When they go inside the next house, we should leave and get far away."

They waited for the opportunity and escaped.

"Let's go over one more street."

The water remained just above knee-level. They moved as quickly as they could, swiping debris out of their way as they walked. Most of the houses and buildings were completely destroyed or had only partial walls remaining. There were no roofs on the houses in that block. There were no people inside any of the structures.

Dolores didn't know how far they had walked. The day was ending. They had eaten, but they hadn't made any progress searching for Emilio. She didn't know how to find him or what to do next.

They turned down another street.

"It looks like people are going inside a building down there. It is guarded by soldiers. We'll be safe. Let's go there," Ernesto said.

The building was a temporary shelter. It was in a church that was elevated just enough that it hadn't taken on as much water as the surrounding buildings. With the help of the National Guard for transportation and security, volunteers were able to clean it out after the first day of the storm. On the outside, a large banner with a red cross hung across the door. National Guardsmen were posted around the outside. It was the first shelter to be set up in Brownsville. It was the closest shelter to the International Bridge and was near the university campus. Most of the campus had been destroyed. The homes and businesses nearby had been reduced to rubble. Only the shelter, a church, was intact.

"Let's go inside. Emilio might be there."

Dolores said a silent prayer for Emilio and opened the door of the shelter.

CHAPTER TWENTY-EIGHT

EVA WAS SICK ON HER stomach. She couldn't sleep, and the wind howled so loud that it kept her awake. What had happened to Steven? There was no way to find out. She had no idea how to look for him or how the Mexican police or prison system worked. Steven had told her the police were crooked in most of Mexico. Perhaps this was a mistake, and the crooked police had arrested him; but he was innocent. Maybe he was framed by the cartel or the police?

For a brief moment, her mind wandered back to sitting in the cathedral and looking at Steven sitting there. He had to believe in God and have faith. He must be a good man. He wouldn't purposely do something so wrong as work with the cartel. He couldn't. Eva refused to believe Steven was evil.

Why? Why did God do this? Why did Eva keep having bad experiences with men? Why? Eva hung her head and cried. She sobbed. She longed for that feeling of serenity and peace she felt when she sat in those old churches in Mexico. She felt like she was in the pit of despair and wanted more than anything to feel the presence of God right now.

This experience made her question her own faith. She felt weak. She wanted to be strengthened by God. She knew other people drew strength from Him. She needed to feel that. She wanted to pray. She wasn't sure she even knew how to do that. She was just so sad and empty inside.

In her sorrow, she was glad she didn't have another class scheduled until Wednesday. She knew she couldn't concentrate until she learned more about Steven. She couldn't think of anything else. She was depressed. He was a good guy. He had to be. He believed in God. He was so nice and polite. She was pretty sure she was falling in love with him. *Why, God?* Why did this happen to her? Why did this happen to Steven? She couldn't stop her thoughts of hurt and anger. *Why?* Her mind bounced all around between anger and sorrow. Then, the sorrow overtook her, and she cried herself to sleep.

The text message alert and light of her phone woke her in the middle of the night. She picked up her phone and read the text.

"Classes cancelled Tuesday and Wednesday due to weather. University closed until further notice."

She sat straight up in her bed.

"What?" She read the text message again. She was so upset about Steven being arrested that the news of the storm didn't phase her. She got up and made her coffee. It was four in the morning. She felt like she hadn't slept. She tossed and turned and was still sick at her stomach.

She sipped her coffee and turned on the TV.

"If you're just waking up to this news today in the Rio Grande Valley, please be informed we are now under a hurricane warning. Hurricane León increased in speed and will now take a more western track. As you can see, the hurricane tracker put the paths here. Most of the models are now showing it will hit between the southern tip of Texas, in the Brownsville area and Corpus Christi. Be aware, the causeway to the island has already been closed. If you are on the island, you'll have to ride this one out.

"Now, the Saffir-Simpson Scale shows this has been upgraded to a Category 3 storm with sustained winds of 125 miles per hour. This will hover over warm water for a bit longer and could be upgraded to a Category 4 by midmorning. Category 3 and 4 are both considered major hurricanes. These winds can cause significant damage. We'll likely lose power and water if it heads directly to Brownsville.

"We are already seeing the impact as the rain bands of tropical storm strength are pounding the Rio Grande Valley. These winds and rains have been with us for the last two hours, and we have measured five inches of rain in that amount of time. We are already measuring winds of fifty-five miles an hour here with the initial bands, which is why the causeway bridge had to be closed so early.

"Another alert here, the Texas Highway Department and Texas Department of Public Safety have issued a notice that Highway 77 and Highway 83 are already closed due to significant rainfall. These highways out of town are already flooding. Don't attempt to get on the highway at this point."

Eva switched the channel to the Spanish network. There was nothing but a snowy, gray picture on that channel. She turned it back to the local channel.

"Keep it right here on Channel 5, and we will keep you informed."

She didn't know what to do. She wasn't able to travel out of harm's way. She could hear the wind howling outside. The fronds of the palm trees were beating the windows. She peeked out the window and couldn't see anything. It was still too dark.

She got a second cup of coffee and returned to the news.

"This just in. We've been informed that the levee near the University and the International Bridge is being watched. There remains concern about the cracks that were discovered recently. Texas state troopers and the Army National Guard are on standby and monitoring the levee situation. It is expected to hold, but they are keeping an eye on it."

I'd better make sure my phone is charged and unplug my computer in case of a power outage or surge, she thought.

She unplugged her computer and grabbed her phone charger from upstairs. She would keep her phone plugged in as long as possible so she would have use of it during the storm if she needed it.

She returned to the TV.

"Take a look at the eye now, folks. We are seeing some better organization here," he said as he outlined the area. "Which means that Hurricane León could very well be gaining strength. As we told you earlier, we expect this may go up to a Category 4 by mid-morning."

Eva looked out her window again. Still dark. She wanted to know if the water was rising and if she needed to go upstairs. She couldn't tell.

I better get dressed, she thought. "How do you dress for a hurricane?" she asked herself.

Her phone rang. She hoped it was Steven or perhaps Maria. She looked at the caller ID.

"Hi, Mom," she said.

"Good grief! That hurricane is headed straight to you! Are you still home? Have you packed? Where are you going? You're going to evacuate, aren't you?"

"Calm down, Mom. They're not sure if it is coming here or Corpus Christi. So far, we just have a little rain and some wind."

"Now, you listen here, missy, I am sitting in front of the TV, and I can see the storm heading your way. Now, you get out of there. You hear me?"

There was a sound of sheer panic in her mother's voice. Eva knew her mother was seriously worried,

"Okay, Mom. I'm sorry." Eva attempted to hide her sobbing. She held it in so her mother wouldn't be alarmed.

"Eva? Are you there?"

She composed herself and replied calmly, "I'm trying to figure out how to get out of here. It may not be possible. The highway is closed due to flooding. If the water gets higher and comes into the apartment, I'll go upstairs. I'll be fine. I promise I'll call you as soon as I know where I am going or more about the hurricane. Now, you take care, Mom. I gotta go."

"Okay. Call me now. Promise."

"Promise."

The tears rolled down Eva's face. She wasn't sure what was more upsetting—Steven, the storm, or perhaps talking to her mother for the last time. She was shaking and unsure what to do next.

* * *

Eva looked out the apartment window. There was sufficient light to see outside through the heavy rain. The palm trees were wildly moving in the wind.

She heard some banging noises and drilling. Across the complex, on the other side of the swimming pool, it looked like the maintenance men were trying frantically to get hurricane shutters up. The wind was causing them difficulty. The thin plywood boards were hard to fight with and keep in place while they were being secured to the frame of the window. Finally, the pair of maintenance workers gave up and ran for cover. Most of the apartment windows, including Eva's, remained unprotected.

She began shaking with fear. Tears were streaming down her face. *Get yourself together,* she told herself.

She watched out the window. The light allowed her to see the water completely covering most of the apartment's landscaped beds, and the parking lot was overflowing. The water was covering most of the tires of the cars in the lot. The street in the front of the apartment flowed like a river. There were no cars driving by. The wind blew the palm trees into an almost-permanent sideways position. Other tropical plants were beaten down completely. She could see a corner of the swimming pool past the flower beds. The pool was overflowing out onto the lawn and the parking lot.

Eva turned on the news again. She was thankful she still had power.

"Please take caution if you go outside. You shouldn't try to drive at this point. The roads are flooding on the major highways and residential streets. Also, remember, do not call 911. They can't help you now. They're not able to negotiate the streets at this point in time. I am receiving reports that the 911 calls are jamming up the remaining phone lines. So again, you're on your own. Don't call 911.

"If you are just now tuning in, we'll show you the track again. Hurricane León, now a Category 4, has taken a direct aim toward Brownsville. It has slowed in speed just a little. Right now, it is churning out about ten miles off the coast. Unfortunately, this slow-down means it will be producing even more rain. It means even more flooding. Please take precautions. We are receiving some reports of power outages and expect that to continue. We also want our viewers to be aware that there may be a loss of cell phone service if the wind damages the towers. If you have not already drawn up plenty of water, do so now. Fill your bathtubs as well. You'll want that for cleaning purposes. The water may not be drinkable for several days."

Eva ran into her kitchen. She pulled out every jar, jug, and container she could. She filled them all. She filled every glass in her cabinet. She poured out the milk in her refrigerator, rinsed out the jug, and filled that, too. She filled both of her bathtubs.

I won't let this storm do me in. I can get through this.

Back in front of the TV, she switched to the Spanish station to see if it was working again. It was. The news showed the streets of Matamoros and then Reynosa. Matamoros had extreme flooding. She could interpret the reporter talking about problems with water drainage off the street. The news then switched to the border fence. The fence was being blown at an angle. The Border Patrol and the National Guard were attempting to reinforce it, but they looked unsuccessful. The report scanned down to the river. The river water was out of its banks. The water was swiftly rolling down the river.

Eva switched back to the local channel.

"And we remind you to stay away from windows in case flying debris should break through the glass.

"Okay, here's the latest data from the reconnaissance plane. It's not good news for those of us in the Rio Grande Valley. The sustained wind is now measured to be 146 miles per hour. This means this storm has the potential for catastrophic damage when it makes landfall. We are expecting this track to hold so that the eye will move just south of Brownsville. This means we will receive the brunt of the wind and the rain. Power outages are being widely reported. Please, if you are still receiving power and are watching us, take cover and do not go outside. If the water begins to rise, get to a higher spot. We expect landfall to be within the hour or two."

Another news anchor came on the air and said, "We have some live footage now from our sister station in Matamoros. Let's take a look on the other side of the river to see what is happening there."

Eva watched closely and saw the streets were flooding badly. Cars were floating down roads. Debris and chunks of structures were piling up. She felt sadness for Mexico and hoped that Steven was safe somewhere.

The video switched to another street. People were trying to swim in the water. It moved so rapidly that one person went under the water and did not return to the surface.

This is horrible, she thought.

She looked out her window. The sky was a strange color, and the wind and rain were fierce. The water had already risen above her front step and was making its way to her door.

The wind dramatically increased. Eva heard crashing and breaking noises outside and saw the pool furniture flying around. A continuous, howling wind was frightening. The sound was unnerving. It was relentless. It was deafening. A crash of glass signaled entrance of the palm tree into the bedroom. The rain hammered the windows and sprayed inside the broken glass on the floor.

Then, a flicker, and her power was gone. She was sitting in a semi-dark room. The sound the wind made was like nothing she had ever experienced. It made her feel like she was in the bottom of a very deep well. She imagined the height of the storm clouds, and she felt insignificantly small. She was frightened. She didn't know what to do. She couldn't stop shaking and crying. She reached for her phone.

She needed to talk to her mother again. She missed her. She wished she was with her mother in Virginia, safe and dry.

"Mom," she said.

"Yes, is that you, Eva? I can hardly hear you. Are you okay?"

"Yes, I'm okay, Mom. But the storm is about to hit. I just wanted to tell you that I miss you, and I will come up there to see you soon. Tell my sisters I miss them, too."

"Oh, sweetie, I will. You take care of yourself. Call me soon. Eva? Eva?"

"Okay, Mom. Mom . . . "

Her cell service was out. A recorded message came on stating, "Due to high usage, your call could not be completed."

"Oh!" Eva shouted.

She looked toward her front door. Water began seeping in under the door. It then began seeping in on the sides of the bottom of the door. Her floor was beginning to get wet. The water inched up. Eva ran upstairs with her phone and her computer. She didn't know what to do. She covered her ears to stop the howling noise and the crashes and cracks of roofs being torn away all around her, trees falling down, and powerlines being blown over. She pulled her mattress over her head.

Not too far away from Eva, the levee began to give way. A border fence began to crumble. And a river, out of its banks, could no longer be guarded. The borderlands of Matamoros and Brownsville became one giant, flooded region. There was no distinction between Mexico and the southern tip of Texas. Miles and miles of destruction from water and wind damage produced lakes of brownish gray water, mowed down buildings, tore down bridges, flooded roadways; and in that moment, the expanse of land that included Matamoros and Brownsville was destroyed.

CHAPTER TWENTY-NINE

IN THE RISING WATERS AND raging wind, Eva's roof was ripped off the apartment. The walls were pulled outward and fell into the water as she held on to a heavy dresser that eventually was blown down into the water along with Eva. She thrashed and struggled in the water as she tried to swim. Objects were moving all around her in the water and banging her arms, face, and legs. Lightening flashed, and the wind growled. She turned her gaze upward, and for the first time in years, she asked God for help.

"Please, God. Please, help me. Please, don't let me die," she pleaded. "I need You, God. Please, help me."

She couldn't save herself alone this time. She needed Him. She cried as she flailed around in the water. She couldn't see where she was or anything around her. She was gulping water and trying to keep her head up.

"Please, help me, God. Forgive me for leaving You out of my life. Please, God."

After a while in the swirling and pushing water, she bumped into a wall and held on to what she thought was an open door of some kind. She held on as the door moved back and forth. She prayed and held the door tightly.

Somehow, Eva pulled herself inside the structure that was only slightly flooded inside. She was able to climb up on to the top of a cabinet. She waited and shivered with fear as the wind blew all around and the rain hammered the tall windows that were intact. She looked at the walls of the structure, saw large letters, and read the statement:

> *Come to me, all who labor and are heavy laden and*
> *I will give you rest.*
>
> Matthew 11:28

She cried, "A church!" And she sobbed as she looked at another wall that had the words:

> *You will seek me and find me,*
> *when you seek me with all your heart.*
>
> Jeremiah 29:13

She wept and waited. "Thank you," she whispered, looking upward. She sobbed and shivered.

As the rain subsided and the wind decreased over time, she began to feel like the worst had passed. She realized her cell phone was in her pocket. It didn't work.

The rain ended, and it began to get dark. She was exhausted. She laid down on the top of the cabinet and tried to relax. She wasn't sure if she slept. She was in and out of alertness. Hours had passed when she heard the first voices. Two people made their way inside the church with flashlights.

"Hello?" a woman asked.

"Hi," Eva said, sniffling. "I was in the water and managed to grab the door and stay in here during the storm."

"Bless you, child. Are you hurt? I see you are bleeding."

A man entered the church. "Hello. Oh, so glad you found us, and you're safe. I'm the pastor here—Pastor Joseph. You can stay here as long as you need. We've asked the Red Cross to come in as soon as they are able and use this building for a shelter. It's the only building left on the block. When the water goes down, you'll see how elevated our building is. It kept out some of the water. This building seems to withstand all of the hurricanes."

Eva began to cry even more.

"Are you okay?" the woman asked. "Let me help you get cleaned up. My name is Elena."

"Hi, Elena." She sniffled again.

Elena found a cloth and helped dry Eva's face and looked at her cuts.

Soon, the pastor was joined by two other men who got the water off the floor and swept the mud out. Elena lit candles and found the emergency supplies in the cabinet. She went to the shelves in another room and got down cots, blankets, and sheets that were still dry.

Elena tended to Eva's wounds and got her some dry clothing. The building was damp; but with the windows open, it began to dry out.

"There," Elena said as she put the bandages on Eva's cuts. Elena gave Eva a hug and asked, "Do you live nearby?"

"I'm not sure. I suppose my apartment is near, but I couldn't tell where the water took me."

"You can stay here and rest up. Once the Red Cross can get in, we'll have fresh food and water. For now, just rest on the cot as long as you like. You are safe."

Once again, Eva began to cry.

"It's okay. You are safe," Elena repeated.

"I thought I was going to drown. I said so many prayers. God brought me here."

"Yes, and now, we can take care of you."

Eva cried a little more and slowly calmed herself. She felt that she had been given a second chance at life. Silently, she prayed and thanked God for saving her. She realized her life before was superficial and shallow. She missed so many important things. She almost lost her life—a life that didn't really have meaning—not deep meaning anyway. She put her head on the cot and covered up with a blanket. She heard the people talking quietly in the background as they got out additional supplies and greeted a few people who found their way to the shelter. At last, she fell into a deep sleep.

Eva sat up on the cot. She looked around the church and saw that other people were there. Some people were bringing boxes inside the church. The boxes had food, water, and first aid supplies. Elena instructed the volunteers where to place each box. She wondered how many people were now safe in the church.

Eva suddenly felt pain. Her body ached. The bandages on her arms and legs needed to be changed again. She managed to stretch her stiff and aching body and stood up. She walked over to a first aid station that was set up while she slept. She waited her turn.

A woman sitting next to her asked Eva if her cell phone worked.

"No," Eva replied. "It got wet. But I'm holding on to it anyway. I want to call my mother when I can get it fixed or get another phone somewhere. If the service is restored by then."

The nurse came to Eva and said, "Eva, come on back. I'll change those bandages for you."

Eva feared everything she had was gone. Her apartment was destroyed. But she managed to hold on to her phone. She had survived the hurricane. Her life was spared. For that, she thanked God. She knew that He alone helped her to find the church and get inside to safety.

"There you go," the nurse said. "That should hold you for today. We'll change it again tomorrow. Don't want to risk infection. The flood water was pretty dirty."

"Thank you," she said and gave the nurse a hug.

Slowly, other survivors began to arrive at the shelter, and they were processed by the volunteers. They were then directed to have their injuries examined or to go to the food and water station.

Eva walked to the food area of the shelter. The local grocery store where she had shopped in the past donated all of the food that was not destroyed in the hurricane to the shelter. There was no refrigeration in the grocery store or the shelter. She was appreciative of the food that was there.

"Is there any fruit?" Eva asked the volunteer.

"We have a little star fruit and a few bananas. I might have some apples."

"Thank you," Eva said as she picked up a slice of star fruit and a banana. Thinking of Steven, she began to cry a little. She wiped her tears and read the Bible verses on the wall. She prayed silently, thanking God for saving her. Someday, perhaps God would reveal the meaning of what happened with Steven. But for now, she was thankful to be alive.

The front door of the church opened, and others entered the church.

"Welcome," said the volunteer. "Come in. You can rest here. We have food over there." She gestured to some tables filled with food. "What are your names?"

The woman spoke in her native language—Spanish—and responded, "I am Dolores, and this is my brother, Ernesto. We are looking for our younger brother, Emilio."

In Spanish, the bilingual volunteer replied, "I'll get the list of names here, and you can add yours. Then, you can check through all of these pages to see if Emilio has checked in."

Dolores took the list, added their names, and searched through the pages for Emilio's name. He wasn't there. She checked again to be certain. No Emilio.

Dolores looked at Ernesto and shook her head.

"Let's rest, Ernesto, and get something to eat and some fresh water."

At the food station, Dolores asked what food was available. The volunteer told Dolores the types of fruit and other foods.

Eva turned to Dolores and said in Spanish, "The star fruit is good." Then, Eva introduced herself to Dolores and Ernesto.

Dolores and Ernesto took a few pieces of fruit and *pan dulce* and sat at a table with Eva.

Dolores took a bite of her fruit and asked Eva, "Do you live here?"

"Yes. I think my apartment was a block or so over in that direction," Eva said. "But it was destroyed."

"We're new here. We've lost our younger brother."

Eva asked, "How old is he?"

"He's fourteen. We lost him right before the storm hit. We were kidnapped by the cartel in Matamoros. They separated us in different vans."

"You're from Mexico? And you were kidnapped?" Eva asked.

"Honduras. We traveled by train to get here."

"That was a long ride from Honduras."

"Yes, but we saw a lot of Mexico on the trip. We were almost in the United States when we were kidnapped. Somehow, after the storm, in all of the water, we ended up in the United States."

Eva said, "The volunteers told me the fence and bridge are gone. All of the Border Patrol and the National Guard have had to be repositioned to help find victims and rescue people. So, right now, there is not a border, just a very large lake out there."

"That's not good. There are many bad people coming over now. We ran from gangs and the cartel along the way. Since we have been in the United States, we have seen Salvadorian gang members and the cartel. We have witnessed them hurting people, stealing, and kidnapping right down this street. We'd hoped to be safe here. And now, I'm afraid it might be the same as Honduras. The cartel and the other gangs are here. The government didn't help us in Honduras. I hope your government will help to get the criminals out. They must keep them from ruining this country like they have done in Honduras and Mexico."

"Well, you are safe now, in this shelter. But I understand your fear about the cartel. When I was in Mexico not long ago, I saw evidence of the cartel. It's not good. I'm not sure what will happen on the border now. There's no way to see where the border is supposed to be. So many people on both sides of the border have no home. And thousands on both sides of the border have died."

Dolores began to cry.

"I'm sorry," Eva said. "I didn't mean to upset you."

Ernesto put his arm around his sister and said, "We'll find him."

Eva felt such sadness for Dolores and Ernesto. She wanted to help them but did not know how.

"Dolores and Ernesto, I am not sure how I can help, but I would like very much to try and find your brother."

Dolores sobbed, and Ernesto teared up as he hugged his sister. "We will find him."

Dolores bowed her head, said a quiet prayer, and made the sign of the cross on her chest. Ernesto hugged his sister again.

Eva smiled as she observed Dolores praying. Eva wanted that kind of faith. She patted Dolores' hand. "You two need some rest. And you can visit the nurse's station over there and get checked out. There are some showers down that hallway. After a day or two of rest, and when the water goes down, we can look for Emilio."

"You will help us?" Dolores asked.

"Of course," Eva replied.

Dolores hugged Eva and said, "Thank you."

Ernesto said, "Thank you, Eva. I'll go to the nurse. She can help me with the blisters on my feet."

Ernesto received the care he needed and also showered. He then found a cot and rested.

Dolores had a shower, got her scratches bandaged up, and rested.

* * *

While Dolores and Ernesto slept, Eva asked the volunteer how to help Dolores and Ernesto find their brother.

"He's only fourteen, and he was kidnapped in Matamoros before the storm. He may have escaped, like Dolores and Ernesto did."

"They don't know if he is in the United States?" the volunteer asked.

"No. They told me when they arrived, they didn't know they were in the United States until they saw the houses on these streets and what they described as the university campus—or what is left of it."

"It sounds like the younger brother may not know where he is, either. There's been a lot of looting and other criminal activity in the area. It is very dangerous to go out there. I would suggest they wait until the water is gone and they can get some help finding their brother."

"Dolores told me that he has likely not eaten in a while and is probably weak, if he is still living."

"I'm sorry I can't be of more help," the volunteer said.

Eva, undeterred, went to the front door. A National Guardsman was standing there.

"Excuse me, sir,"

"Yes, Miss?"

"The last two young people that came in here have lost their fourteen-year-old brother. Do you have any way to ask if a young boy named Emilio has been found? Maybe in one of the other shelters?"

"I will radio in and ask," he said.

"Thank you."

The soldier walked to a large Humvee with radio equipment, parked in an elevated spot that had only eighteen inches of water. He talked on the radio for a few minutes.

"No. I'm sorry, but they have no one by that name in the other shelters."

Eva was disappointed.

"I was told the coast guard has patrol boats out now looking for anyone to rescue, but there aren't enough boats to cover such a massive body of water. Luckily, the Cajun patrol and other volunteers with boats have arrived in McAllen. The National Guard soldiers and available local law enforcement officers will accompany the volunteer boaters. They are sending out several airboats and other shallow bottom boats to search and rescue. The airboats are already headed this way. It may take them another day or so to get here. They are having trouble with fuel along the way for some of the motor boats. Several have departed already, heading to Brownsville. I requested that they look for Emilio near the border area."

"Thank you so much. Is there anything else we can do?"

"Not at this moment. Oh, they wanted to know if Emilio spoke English and how they will know to identify him if they pick him up. Told them I will radio back."

"No, he doesn't speak English. They can ask his name; and if he says Emilio Sanchez, then ask if his sister's name is Dolores, and his brother's name is Ernesto."

"Okay, I'll let them know, so they can notify the airboats heading this way."

"Thank you."

Eva returned inside, and Dolores was sitting on the cot. Ernesto was sleeping soundly.

"Dolores, I spoke with a soldier, and he is helping to find Emilio."

"Really? What are they doing?"

"Sending boats out along the border—or what was the border—to look for him."

"Thank you," she choked out and then began to cry again.

"It'll be okay," Eva said as she hugged her.

Two days went by slowly, and the water remained. Pastor Joseph held a small service each day, and the people in the shelter sang and prayed together. Eva felt closer to God than she ever had. She hadn't experienced such a warm and loving feeling in her life. She visited with Dolores and Ernesto during their stay together in the shelter. She felt a strong connection to them as if they were her family. She felt a sense of needing to protect them, like a younger brother and sister. They were all survivors. They had that in common. It seemed as if she had known Dolores and Ernesto for years rather than days.

Eva wanted to learn more about them and their family. She wanted to help them in any way she could. Eva knew they were in an unfamiliar country and had no personal resources. She knew God would help her to help these young people who had already survived so much tragedy.

Later that day, Eva asked Dolores, "Do you have plans? Have you thought about what you are going to do once the water is gone?"

"No. I want to find a family or a place to stay and find work."

"I'm not sure how much work will be available in this area. I'm not even sure when my university will be back in service. But we might be able to get some assistance and a shelter to live in for a while."

"I don't know any English or how to ask for help. I don't know where to go," Dolores tearfully replied.

"Don't worry," Eva said and patted her hand, "I can help you. I am in the same situation, really. I don't think I have an apartment anymore, so I will need to find some place to live. We can look together."

"You would do that?" Dolores asked.

"Of course," Eva replied. Somehow, she knew helping these young people from Honduras was what God wanted. She believed that was why she was saved in this church. She believed that is why Dolores and Ernesto wandered into the church. Eva wasn't sure about much in her life, but she was sure about this.

Dolores hugged Eva as if she wouldn't let her go. She cried quietly and whispered, "Gracious a Dios."

* * *

Volunteers from all over the country began to show up. Substantial loads of food and supplies were provided. People across the United States sent clothing and other necessities. Eva, Dolores, and Ernesto received new, clean clothes, towels, shampoo, soap, toothpaste, and even a little make-up.

The volunteers brought in news, often not good. The total body count was over three thousand and still climbing. There were no functioning hospitals in the immediate area, and all of the McAllen hospitals were overflowing. Patients were seen in makeshift tent facilities. Doctors and nurses volunteered for weeks at a time to assist. Many critical patients were air-lifted to San Antonio, Austin, and Dallas. Houston hospitals were overflowing from patients from Port Aransas and Corpus Christi, where the hurricane, then a Category 2, finally sputtered out and went up the state of Texas.

On the fourth day that Dolores and Ernesto were at the shelter, an airboat came to the front door. A weary, bruised, and scratched up Emilio was helped out of the boat and up the steps to the front door.

The volunteer opened the door. "Welcome," she said.

In Spanish, he said, "Hello. I am Emilio. I am looking for—"

"Emilio!" Dolores screamed. "Emilio! My baby brother! Oh, Emilio!" She ran to meet him, and Ernesto was right behind her. The three embraced and cried.

When Dolores was able to compose herself, she said, "And this is my good friend, Eva."

"Nice to meet you, Eva."

"Eva will help us find a place to live. She will help us find a place to stay. But now, get some food. The nurse can take care of your scratches and cuts. We will get you some new, dry clothes, and then you can rest." Dolores hugged him again. Ernesto hugged Emilio as well.

Emilio began to cry. "I thought I'd never see you again. I escaped from the kidnappers, and some nice people helped me. Then the storm came and tore down their house. I don't know what happened to them. The water carried us all away."

Dolores hugged him and said, "It is okay. We are together now."

"Eva," a volunteer said.

"Yes?"

"Here." She handed Eva a phone. "A person came by and donated these cell phones. They work. You can call your mother."

"Thank you so much."

Eva punched in her mother's number.

"Mom?"

"Oh, Eva," she cried. "Is that you? Eva? You're alive?" She continued sobbing loudly.

Eva could not understand anything else her mother said. Her mother was crying uncontrollably.

"Mom. It's okay. I'm fine. I'm in a church, and the people here are wonderful. And Mom, what you said before, when you said there's a lot I don't know . . . You were right. I miss you, Mom."

Her mother sobbed more and finally composed herself enough to ask, "When can you come home?"

"It will be a while, Mom. We can't get out yet. I'm not sure about my apartment. I will be able to go look in a week or two. But I have a phone now and can call you every day and let you know what is happening."

"Okay. Please call me."

"I will, Mom, I promise. I love you, and I'll call tomorrow. Can you let my sisters know? Oh, and Mom, can you ask your prayer group to pray for us here in south Texas?"

"We have been praying every day. I will call each of them when we hang up. First, I'll call your sisters. Oh, thanks be to God you are safe. Call me tomorrow. I love you, honey."

"I love you, too, Mom. I miss you. I'll call tomorrow."

"Bye, sweetie."

CHAPTER THIRTY

IN HER SMALL CAPE COD house in Southside, Virginia, Eva's mother turned on the news. The reports were focused only on the damage of Hurricane León.

The female news anchor reported the following:

> "It has now been confirmed that the caravan of Central Americans was on the outskirts of Matamoros when the hurricane made landfall. We have confirmed that more than two thousand were killed in the storm and that another two thousand or so left the area and returned south. Their whereabouts are not known at this time. Mexican and United States authorities have been alerted.

> "The National Guard and other local law enforcement agencies continue to report looting in the area of the hurricane's destruction. Of the looters arrested, it cannot be determined how many are United States citizens and how many are from other countries at this time. Computers and data to identify those arrested are not operational in the area.

> "Now we turn to the United States-Mexico Emergency Summit."

A male news reporter provided the following report:

> "Both the president of the United States and the president of Mexico continue to negotiate the strategy for reconstruction. The terms that have been

agreed upon thus far—let us put these on the screen for you—here we go, if viewers would follow along:

1. *Mexico has agreed to shut down their entire southern border between Guatemala and Mexico, and to stop all freight trains— so called "death trains"—from their northern destinations. All freight trains will go no further than a line or boundary from Monterrey on the east route and to Sonora on the west route. This boundary will be set up and patrolled to make certain that people do not ride the train to these stops and then proceed to the United States through Mexico.*

2. *Mexico and the United States will jointly build a security barrier for the border between the United States and Mexico. Money confiscated from the cartels will be used to fund the barrier.*

3. *In a region twenty miles north of the border of Mexico and twenty miles south in the area impacted by Hurricane León, in a line designated by this picture shown on the screen, will be the free zone, or no border zone, for people to live in the immediate future and may be up to a period of two years. The few remaining people in this region have been displaced from their homes and, in some cases, from their home country. This region includes both Brownsville and Matamoros. It has been confirmed that many of the remaining survivors in this area do not know where they are or how they arrived. This area will be guarded by both United States National Guard and Mexican Federal Security forces. Citizenship will be determined at a later date. Those displaced from their homes in Mexico may opt to apply for American citizenship that will be expedited following security checks.*

4. *Mexico and the United States have agreed to jointly fund the humanitarian efforts for all victims of the hurricane within the region. Additional measures are planned for future immigrants that may attempt to enter the northern border of Mexico and*

the southern border of the United States so that these victims will
receive assistance.

The phone rang.

"Mom?"

"Oh, hello, Eva. How are you doing?"

"I'm doing well. I found out how to apply for a place to live for the short term. What do you hear on the news? We don't have access yet to a television."

"I'm watching the news now. It looks like both governments, the United States and Mexico, are going to work together to get the area of South Texas and Mexico restored."

"Really? That's good news," Eva said.

Her mother laughed. "Yes, and they are calling it 'Rebuild American Again.'"

"Interesting. And how about Mexico?"

"They are calling their plan 'Make Mexico Safe Again."

"Well, they certainly need to do that!" Eva agreed.

"Yes. It sounds like they are going to focus on the gangs and cartel."

"That's what they need to do!"

"Oh, and guess what else?" her mother asked.

"What?"

"The President tweeted this . . . wait, I'll read it to you. 'Cartel, gang members, and other criminals in Mexico and Central America, we are coming for you. You can run, but you can't hide.' And they are reporting that the people of Mexico they have interviewed have applauded this effort to restore Mexico."

"That is good news. It will help if everyone just works together," Eva said.

"Have you heard anything else about funding for us down here? Did they approve our housing money yet?" Eva asked.

"Yes! They announced that earlier, that both the House and the Senate unanimously approved the emergency funding bill."

"That's wonderful, Mom. Oh, I'd better run. Church is starting in five minutes."

"Oh, wait . . . one more thing. It looks like they are sending a member of the cartel to the U.S. to be tried for drug trafficking. Someone named Juan Ochoa. They said he was recently traveling with a tour group in Mexico under the name of Esteban Garcia, or Steven."

Eva's heart sank. *Steven.* That seemed like years ago.

"Eva? Are you there?"

"Yes. Okay, Mom. I've gotta run to church."

"Okay. Talk to you tomorrow."

* * *

Eva sat in the small church in a pew next to Dolores and her two brothers. They listened to the pastor and sand the hymns together. The sunlight streamed through the windows as it had in the churches of Mexico. But Eva was different. She had changed. She now realized she needed God walking with her in her life. She understood that being independent and accomplished in some areas of life didn't mean she didn't need God. She needed Him more than ever.

She watched Dolores as she sang in broken English. Somehow, Eva felt responsible for these young people. They were all starting over. They all relied on God for guidance. Eva knew their future would be better. They had God, and they had each other.

Someday, with God's help, she would make sense out of her life and what happened with Steven. She understood now that she did not need to know why. She only needed to depend on God and trust that He was the One with a plan for her life.

For more information about
Terry Overton
and
Both Sides of the Border
please visit:

www.terryovertonbooks.com
www.facebook.com/allthingspossiblewithhim
@terryoverton6

For more information about
AMBASSADOR INTERNATIONAL
please visit:

www.ambassador-international.com
@AmbassadorIntl
www.facebook.com/AmbassadorIntl

*Thank you for reading, and please consider leaving us a review
on Amazon, Goodreads, or our websites.*

An American businesswoman with a secret past.

An African boy without a home.

Two missionaries with more than one mission to accomplish.

Will all of their wishes come true where the sky meets the sand on the African plain?

When a prominent city official dies in a car wreck, Scott and Angela find themselves tangled in intrigue and deception. Together they search for the truth and discover that not all is what it seems.

When ten-year-old Nate "Weenie" Dooley discovers that his father has left him first, it will take the help of a stray dog, some kind neighbors, a one-man-band, letters from a long-lost-aunt, and a new understanding of God to figure out he isn't really alone.